PENGUIN BOOKS

The Sea Change

Joanna Rossiter grew up in Dorset and studied English at Cambridge University before working as a researcher in the House of Commons and as a copywriter. In 2011 she completed an MA in Writing at Warwick University. *The Sea Change* is her first novel. She lives and writes in London.

The Sea Change

JOANNA ROSSITER

PENGUIN BOOKS

PENGUIN BOOKS

Published by the Penguin Group
Penguin Books Ltd, 80 Strand, London WC2R ORL, England
Penguin Group (USA) Inc., 375 Hudson Street, New York, New York 10014, USA
Penguin Group (Canada), 90 Eglinton Avenue East, Suite 700, Toronto, Ontario, Canada M4P 2Y3
(a division of Pearson Penguin Canada Inc.)
Penguin Ireland, 25 St Stephen's Green, Dublin 2, Ireland (a division of Penguin Books Ltd)
Penguin Group (Australia), 707 Collins Street, Melbourne, Victoria 3008, Australia
(a division of Pearson Australia Group Pty Ltd)
Penguin Books India Pvt Ltd, 11 Community Centre, Panchsheel Park, New Delhi – 110 017, India
Penguin Group (NZ), 67 Apollo Drive, Rosedale, Auckland 0632, New Zealand
(a division of Pearson New Zealand Ltd)
Penguin Books (South Africa) (Pty) Ltd, Block D, Rosebank Office Park, 181 Jan Smuts Avenue,
Parktown North, Gauteng 2193, South Africa

Penguin Books Ltd, Registered Offices: 80 Strand, London WC2R ORL, England

www.penguin.com

First published 2013
001

Copyright © Joanna Rossiter, 2013

Set in Dante MT Std 11/13 pt
Typeset by Palimpsest Book Production Limited, Falkirk, Stirlingshire
Printed in Great Britain by Clays Ltd, St Ives plc

ISBN: 978-0-241-96415-6

www.greenpenguin.co.uk

MIX
Paper from
responsible sources
FSC   FSC® C018179
www.fsc.org

Penguin Books is committed to a sustainable
future for our business, our readers and our planet.
This book is made from Forest Stewardship
Council™ certified paper.

ALWAYS LEARNING   **PEARSON**

For Bill, who, when the pages were blank, saw only opportunity.
To Imber – for giving so much, so quietly.

'But you can say, you can guess, that it
is you yourself, your own roots, that clutch
the stony rubbish, the branches of
your own being that grow
from it and from nowhere else'

Rose Macaulay, *The World My Wilderness*

Prologue: The Sea is Never Full

Kanyakumari, India, 1971

It is there before we know about it. Being born. A Persian rug, unrolling. Our wave, heavy, like death.

'Up! Up!' a voice shouts from outside the guesthouse. It doesn't belong to James. 'It's coming!'

Where is he?

Stone. Bone. Think hard and then harder. That's how it hits the shore. It takes the beach in one breathtaking gulp, palm trees dominoing down and fishing boats scattering as easily as the seeds of a dandelion. Streets fuse into the flesh of the water, like new limbs, new skin, until it morphs into a moving city. Trucks and tuk-tuks roll over and over like shirts in a washer; houses are picked up whole. Then, with sea-soaked hands, the water sets itself alight. Flames – blinding and orange – buoy themselves forward on black, black, mirrorless liquid.

One man runs. And is outrun.

It's not James. James isn't on the beach. James gets away in time. He went, before it came, to pick up breakfast. I was going to meet him on the beach. I was late, faffing about in the room with our luggage, remaking the bed. I don't know where he is. I don't know where he is but I was going to meet him on the beach. The beach. And then it came. He'll have thought better of it. He'll have gone up the hill to get us some *lassi* instead; he'll come running up the stairs any second now. He'll be here. And safe.

It's about to hit the guesthouse. I don't have time to think about how thick it is. I just feel its thickness beneath me. You'd think that it would strike you once, hard in the face. And then it would be over. But it isn't like that. Instead it arrives and leaves, advances and retreats, bringing more of itself each time.

Our room is about to go under. I reach for Mum's letter on the bedside table – it can have everything else. Then I take the stairs two at a time. James's last packet of Player's No. 6 is probably pregnant with saltwater by now. He could have gone straight up to the roof, forgetting to fetch me. Please, God. The staircase is inking up with water, like mercury rising inside a thermometer. Furniture and luggage froth up from the ground floor. Everything keeps moving, stirring; nothing is still.

Guests on the floors below reach out into the rising wreckage as I climb the stairs, eyes hollow with what is brewing beneath them.

'My husband. Have you seen my husband?' The word feels new and unused, still fresh out of its packaging.

'What's the husband's name?' asks the landlord. We're on the roof now.

'James. It's James,' I say, as if it will help.

'It's going to take us!' blurts the American whose room is on our floor. He's still in his dressing-gown and his eyes are glued to a block like ours across the road, which topples and is carried off. But our building stays standing, sacrificing its organs – curtains, windows, cabinets and beds – until we're left teetering on its bones.

I've gone back to the stairs but the landlord is standing in my way.

'Madam.'

'What are you doing?' My voice is hoarse and high. 'I need to go! Let me go!'

'Please, madam. It is not safe.'

I tuck the letter – still in my grasp – beneath the padding of my bra. Then I push past him to the stairs. I'm level with the water now, and looking. Outside the window, all the inanimate things – the cars, the trees, the boats and the barns – have been brought to life, rolling and writhing in the sea. But there are no human faces – not even a body. These it keeps hidden from sight.

I shout his name. I shout it again. The water is goaded, and rises – I can't get back to the roof. It's ripped my feet from the floor and forced me through the window. Down the rabbit hole I go. Like Mum used to say when I stared into space too often and for too long. *Alice is down the rabbit hole*, she'd mouth in code to Tim. She was always afraid that I wanted to get away. There's no choice now. It's taking me. Not forwards, like I expected, but backwards. Out to the ocean; towards home.

The water feels magnetic: the more I strain, the more it pulls. *Did I not tell you this would happen?* Mum would say. *Didn't I warn you not to go away with him?* As if James himself were responsible for my being dragged out to sea.

The shoreline depletes. I'm flailing about, trying to grab hold of the horizon and drag it towards me but it's drifting further and further away. I can't keep this up for much longer. It'll only take another wave. Send another. Anything but drowning. After a while, there's just breath. The sea's lungs swell in time with mine until I find I can't keep its rhythm – chest quivering into a frantic staccato. Every bit of me aches. So I rest. For a second. It's enough for the water to pull me under. I resist its muzzle but it's no use.

There is noiselessness underneath. Nothing but the push and tug of the sea. A giant swell of ocean, colder than the rest, swarms below. I let go of my muscles, my fists. I give in to lightness.

Chapter 1

Pete used to say that a place isn't everything: people can make a home out of a cardboard box, if you give them half a chance. He didn't understand why I clung to Imber as if it were a lost soul. But perhaps if he were here with me now, standing in the dip of the church doorstep, I would see something give way in that flint face of his.

The earth has run its fingers all over the church. Clots of moss bloom in green seas on the roof. Ivy has prised open windows and doors and clawed at the fissures in the stonework. Nesting birds leap up at the smallest of movements – mistaking every sound for a bullet. As I step into the porch, they splash through the glassless windows and ghost through the air above the nave. So immersed is the stone in creepers and lichen that it is as if the church is Nature's own creation; born from the ground like a new breed of tree.

The sight of my mother's note on the door stills my breath. The rain has had nearly three decades to invade the ink but, sheltered as it is by the porch, I can still read its message as if it had been written yesterday.

We have given up our valley where many of us have lived for generations, entrusting it to you for the sake of the war. Please take good care of the church in our absence; to us it is more than stone and glass. We shall return one day and thank you for treating the village kindly.

I often wonder whether, if my mother had known the fate of our village, she would have written something different on the church door. Would the words have come less easily? Or would she have gone on believing, blithely, that our sacrifice was worth all those unborn memories? The ones we would have reared in the cottages, in the fields, in our very own nook of earth.

Today is the first time I have been back in twenty-six years. It should have felt like any other day: the same wrestle with the alarm clock; the same small battles with Tim about when he last heard from Alice, and who is to blame for the gold- not silver-topped milk bottles outside the door. Except I woke early, unsure of whether I had slept at all. I slipped off before the alarm and left him asleep in bed. Outside the house, the light was still threadbare.

I began the short drive in Tim's Cortina through the military firing range – no more than five miles – across land I had not touched since I was nineteen.

Boreham Down slipped by on the left. As I drove, the Plain rose and fell into muddy gullies and chalked ridges, like the peak and trough of a petrified wave.

I could see the bell tower through the windscreen, pressed into the cushion of Salisbury Plain. But the rest of the village was hidden – just as it used to be – below the camber of the Downs.

Shooting targets were pinned, like my mother's note, to the nape of South Down where they labelled the land's anatomy: '1' for the patch where the knapweed grows thickest; '2' for the hill's hip; '3' for the spot that is last to capture the sun; and '4' for the valley floor. The corpses of tanks clung to the side of the ridge, housing flowers and grasses and empty metal cartridges. The hills seemed to have borne their scars well. Somewhere under the grass, I knew there would be bullets, hidden like cysts in the soil. But in this morning's light, I couldn't distinguish the marks of the shelling from the indents made by the rain. The Plain has survived what no city or body ever could.

It is necessary to evacuate the major part of the valley, including your dwelling. The letter was so matter-of-fact. And I had never seen, only felt, the damage that their shells could do. Even before the war, explosions as far away as two miles would cause our windows to quiver and crack, the glass falling from its frame, like a cloud emptying itself of water. For months after we were evicted, I dreamt of rain – metal rain – lodging in the walls of our parsonage and spidering across the mirrors.

I have driven Tim mad with my quietness about this place. It is as if, by not talking, I talk about it all the time. He told me it is because of here – a plain on which he has never set foot – that Alice started to drift. I boxed her in, he said, with my memories. And so I stood and watched as he packed her bags and let her drive all the way to India with a man we barely know. Then I kept silent, so that he wouldn't drift too.

I don't talk to him about Imber any more because I know what he'd think. I'd give him the valley – all its names, faces, places – and he'd imagine it as something golden and lost. It is not golden; it is not lost; if it were, I would long since have escaped its ghost. But I can only ever give him the shell of what it was – a washed-up periwinkle that you hold to your ear to listen to, only to be told that it's not the real sea that you can hear. Just air. A place made of air.

After South Down, the road eased me into the base of the valley. To the right, I could trace the old divides: the stone walling that separated one family's farm from another. The walls reared up high in places and crumbled in others, leaving the fields half finished. The land around the village wasn't tamed in the same way as it had been before. Ivy has been left to run over man-made things, to knead the angles of the outhouses into unliftable curtains of green.

I half expected to see the army keeping guard but they were nowhere to be seen.

Inside the ruins of Seagram's Farm, I kicked a gold-coloured cartridge across the floor and ran a finger along the graffiti on the walls. Names and dates of squadrons littered the chimney breast. *I saw a ghost called Clara* was carved above the hearth.

Past Seagram's Farm, the redbrick skull of the post office gawped across the road at the roofless remains of Parsonage Farm. If I shut my eyes, I could see how it used to be – the roadside all cobbled and complete with a ribbon of cottages, villager knitted to villager, like knots on a length of string. When I opened my eyes, it was like taking the pin out of a grenade: the memory was left in pieces, the walls reduced to the height of my knees and the doorways mangled by barbed wire. Inside the post office, the divide between upstairs and down had all but disappeared so that Mrs Carter's fireplace looked as if it were built to heat the sky. I wanted to cover the place up, as one does a body once the life has left it.

I imagined Mrs Carter standing behind the post-office counter, sorting letters. When she thought no one was looking, she'd halt the flick of her fingers and stare at the window. She was not sad or happy; she just stood there, immersed in thought, until a customer interrupted her and she would carry on with her day. I would not have picked anyone else to receive the news of the eviction first; it was hardly a message to which you could put words. And Mrs Carter, whose hands spent all day ferrying other people's words from place to place, was a silent old soul, not one to speak unnecessarily. Her silence, we agreed, was the only thing fit for that letter.

I was in a queue of customers waiting to drop off my post when she picked up an envelope with her own address on the front. It had a military stamp on the seal – the same as the others she had sorted that morning. She turned away from the counter and we heard her slide her fingers through the paper. She walked out of the room shortly afterwards. I was sent to fetch her: it was not like her to forget about the customers. I found her staring into an empty flowerbed at the back of

8

her garden – the patch of soil where she could make nothing grow.

It is hoped that you will be able, through your own efforts, to find alternative accommodation and, if appropriate, fresh employment, and that you will be able to make your own arrangements as to removal. I took the letter from her, as if robbing a statue of its sceptre, and ran into the post office to break the news to the rest of the village. We were all nosing in on the note – everybody wanted to read it for themselves before they believed it – when Mrs Carter reappeared.

'Don't fuss, don't fuss,' she murmured. 'There's one for each of you in the postbag.'

They moved us out in December, a week before Christmas. I say they moved us – in fact they had very little to do with the evacuation. *It is necessary, it is hoped.* Nobody was going to take the blame.

There was talk of them sending lorries, only some of which came. The rest of us were left to depend on Major Whistler's kindness; Imber Court had a cart at its disposal, which was duly loaded with furniture, pots and pans and a bath full of Mrs Carter's crockery. Mrs Carter tried to stay calm. It was only china after all – not even matching china, she whispered guiltily to me, as she climbed onto the cart; still, if it could survive thirty years of marriage, it could endure this. As the horse turned out of the village and down the track to Heytesbury, the chime of her cups and saucers crossed the Plain. We knew, then, that the crockery would not make it to town intact.

If my father had been with us, we would never have left in time. He would have fussed endlessly over his books. My mother put me in charge of packing them; she could not have borne it herself. I did my best, placing heavier volumes at the bottom of the case so as not to damage the lighter ones. It pained me to think of the books packed away in their boxes without Father to read them. 'Don't you worry, my girl, they're

9

all up here,' he said, giving his head a tap. But I knew better. I had seen the way he pored over each cover, smoothing down the pages with care as he read and returning the book with the precision of a pharmacist to its designated spot on the shelf. Had he not been ordained, I half wondered whether he would have become a bookbinder – not that there was any need for such a thing in Imber. It was a blessing that he wasn't around to see the fate of Imber Court's library, from which he was a frequent borrower. The lack of lorries left the Major carting clocks and books and desks down into the cellars. He would never have said anything but Pete had gone to the Court to ask about moving Albie Nash, the blacksmith, whom he had found hunched over his anvil, weeping. He found the servants cradling piles of books quietly down the stairs like sleeping children. Pete offered to help but the Major reddened and, in a hushed voice, asked after Albie.

My father's books were the last thing we packed. I took them in their boxes and placed them with our other possessions in a pile outside the parsonage door. It wasn't until it came to leaving that I saw how much there was that I couldn't take with me. Walking into my sister's empty room, I tore off a loose piece of her rose-patterned wallpaper and placed it in my pocket; I had always been secretly jealous of it. Having spotted it in a shop window in Wilton, she had pleaded with Father for weeks to buy it for her eighteenth birthday. My father often joked that she would have been better off being born in the city: she battled constantly against the mud that gathered in strips under her fingernails and in clods on the soles of her shoes. And she could not pass through the parsonage hallway without noting the thin grey skin of chalk dust that coated the floor. I used to tell her there was no escaping the land – it was in our name. I don't think Freda liked 'Fielding' much: it was too plain. The name was a better fit for me: I spent more time on the Downs with Pete than I did in the house.

With the scrap of my sister's wallpaper in hand, I took in the view of the Plain from her window – another thing that I couldn't take with me. The grass looked bleak at this time of year, stretching its rags over the chalk. It used to pain me so much to see it like this that I would pull out Father's botany pocket book and reel off the names of the flowers that sprouted there in the summer, as if the colour in their syllables could stir up some magic in the bones of the hill and beckon in spring. I would miss the shiver of ash trees that flanked the right side of the garden. The fullness of their branches in the summer almost masked the Plain from us entirely.

Having taken up his post during the summer of 1931, my father could not understand the need for the trees; he loved the view of the plain as much as I did and was in half a mind to take an axe to them. But the other villagers were quick to warn us against it and, come winter, we were glad of their advice. The winds rattled the house to its core throughout February and we became used to these small fracas, putting up shutters and sometimes even taking refuge in the cellar. Later, when the bombs fell in Wilton, I thought of Imber's winds and how we rode them out underneath the house with nothing but a candle and a song from Freda.

At the window that day, I tried to convince myself that I'd soon come home to see the ash trees clothed again, drinking in all of August's light; I would come back for my father's sake. But the gap in the line of ashes – where we had felled his tree – told me otherwise. Like the shadow of a sinking Zeppelin, the war had started its descent. Only Martha Nash was resolute in her insistence that we would return within two years. She had to be, I guess, for Albie's sake.

After I had finished packing I left the parsonage in search of my mother who, I knew, would be in the church. I found her in the tower, staring up at the bells.

'They will look after it, won't they?' she asked after a while, running her eyes down a bell rope to meet mine at the base of the tower. Her birth, her marriage and the beginning of each week had been marked under the peal of these five instruments. 'No one ever wishes for death, Vi-vi,' she told me, 'but there was always comfort in knowing you would bring me here when it did come.' I didn't like to hear her talk as if we weren't coming back. She wasn't old. She had no reason to think she would not return in her lifetime. Not like Albie. But ever since the accident she had handled her days so carefully, aware that they could evaporate at any minute.

'Will they let you bury me here?' she asked me. She had always been like that, posing questions that were beyond my reach, as if she were the child and I were the mother. I would scramble in vain for an answer and always came up short.

The Major's wife appeared at the door. 'Are you the last?' Her voice skimmed across the nave.

'We're just waiting for the AT3 girls to come back from Lang ton,' my mother replied, standing up.

'Where are they housing you?' she enquired.

'We don't know. Somewhere in Warminster, I expect. Perhaps Wilton.'

'Oh, Warminster . . . I see.' She picked at the doorframe as she spoke. 'I'm sorry to have disturbed you. Only I thought you might like to leave a note. I have paper.'

'A note?' I queried, my mother squeezing my hand as a way of telling me not to pry.

'Yes. I thought he would want –'

My mother stared at the slip of paper that was held out to her. 'But . . . what would he have me say?' she asked, her question floundering in echoes around the four walls of the tower.

The years have yellowed the note, curling it up at the edges as if to check what is underneath. I push the church door open, the last word, 'kindly', on repeat in my ears. The hinges turn in their sleep and I stand in the base of the tower – this time without my mother. The air next to me where she would have stood is as cold as a tomb. There are four bells missing from the cages above; only one remains. The wind's chorale enters the tower from the Barrow. It disturbs the ghost of each bell and carries their peal in silence across the Plain.

Chapter 2

We kept them away for so long. There was no reason – other than a war – for us to let them in.

Mama said that, even if there had been no evacuation, there would have been other wars, other threats that would have overtaken us. But in my mind we had a course mapped out, which, once lost, could not be caught again – only ghosted. The men and women we would have married, the children they would have given us: everything remains locked in some parallel womb of impossibility.

If it hadn't have been for the war, we would still be hidden in the Downs with Father, coaxing our living out of the land. Each meal – dark with the earth from which it had been drawn – would have been as hard-earned as before. And the water would have tasted all the richer for having half a mile's walk sweated into it.

The army could not comprehend why we wanted to stay. Winter floods and withering summers plagued the valley floor; Imber's water arrived in abundance or not at all. It was not uncommon for the Dock that ran through the village to dry up completely in the summer. Then, come wintertime, we would watch it bleed and swell into the floors and furnishings of the cottages bordering the stream. The land was of little use for anything other than sheep farming, a hard vocation at the best of times. The military watched the fluctuations in the weather; they saw how little the seasons yielded us; they watched from all four sides of Salisbury Plain. Then they crept in on us, preying on the precariousness of our harvests and buying up our farmers' land, piece by piece, plot by plot.

But even if the crops had died out or the water had dried up, we would have survived on other things: long draughts of air sprinting across the Plain, the sunlight snagging itself on each chalk milestone; the spasm of a newborn lamb in our hands. I think of this impossible valley so often that the light there has yellowed; the trees have grown fuller and the flowers have turned to glass. The more I paint it in my mind, the stiller everything becomes. But we were not so hidden, not so set apart, as to be forgotten by the war.

Aside from fetching gas for our lamps, we had very little cause to travel to town before war broke out. Seven miles from the next village, we were not in anybody's way; and Imber had preferred to be left to its own devices. It was a meek existence and one that we did not complain about. Even our parsonage, a sprawling yawn of a house that rivalled Imber Court for size, did not have its own water or electricity.

My father preferred it that way, he hated how the grandness of the house set us apart from our neighbours and caused them to treat our family with a deference that we neither deserved nor desired. When Imber Court offered him the use of their outside tap, he continued to send Freda and me to fetch water from the well so that we would not be seen to be distancing ourselves from the rest of the parish.

Mama stopped short of putting her head in her hands when on one occasion, while dining at Imber Court, he took issue with Major Whistler's complaint about the chalky taste in his tap water. Father was at pains to remind him that the rest of the village had to walk half a mile to quench their thirst. Mama laughed away his affront as best she could. Yet behind closed doors my father knew his place. He instructed us on a regular basis never to go and play in the grounds of the Court unless invited by the Major. My mother would add, with a wry smile in his direction, that if we were fortunate enough to receive an invitation, it would be thoroughly improper to mention their tap.

My sister loved nothing more than to go and play in Imber Court. She thought the Whistlers a rather superior breed, which she should emulate wherever possible. She mimicked their mannerisms and their tone of voice and even purchased a pair of clip-on earrings that she thought resembled Mrs Whistler's. When the other girls called her a copycat, she bought a different pair to distinguish herself – as if they wouldn't guess and smile archly behind her back. She hated having to go to school with the rest of us and begged Father for a governess, like Mrs Whistler had had when she was younger. She needn't have bothered asking: Freda would not have been given her way even if we had possessed the savings for such a thing. My father wanted us elbow to elbow in the local school with the rest of the village, where we belonged. It was hard on Freda – at fourteen, she had been the eldest of Imber's schoolchildren and the brightest, and Mrs Williams, the mistress, had quickly run out of ways to keep her occupied. She had treated her more like an assistant than a pupil. It had angered me to watch my sister turn from her own books to help the labourers' children with their writing. The little ones loved her for it but I saw only her pride at having been singled out. She used to tick them off terribly for not paying attention. It was no wonder their heads lolled with sleep in class when they had been up before the sun, tending sheep on the Downs. Freda thought all farmers lacked wit and sharpness and was not afraid to say so. She had not seen, as I had, the maturity with which an Imber boy could whistle orders to his dog and keep an entire flock in check. She was too busy copying Mrs Whistler's jewels.

I resented having to scrub my hands and face after school and put on my best dress to go to Imber Court, particularly when they asked us to play tennis. Mrs Whistler loved to see the old court being used by the children but I was bewildered as to why anyone would want to fill an entire afternoon by hitting a ball back and forth over a net. She seemed to have forgotten that, in the rest of the village, there were harvesting and rabbiting and shearing to be done. I sat at the side of the court for most of the matches and let Freda play with the Dean children from Seagram's Farm. She used to dance through her games, stretching out her long limbs and nursing the ball neatly over to the opposite side of the court; I was convinced Harry Dean let her win only because she was pretty. It became a ritual of mine to ignore the pop, pop of the ball on the grass and pick out underneath it the slow grind of a tractor somewhere on the Downs. The farm workers told me that tennis was an idle sport for people who had nothing better to do. I wanted to be out in the fields with them, in the midst of the seasons, ushering livestock through winter and spring and reaping the rewards of summer. I wanted to be with Father, not playing silly games with the Deans. He would be the first to roll up his shirtsleeves and lend his help in the lambing season to any farmer in need of it. I would beg to go with him in the hope of trying my hand at birthing lambs and loading the mangers in the barns with hay. Provided I wasn't engaged for an afternoon at the Court, he would always give in, despite protests from Mama. We would push a bottle of hot tea into one of Father's woollen socks and pass it around the labourers when we found them on the Downs.

He didn't treat me like a normal little girl. He knew I was different from Freda. When the military widened the road through the village and channelled the Imber Dock through stern, concrete pipes, Freda caught me red-handed, up to my knees in mud, trying to crawl from one end of a pipe to the other. I tried to explain that the schoolmistress's son had dared me to do it but Mama was furious when she found out. She said I had disgraced myself in front of the entire village. Father, however, ran a hand through my muddied hair and told me not to get caught next time.

He might not have cared about having his own well, but he was not averse to craving some of the superfluities that life in Imber did not afford: he longed for a telephone line. The dark arcs dissecting the skies of Salisbury and Warminster fascinated him; I often caught him running his eyes along them on our journeys into town, as if he were trying to listen in on the conversations sealed inside the wires.

Not even Imber Court had use of a telephone. When a line finally arrived, it was installed with Mrs Carter in the post office. It was to be a public telephone, which, much to my father's glee, we were all at liberty to use.

On its first day of operation, the queue for the telephone stretched all the way down the road to the smithy. My school friends Pete and Annie were sent across to Chitterne to receive calls from those of us who could not think of anyone beyond Imber to telephone. I remember nervously slotting in the pennies, waiting for the voice of the operator and pressing button A with a giggle, just as Mrs Carter had instructed me to do, as soon as I heard Pete's voice all small and compressed and ticklish in my ear. But when I think back to those first words whistling through the wires to places beyond the Plain, I can't help but feel that we entered into an irrevocable bargain: wired for ever to the outside world, we could never again know what it was to be fully alone.

I have begun to trace the roots of the evacuation back to that sprawl of unsightly wires. What if we had stayed separate? Kept ourselves to ourselves. Maybe then they would have left us alone, firing shells from one side of the valley to the other without even knowing we were there.

It would be different if Annie and Pete were around: they would anchor me, stop me keeping everything behind glass, in a snow globe, as if it can never be retrieved. But they're not here. Annie married a northerner, and Pete – it's enough to say he's gone too. They did not suffer the trouble that I had in moving away. I can still imagine their faces pressed into the black lacquer of the telephone receiver, Pete holding the earpiece, Annie trying to grab it from him, as they made their first call.

Annie, a small, pale sprig of a girl, was scared stiff of my sister. She was in awe of the dresses that she wore at weekends and would do anything she could to avoid being frowned upon by her at school. She found it difficult to keep up with the others; I would watch helplessly as Mrs Williams called her to the front of the class to solve sums and conjugate verbs: she would always flounder over the answers and I wished Mrs Williams would stop asking her in front of everyone. I'd try to mouth the answers to her. But Freda always caught her squinting in my direction, which only made it worse for Annie. She feared Freda's scorn more than she did the schoolmistress. Annie didn't have any sisters of her own; if she had, she would have realized that, by choosing to become my friend, she was placing herself directly in Freda's line of fire.

Nevertheless, we became inseparable. Everybody else thought her a foolish, bashful girl but I saw her spirit. Annie had a good heart and that, to me, was more important than arithmetic, spelling or a well-trimmed dress. With Annie by my side, I felt as if I could do anything. Imber gave us the confidence that we might have lacked in larger, grander climes. Only in Imber could a parson's daughter roll up her skirt and dig a hole, take a pair of shears to a sheep or play cricket. I hear stories, now, of girls who wept at the end of the war; they said the fighting bought them their freedom. But I was already free. I didn't need their explosions, their calculated invasions, the gradual erosion of what I had known.

Pete understood why I needed Imber. He knew I depended on it in a way that he never had to. I'd catch him looking at me knowingly when I tried to help with the thatching or stone walling. In any other place, I would have been made to stay inside, like a proper parson's daughter. It unsettled me – the way he seemed to want to try to work me out with his eyes. But he was too quick-witted to be made an enemy so I swallowed my inhibitions and made sure he was my friend.

Out of all the boys in Imber, Pete was the most practical – he fitted into other people's families like a key cut for a door; it didn't matter if it was lambing or ploughing or firing a gun, he picked it up quickly and became the best there was at it. It was the same with places: I took a long time to settle into Wilton after we left Imber but it was only a week before everyone knew Pete. He possessed an ease with the outdoors that showed itself in his shoulders and limbs, a strength that everybody knew he would carry with him into adulthood. I tried to ignore his good looks by joining in with the jobs he performed around the village, casting myself as an ally rather than standing back and asking to be admired, like the other girls. Annie was the worst: she played with her hair and pretended not to hear his questions, just so he would ask them again. He was not the kind of boy with whom I wanted to fall in love; every girl in the village had her eye on him – I hardly needed to add my admiration. But I couldn't help myself. I knew I saw something in him that the others failed to see: the way he raised his eyebrows in a questioning fashion every time somebody spoke to him. Or the manner in which he stood listening with one foot always slightly ahead of the other, as if he were about to bolt at any minute. He was always poised, never settled. He worked the land with vigour, as if striving for something.

I was never presumptuous about his opinion of me. Even when I happened to meet his eye, I was quick to stifle the thought that he had looked at me first. It was fanciful. I was making it up.

The only small indulgence that I allowed myself was his letters. Back in Imber, Annie and I would write a letter a week to Pete even though he lived only half a mile away down Dog Kennel Lane. Mrs Carter must have thought we were mad, spending all our pocket money on stamps and ink and envelopes that would travel just a few hundred yards up the road. It was Annie's idea to send him letters. At first, I convinced myself that I was intervening simply to save her from embarrassment. I would correct her spelling and ensure that she limited herself to the facts of the day: the weather, the lambing, the bus ride to Warminster. Eventually she persuaded me to write my name next to hers after 'Yours'.

'You might as well, Vi! They're your words, after all.'

If it was going to have my name on it and he was going to be reading it, it had to be perfect. The very idea of his eyes scanning the paper made my stomach swell and my head giddy. I gave in on the condition that we wrote the entire letter again.

'But we've just spent all afternoon writing the first one!' she exclaimed.

I took out a fresh sheet of paper and tried to quell a blush.

'You like him too, don't you?' She giggled. 'I don't blame you. You're the last girl in the village to give way.'

Pete showed no sign of having received the letters at first. But then, after we had written three or four, he began to write replies.

'The Parsonage?' Annie lamented, as she read the address on the front of his first envelope. 'But it was my idea to write to him.'

I kept quiet.

'Look,' she said, running a finger over his first line. 'Dear *Violet* and Annie. Why's your name first?'

'I'm certain he didn't mean anything by it,' I murmured.

'Yes, but your name's first and that means he *thought* of you first.'

'That's daft,' I told her, wishing it wasn't.

'It's your hair, Vi.' She sighed. 'You've always had the most beautiful golden hair.'

Annie was by far the prettier of the two of us, a fact that I kept to myself. I secretly envied her saucer eyes – greener and curvier than the pond at Steeple Langford. The pink in her cheeks rooted in just the right place whereas I tended to flush even on the coldest of days. She was elfish and mysterious-looking – the kind of girl whom shepherds and farmers stood back from, afraid to touch. My principal advantage was not my hair, which, contrary to Annie's belief, was never anything other than a half-hearted brown: it was my breasts, crude and huge. I hated them. And I despised the kind of stares they attracted, despite my efforts to cover them up. Boys, and even girls at times, struggled to look me in the eye, as if my face were buried somewhere in my chest. Annie was never jealous, not in a scheming way at least. She just talked about how unfair it was, pinning her chin down over her neck to see how hers were getting on.

Anyone would think the girl had grown up without a mirror. And the not-knowing made her all the prettier. In the beginning, before the letters, Pete liked her more than he did me. I'm sure of it. But she did such a good job of acting aloof around him that I was the one he thought he could have. I was sure that he mistook the letters for my idea, not hers, and that was why he had addressed them to me. It had been fickle of me to agree to write them in the first place. But the memory of my name at the top of his page kept returning. I tried in vain to swallow my curiosity. He didn't mean anything by it. Of course he didn't. It would be foolish to get carried away.

Words didn't come easily to Pete. Or perhaps he was deliberately sparse with what he said; I couldn't determine which. His letters were short and frequently borrowed sentences from other people. Sometimes he would find a poem to copy out for us in the library at Imber Court. The lines from Keats were my favourite. *Bright Star, would I were steadfast as thou art.* Annie and I would dissect his quotes, pulling each other's hair out over who was the bright star, basking in the myth that there was an art to the poems he chose. In truth, he was just as inclined to copy out a verse about a heroic battle as he was a stanza on a forlorn lover.

Besides, they never told me what I really wanted to know. What did he think about when he was up on Salisbury Plain for nights on end, watching the sheep? Did he think of me? Did he ever spare a thought for his mother and father?

He had appeared one day, at twelve years of age, with nothing in his pocket but a bus ticket bought in Hammersmith and the clothes on his back. He had offered himself as a labourer to any family who would give him food and lodging. Mr and Mrs Archam as good as adopted him. They had lost a son to pneumonia two years earlier and Pete was a gift – a welcome pair of extra hands and a face to fill the empty chair at their dinner table. Rumours of a new arrival spread quickly through the village and I wasted no time in running down Dog Kennel Lane with Annie to see if he was worth making friends with.

We found him alone in the Archams' farmyard, scuffing his shoes across patches of dried mud, hands in pockets, head crooked over his shoulders. He was scanning the ground for something, although I could not decipher what. Every now and then, he would bend down to pick up a stone and then throw it away again after a quick examination of its feel and shape. Finally, he stood up straight, eyes fixed on one particular piece of flint in his hand. Then he marked a circle in the mud around his feet, his arm arcing like a rudder through water.

'Maybe it's a game that children in London play,' whispered Annie, from our hiding place behind the cattle shed.

'Perhaps he's not from London . . . He could be a spy for all we know!'

'I say!' Annie shouted over to him, with no warning. 'Are you a German?'

'Sssh!' I hissed, pulling her further behind the shed. We watched as Pete flinched and glanced towards our hiding place. Looking around in vain for an escape route, we emerged sheepishly from our hiding place.

'I'm Violet,' I said, offering a hand.

'Pete,' he replied, not taking it. He clipped the t in his name so that it came off his tongue as hard and impenetrable as the stone in his palm.

'Where are you from?' asked Annie, folding her arms. 'Because nobody around here seems to know.'

I tugged at her pinafore. 'Come on, we'd best be back before dinner. Pete here will need to unpack his things.'

'Unpack?' he scoffed. I felt myself redden.

'Oh, of course,' bleated Annie, 'we heard you arrived without a scrap. But don't worry, Violet and I can find you a toothbrush and a blanket, if the Archams don't have anything for you. Isn't that right, Vi?'

I nodded, looking awkwardly at the space beyond his head. The feel of his eyes on me made me want to leave the yard.

'I'll make do,' he muttered.

'What's it like in London?' asked Annie, unabashed.

'Annie, let's go,' I pleaded, tugging at her sleeve, then turning away in the hope that she'd follow. Despite my best efforts, Annie stayed put, leaving me to flounder between the conversation and the yard gate.

'I bet there are crowds of men with umbrellas and canes.'

'Beats me. I'm not from London.'

'Then how come your clothes are all sooty?' she protested. 'You're not a farmer – farmers don't have that sort of dirt.'

'All right, Sherlock,' said Pete, with a smirk. 'If you must know, I'm from Bermuda.'

'Bermuuuda?' parroted Annie. 'Never heard of it.'

'No surprises there, then. You've probably never left this village.'

'Actually, there's a bus that goes to Warminster every week and Violet's father has even lived in *Oxfordshire*, hasn't he, Vi? He's the parson, you see.'

I seized my chance and retraced my steps back towards them. 'Come on, it's late, Annie. Leave him alone. Who cares where it is?'

'I'll bet you sixpence you haven't heard of Bermuda, Miss Violet.' The sound of my name caused my chest to tighten.

'Oh, don't be so sure of yourself!' blurted Annie, before I could squeeze her hand to stop her. 'Violet's ever so good at geography. Mrs Williams says she's the best. She's even better than Freda!'

'All right, then, let's hear it.' He discarded the flint he was holding and clapped his palms together.

'You aren't from Bermuda,' I said flatly.

'Looks like I'll be keeping my sixpence then.' He smiled. Annie looked crestfallen. I could tell she had been envisaging the jar of sherbet lemons on the grocer's shelf at the back of the Bell Inn.

'That's not to say I don't know where it is,' I added. Annie's eyes lit up. 'It's in the Atlantic. Father says they have the most awful storms there – whole towns have vanished overnight in the wind.'

Annie narrowed her eyes at Pete. 'Is it true?' I did not know whether she was referring to the storms or to Pete's dubious claim.

'If I were you, girls, I wouldn't indulge him any further,' said a voice from the entrance to the yard. I turned to see my sister in a tea-dress and wellington boots, leaning nonchalantly on the gatepost. 'You're late for dinner. Father sent me to fetch you. You as well, Annie – your mother will be wondering where you are.'

Annie scuttled over to my sister as if she were her mother.

Freda, you're such a show-off, I wanted to shout. My sister had a way of waltzing into situations and putting her stamp on them with seemingly no effort at all. I disliked her keenly for it. Even when we were older – and I had plenty of reasons to think her foolish – I never escaped the feeling that she had the better answers, and the better secrets.

I braved one last look at Pete. He was staring past me towards the gate to where my sister and Annie stood. The light left with the three of us, and as we made our way back down the track, I turned to find the yard empty: Pete had gone, leaving only his circle, which rested like an uncracked code in the dirt.

Already, I sensed that he wasn't one to be pinned down – not an easy lad to love. As soon as we were evacuated, he parted ways with the Archams and went to work as a farmhand in Coombe Down. Mr Archam never recovered. Annie told me the doctor's notes had stated that he had died of a broken heart. But stories like that always did have a way of swelling on her tongue. Whatever caused Mr Archam's passing, it would have been a lonely death without Pete by his side.

Chapter 3

Something cuffs itself to my wrists, hoisting me out of the water and giving me my air back. Rasps and rasps of it. I can't take it in properly – each breath a stammer. There's something sharp scraping across my belly. My shirt is rucking up. I'm being dragged out of the sea.

'Help' is my first word, frail, half formed. I don't understand the reply I'm given. Tamil or Malayalam, maybe. It's a man's voice. There's a rough, rusting surface beneath me that feels powdery and metallic on my fingers. It fits unevenly under my shoulders, the metal arching into sharp peaks and troughs. But we're floating. And that's all that counts.

The voice is shouting now but I still don't understand. The saltwater dissipates in stinging blinks; I begin to make out the man's shape. He's soaked to the skin, like me, in a checked *lungi* and plain shirt, hair wired with grey. His face, creased with years, is washed into blankness at the sight of me and everything that's gone before us.

'*Vana-kkam,*' I reply. One of the few words I know in Tamil. *Good morning.* I must sound ridiculous. He's smiling. At least that's something.

'*Ongelal payse . . .*' I don't catch the rest. And even if I did it would be useless.

'I don't understand. I'm so sorry.'

He tips his head from left to right and back again. Then his hands rise and leap into action, eyes widening as he gestures towards the shore. He mimics the wave coming in as he speaks, then knocks the metal underneath him with his knuckles, drawing out the shape of a square in the air with his two index fingers. He points to his chest and bangs the metal again, rattling out his sentences at such speed that I'm sure I wouldn't catch everything even if we did speak the same language.

'Your house? This is your house?' I watch him draw the shape in the air again and point down at the sheet of metal.

'House!' He nods, rapping on the metal for a third time. I force myself to sit up and look down at our makeshift raft. It is nothing more than a sheet of corrugated iron – a roof. Something catches his eye and he grabs me by the wrist, like he did when he rescued me. He points to my ring, then down at the house and then back at the shore, face stiffening.

I catch only one word from what he is saying: *Manaavi*. James and I learnt it yesterday – our wedding day. He said he preferred the sound of it to 'wife'. I meet his stare, which is taut, unblinking. Raising my hand, I point to my ring and then to the shore, just as he did. *'Kanavar,'* I whisper, 'my husband.'

I talk in English, telling him about James and our wedding – how not even my parents know what we have done. How I don't know where he is – that I need to go and look for him. He speaks Tamil back to me, accompanying his words with broad, bold hand movements, which I watch, eager to interpret what he is saying. I try to discern the verbs and nouns from his tones, holding each sound in my head and attempting to dissect it. In the end, I have to let his sentences go – they don't yield their logic easily and the words blur together. He turns away from me after a while, frustrated at not being understood. We resume our gaze at the sea.

We try to paddle our way back to the shore but the beach soon slips beneath the horizon. I think of James, adrift maybe, like me, waiting on the mercy of the tides. It's no use. We cannot resist their pull. We can only lie with our arms dipping like nibs into the water and go wherever the currents decide.

Minutes pass like hours, hours like minutes. Time dries in our throats. Flotillas of drinking water appear on the horizon if

I stare at it for too long. The sun becomes what I want it to be – a giant parasol cocooning me like night – instead of what it is: unbearably bright and scorching. And all the while we're floating, riding the roof as if it were the saddle of a horse, never still.

Night comes. And then day. Time gathers. And gathers again. Waves bloat and expire.

The heat invades the gap between my waking and sleeping. I'm afraid that, if I don't find a way of waking myself, my mind will drift off with my body to a place with no anchor – no hard, still point on which to tie thoughts; only thirst.

In a last-ditch attempt to keep myself awake, I press my hands together in a sideways prayer and extend them towards my companion. I motion for him to copy me so that our middle fingers are just touching. He frowns and I go in for the slap, clapping my palm onto the back of his outstretched hand and letting the sound ring out across the water. A clean slice through the ears. Finally I am awake.

He whips his fingers away and cradles them against his chest crossly. *'Yenna seyringa? Athu vallithidhu!'*

I smile and hold out my hands again in the same position. He shakes his head and pushes air towards me to dismiss me. But I keep my hands where they are and wait.

'Come on,' I rasp – throat dry from the saltwater. 'It'll take our minds off it.'

After a few minutes, he mutters something and presents his hands to me again. Before I can ready myself, he has launched into a swipe that sends a sting up my arm. 'See!' I laugh, with a flinch.

He smiles and tilts his head from side to side. Then he points to his chest. 'Ravindra. Ra-vin-dra,' he repeats, separating the syllables for me.

'Alice,' I reply, offering a hand. He doesn't take it and instead presses his palms together under his chin.

'Aleece,' he echoes, trying out the word on his tongue.

I speak his own name, attempting to roll the second *r* as he did but not quite pulling it off.

He settles down again on the roof. It is not long before the silence returns. The heat has baked my clothes dry. James's shirt, which I pulled from under his pillow and threw over myself before I left the hotel room, is stiff with a thick skin of silt. I try to think of where he might be – if he made it to higher ground.

Did he even see it coming? Or did he just carry on in the heat with his back turned, oblivious to the water twisting into a fist behind him? The day had lulled us both with its blue sky and lush greens; we hadn't thought it might collapse. We should have guessed our time might be gone before we had the chance to measure its weight.

It seemed so beautiful – the notion of us driving for thousands of miles over Persian ruins and Kashmiri meadows. I fell in love with the trip before I fell in love with him. The idea of it. And those startling eyes of his, which seemed already to have a bazaar of stories hidden in them before we even set foot in Istanbul. I knew it would infuriate Mum. His hair. His lack of ambition.

We pooled our savings – from the sale of his photographs and the money that I had collected from waitressing at Isabel's – and bought a second-hand Mercedes 319D. He knew the van would only get us as far as Pakistan, Kashmir at a stretch. But he said that if we billed the ride as 'Istanbul to Delhi', we would soon find paying passengers. And he was right: every seat was taken within a day of us arriving in Turkey. The cities along the route were barely even names to me. I had no pictures to go by. Only stories from the long-haired campers that I had met on the Isle of Wight: how Ararat humbled you and Gulmarg made you free.

We could live hand to mouth, they said, and eschew the routines that shackled us at home – forget the mothers and fathers and the pasts that were not ours to bear. James said life didn't have to be linear – a constant accrual of wealth and age. We could care only for the shoes on our feet and the shifting patch of earth that was our bed. I thought of Joni and the promise in her guitar. We'd wear the day until the night came, enjoy the sun-show while it lasted.

I didn't understand – then – what the wave would bring. That the cold horror of an irrational ocean would erase every mile of carelessness we had etched between Turkey, Persepolis, Lahore and Delhi. That it would throw into doubt the solidity of the future – and sear instead its uncertainty on our thoughts.

I'd always thought of journeys as choices – between staying and leaving, between one direction and another. But here, boats have been thrown violently off course, fishermen dragged by unstoppable currents; and letters have been delivered deep into reefs where there is not a soul alive to read them. I'd thought James, like our journey, was a matter of choice: someone I could fall in and out of love with as I pleased. A person I could marry one day, without a thought for the next. But now it has nothing to do with me: our togetherness – or our separation – is in the hands of the sea.

After we met at the festival, James did everything for me – he found me the job at Isabel's, moved my things from Mum's house to London and fixed me up with a place of my own near Mornington Crescent, just a handful of roads away from his. We did not act tentatively – as new acquaintances ought to have done.

James was accustomed to the city – the way it invaded you with its ebb and flow of clocks and habits. He was not shocked, as I was, by the siege of wet weather, the paper chain of identical days. Nothing to him was ever permanent; soon enough he would find a way to move on.

I got home from work early one day – I always left the café

before he left the studio – and began plotting the trip he had talked of on the Isle of Wight: something to sustain us. By the time I heard the doorbell, I had covered the kitchen table with the maps I had bought in Stanford's. I pulled back the latch to find Mum, not James, bedraggled on the doorstep in her old Dannimac jacket and wellingtons. *Nobody in London wears wellingtons*, I remember thinking.

'What are you doing here?'

'Alice, thank God you're all right.'

She embraced me but I stood still, arms folded. 'How did you get this address?'

'It doesn't matter. What matters is you're okay.'

'You shouldn't have come.'

'I couldn't just wait for you to come home . . .'

'I'm not coming home, you know that.' I paused, door half closed. 'And don't think I'm letting you in.'

'I don't expect – I just wanted to talk to you.'

'There's nothing to talk about.'

'Please, Alice, just one minute.'

I moved from the doorway with reluctance and she slipped hesitantly inside the flat. I could feel her eyes on the walls and furniture. I flicked the kettle on while she waited in the living room. It wouldn't be long before she saw the maps. There was no point in trying to move them.

'I rang,' she began, 'to tell you I was coming. The line wasn't working.'

'You didn't think I'd give you my actual number, did you?'

'Alice –'

'You're lucky you didn't get through. I would have made sure I was out, otherwise.' I caught her eye momentarily. She looked wounded – more so than I'd intended.

'What are these?' she asked, with *faux*-composure, pointing to the maps.

'Maps of Iran and Pakistan.'

'Quetta . . . I've never heard of such a place. Is that where he's taking you?'

'I'm not being *taken* anywhere.' I passed her a cup of tea, milky with two sugars, the way she likes it.

'You won't be able to fly, at least not until you get a proper job.' She pressed her lips together to stop herself saying more.

'Actually, we're going to drive. There's a route that will get us all the way to Delhi – through the places we've dreamt of seeing.'

'But –'

'We're thinking of turning it into a tourist operation. Regular trips – there's quite a demand for it, you know. Among our sort.'

'You're not serious –'

'Deadly.'

She put her tea down on the maps and looked at me with incredulity. 'But what about the café?'

'What about it?'

'They might make you permanent. That would be something at least.'

Permanent. An indeterminate number of hours spent brewing tea and wiping surfaces began to ink itself onto the map of Delhi that I had in my mind.

'Mum, I'm a French graduate. The café is hardly the be-all and end-all. I want to see things, like James.'

She picked up her tea from the map again, leaving Tehran imprisoned in a milky ring. 'But you've only known him a couple of months.'

'It's not important how long –'

'It's mad, Alice, that's what it is.'

'I've got James, I'll be fine.' I turned from her and spoke into the sink, pouring the rest of my tea away. Then I flicked the switch on the kettle again to make a cup for James. The sooner she was gone the better.

'He probably didn't mean it,' she began again.

'What?'

'He probably made promises . . . Some men are like that.'

'You don't know anything about him.'

'I know more about his type than you think.'

'Oh, here we go, back to Dad.'

'That's not –'

'Why can't you just accept that I'm happy?'

She paused, seemingly flummoxed by the question. I stood, breath held, waiting for another outburst. 'Please don't go away,' she whispered.

The water in the kettle reached its crescendo and I began to pour it over the teabag in the mug. 'I'm going, whatever you say, so you may as well be pleased for me.' The liquid slopped over the rim and spilt on the surface.

'Never mind,' she murmured, crossing the kitchen, picking up a cloth and pushing it over the mess.

'I can do it,' I snapped. Something seized me – her impertinence, my anger. So I turned and quit the room. I grabbed a jacket in the hall – not checking if it was hers or mine – and slammed the front door behind me. Outside the apartment, I took a right turn and walked briskly to Regent's Park. The gates were locked and I was left peering through the bars at the grass: sparse and wet. *She had no right.*

Back at my flat, James had arrived and chopped onions and garlic in my absence. He took me out dancing on Fridays but on Tuesdays we always ate together. Sometimes I cooked for him at his and sometimes he came here. I walked towards the kitchen. He was browning onions in a pan with the record-player on. One of the folk songs we had discovered on the Isle of Wight sifted through the living room when I re-entered: James was humming something about being a river, which made me smile in spite of my anger at Mum. I removed my jacket, noticing hers had vanished from the rack. It must be gone eight: what if there were no more trains bound for Wiltshire? I knew – in a way that she wasn't aware of – how much courage it would have taken her to come to London. On her own, not knowing if I would let her stay. I walked to the kitchen, looping my arms around James's waist from behind. He let go of his breath and took my hands. His touch still came as a surprise to me – as if I were learning of his feelings for the first time.

My skirt has dried in uneven pleats, mud trapped between each fold. Ravindra retrieved it from the water after he rescued me. When I came round, he covered his eyes and shouted Tamil at me until I had pulled it over my legs and made myself decent again. It is an old one belonging to Mum – borrowed once and never given back. I grabbed it from the suitcase without thinking before running from the wave. The coral-pink pattern is barely visible under the mud. I picture her wearing it, standing in the garden with laundry at her feet and an empty washing-line above her head, eyes lost in some arbitrary branch of the magnolia tree. The smallest of my mother's tasks were always accompanied by the longest of pauses – pauses that seemed to lengthen as she got older. I remember the photographs of her days helping with the silage in Imber. She wore boyish overalls and a big grin; her hands seemed dirty and busy; and she stood as if it were a struggle to keep still for the camera. By the time I was born, the busyness had left her. And my only role, it seemed, was to wake her from each pause and remind her I was there.

As well as my clothes, I have his hollow O on my fourth finger. I remove the ring and peer through it – a window into more sea and more sky. I still haven't grown used to its grip. I am always aware of it. Out here, with only the sea to hear me, I'm starting to wonder what it means – this circle. Out here, I can say freely that perhaps I married him for the push – to push us on to something new: a bright, uncharted territory that wasn't anything like the past.

If I make it back home, it'll be the first thing she notices. She'll grab my hand, see the gold and say I'm headstrong and foolish. That I kick my way through life. But it's not her place – she has no right – to tell me how to act.

Ravindra is sleeping. I reach under my shirt and feel for Mum's letter in my bra. There is nothing left of it. Somewhere inside the seasons of the wave, the ink is being washed from the paper. Each of its sentences is released eel-like into the water. *She is what I would have given you, had I been a better man.*

Chapter 4

We were the first family in the village to hear about the war – the only household other than Imber Court to own a wireless. Freda and I were peeling potatoes in the kitchen with Mama, having just returned from the morning service at the church. I tried to peel mine into one long strip so that it copied Freda's hair, which helter-skeltered down her face opposite me. Her hair was curly; mine was straight; we both wished we had been born with the reverse of what we had been given. I could hear Father pacing the floorboards of the neighbouring study, dissecting the sermon he had just preached.

'Throw me a potato to deal with, Freda. It will take my mind off it,' he called down the corridor towards the kitchen. Freda stood up and tried to throw one under-arm through the doorway towards him. It barely reached the threshold between the kitchen and the hall, nosing at the wall sluggishly.

'Freda, you throw like a girl!' I laughed. She sat back down at the kitchen table, thrusting her arms together in a fold across her chest, then immediately standing up again to tuck her skirt underneath her in case it creased. I took a potato from the tub in front of us and raised my arm.

'Don't you dare, Violet!' My mother turned from the sink. 'One is enough!'

I swung my hand into a cricket bowl as she spoke and watched the potato fly towards Father. It bounced at his feet and he caught it low off the ground.

'See! That's the way to do it.' I smirked at my sister.

'I don't know what you're so proud of, Vi. Mama told you not to.' Freda dropped another bare faced potato into the bucket as she spoke so that the water in it splashed me. Ignoring my indignation, she stared mournfully down at her hands. 'Mama, why can't we keep a cook? Look at the state of my fingers! People in town will think you've sent me to the workhouse.'

I rolled my eyes at my mother, who caught my meaning but refused to be drawn, instead walking across to the stove to stir the stock.

'I'm being serious, Mama!' Freda moaned. 'Why can't we have a cook?'

'Freda, that question has grown rather tired over the years, has it not? You know very well my answer.' Mama drew circles in the liquid with her spoon and, rather than turning to face Freda, directed her words into the pan. 'The living here is plenty,' she continued. 'It always has been. And your father couldn't possibly impinge any further on the diocese. Many of his colleagues at Wycliffe would consider themselves blessed to be in his position.'

'I heard Edward Bramley practically lives in a shed at Berwick!' I chipped in. Mama gave me one of her chiselled looks and I lifted up my hands in innocence.

'And so, Freda, no, we shall not keep a cook, or a parlourmaid for that matter.'

'Do you mean to say, Mama, that Freda will be peeling potatoes every Sunday for the *rest of her life*?' I brought my fist down on the table in mock outrage.

'Enough,' clipped my mother. She put down her spoon, rubbed her hands across her apron and glided down the corridor to the study. Father had propped himself up absent-mindedly against the doorframe and was studying his potato intently, as if its divots and moles were islands on a globe. 'Jack, you shouldn't encourage them to throw potatoes.'

He met her stare as she spoke and, once she was close enough to him, placed his two hands on her waist. I watched the muscles in her back relax through the white of her shirt. Even though she was facing away from us I could tell he had freed a smile from her. 'I stumbled over my point about St Peter walking on the water. I know I did. Did it make sense?' he asked her.

'It made perfect sense! What does it matter now, anyway? It's been and gone.'

'It matters to me.'

'Don't worry, my love, it came across well, didn't it, Vi-vi? Freda?' She turned back to the kitchen to look at us.

'It was brilliant, Father. Even the Major liked it!' I shouted through.

'It's quite a distraction to have him in the front pew,' he fretted to Mama. 'I know he needs to be there as much as the rest of us but – oh, I don't know, it is a trifle off-putting. I never felt that way with Tom Dean . . .' and on he went. My mother sauntered back to the kitchen as he spoke. She glanced at me and pretended to turn the wireless switch, showing me what I must do. So I meandered into the study and looped my arms around my father's shoulders.

'Can we listen to the wireless, Father? Please?'

He sighed and then, after a pause, gave me the answer I had hoped for.

'All right, then, darling, it'll probably take my mind off it.'

Mama, aware of her victory, returned to the stove and hummed contentedly to herself.

The usual fuzz sounded as I turned the dial. It took a good few minutes to settle on the right station. None of us expected to hear the Prime Minister's voice. *This morning, the British Ambassador in Berlin handed the German government a final note* . . . My mother came running in with Freda, who still held a potato – cold, like a lump of meat – in her hand. We all stooped to get closer to the speaker . . . *Consequently this country is at war with Germany*

Is. At. War. With. He had separated the words, each one boulder-heavy on the ears.

My father took hold of my mother's hand. *I know that you will all play your part with calmness and courage . . . You will report for duty in accordance with the instructions you will receive.* Freda held her breath and glanced across at Father. *Now, may God bless you all, and may He defend the right. For it is evil things that we shall be fighting against: brute force, bad faith, injustice . . .* They were grave words and, for a while, I believed they were only meant for far-away places – sprawling capitals like London, Paris and Berlin. Fighting *against* bad faith. I pictured St Peter stepping out onto the water to fight off his doubts.

Bad faith. Someone somewhere had started to sink.

I waited. And waited. But the war did not arrive – at least, not in the guise that I expected. Rationing tightened its grip on the village as the months went on. But, aside from our meals, it was easy to forget that anything had changed. Most of the village remained at home to farm the fields. The events in Europe seemed, at first, to be sealed inside the wireless, like a story we listened to at night.

Pete, who by now was some years settled in Imber, began smuggling all sorts of paraphernalia into the village – things a thousand coupons couldn't buy. Whisky, tobacco, bags of sugar the size of your belly. I don't know who he got it from and what he did with all the money – squirrelled it away somewhere, I suspect. He showed no sign of being any better off than the rest of us. Yet he must have been – the amount people would pay for sugar. He wasn't best liked by Mrs Tippets at the grocer's. Ever keen to play her part in the war effort, she dealt strictly with our coupons, measuring our supplies to within a hair's breadth of the nearest ounce. When Pete began undercutting her prices and handing out whole bags of sugar to whoever coughed up enough coins, Mrs Tippets's trade dwindled and, the only grocer in the village, she grew suspicious. He was banned from the shop and it was only her deep-seated loyalty to the rest of the village that prevented her calling in the warden. Pete was looked after, though. Imber's wives hated the thought of a farm boy going unfed: it wasn't long before he had enough dinner invitations to last him a month. Even the most patriotic among us were wise enough to know a good thing when we saw it. When Mrs Tippets's back was turned, respectable farmers would ply Pete with meat and milk eked from their coupons, knowing he would reward them with whisky when he next got his hands on a barrel.

'What's a boy like you getting involved in things like this for?' my mother would ask, when he turned up at her door with sugar. She would glare at me as if it were my idea.

'Hold your hand out, Mrs Fielding,' he'd say, and, rolling her eyes, she'd oblige. Then he'd hoist up the sack and pour a pool of crystals into her palm. 'If you're not at ease with buying some, then at least have a taste.'

She'd lick her finger, dip it into the heap on her palm and a patch of sugar would stick to it. Then she'd lift her finger to her mouth, shutting her eyes to savour the taste. 'You'll be the death of me,' she'd mutter, rummaging in her skirt pocket for a few coins. And I'd be there breathing a sigh of relief behind her. She could easily have reported Pete to the warden or, worse still, refused the sugar. Annie and Pete would have been going on about cake and biscuits for weeks while Freda and I made do with bread pudding.

I went with him once, all the way to West Lavington to smuggle supplies sent from Devizes. I shouldn't have gone but I wanted to know how he did it. We met at two o'clock in the morning. The sky was low and thick – no stars. It was so dark that even the lumps of chalk lining the path appeared blackened in the night. I could not trace the noises I heard – a disturbed bird, perhaps, or the blur of the wind through a copse. If it were not for the scuff of the track under my feet, I could have been forgiven for fearing that we had cut ourselves adrift from the land and were stranded on a barren stretch of anonymous sea. How Pete worked out which direction to take, I will never know.

Once we had found the edge of Salisbury Plain, we climbed a hill – I could not say which one – and wove our way through a wood that backed onto a snatch of cottages. Pete picked his route with ease, his feet pressing noiselessly on the foliage beneath us. I, on the other hand, made quite a racket, snagging my skirt on the bushes and rifling through the undergrowth. But he was patient, waiting for me to reach him, then shepherding me through to the other side. I felt his hand on my back, as we emerged from the trees, lingering slightly longer than required.

In the churchyard, he retrieved a sack from behind the grave of a Mr Alfred Stash.

I started to giggle. 'It's a little bit . . .'

'What?'

'Margery Allingham.'

'Who?'

'You know, Albert Campion, *Death of a Ghost* . . .'

He let out an impatient sigh.

'Oh, you know what I mean! Hiding your loot behind the grave of a man named Stash. It's . . . well, it's obvious!'

'What do I care what the poor fellow was called? I just come to where I'm told to come.' He lifted the sack onto his shoulder as he spoke. 'Anyway, keep quiet, won't you? You'll get us caught!'

He set off into the thicket and I followed. At the other end of the wood, a half-moon emerged from behind the clouds. It lit Pete's back with a watery light and set it against the expanse of the Plain – 'second-hand sunshine', my father used to call it. The Downs now decorated the horizon with dense silhouettes, making it easier to find our way home. I watched Pete cradle the sack across the fields as if it were a sickly lamb that needed taking to the barn for warming. Then I picked up my pace to close the gap between us, all the while wondering what was inside the sack.

Pete wasn't the only one going behind the wardens' backs when it came to rationing. Word spread through Imber that the Sheltons, who leased the land up the side of Long Barrow, were planning to slaughter an extra pig.

To this day, I do not know who called the warden. Everybody agreed that the Sheltons' idea was unpatriotic, but we weren't about to take the side of some toffee-nosed official sent by the military to check on us. Besides, the Sheltons had six little mouths to feed and a seventh on the way. They needed all the food they could get.

When the warden stopped at the parsonage to ask for directions to the Sheltons', I ran ahead to the farm to alert them. I took the back route, looping through the ash trees at the end of our garden and sprinting down the gully that ran immediately parallel to the church. In the summer the smell of hay starched itself into the air here; it seemed to reach right up into the attic of your head when you inhaled it, forcing you to remember it long after the season had gone. I had turned up my nose at it when I was younger. But after the evacuation, I used to walk all the way up to the farms at Compton Chamberlayne just to fill my lungs with its dryness.

'Mrs Shelton!' I exclaimed, arriving breathless at her garden gate. 'Forgive the intrusion. I thought I should let you know that the warden is on his way. You have about ten minutes to hide the pig.'

'Pig? Goodness, my girl, what makes you think we're keeping back a pig?' She smiled at me in a way that told me the rumours had in fact been true. To my amazement, she remained kneeling before her vegetables, as if I had interrupted a prayer she wished to finish. There was no frantic rush. She simply angled her trowel back into the ground and unearthed another leek. Soon enough, the warden arrived at the gate, eyeing me suspiciously.

'Aren't you Jack Fielding's girl?' he asked.

'Yes.'

'I spoke with your father earlier.' He narrowed his eyes.

'Violet wanted a leek for some soup, didn't you, Violet?' Mrs Shelton held out the soil-coated vegetable towards me, as if passing on the baton in a relay.

'Yes . . . Mama's got the chills. Nothing a bit of warm broth can't cure.' I took the leek from her with both hands and she turned her eyes back to the ground.

'Mrs Shelton, if you please, I have come to check the farmhouse,' began the warden.

'Whatever for, sir?' she asked, not looking up from her trowel.

'I have been informed that your family may have become embroiled in some clandestine activity.'

'Clandestine,' she murmured. 'I can't think where you might have heard such a thing.'

'We have eyes and ears in all sorts of places, Mrs Shelton. Eyes and ears.' He placed his hands behind his back and peered towards the front door of the farmhouse. 'Is Mr Shelton at home, I wonder? I hope it won't be necessary to obtain a warrant.'

'My husband is working in the fields. And, sir, there is certainly no need for a warrant. We are all friends here. I will show you around myself.'

'Thank you,' he replied, straightening his back.

She rose from the vegetable patch in one single motion and wiped her blackened hands on her apron. The warden followed her inside the house while I sneaked round to the back to spy on them through the dining-room window. I could just make out three of the six Shelton children gawping through the oak banisters in the hallway, faces dirty from an afternoon's work. The warden checked everywhere for the pig – he even rolled back the dining-room rug in search of a trap-door. Once he had finished with the house, he conducted a methodical search of the barns, only to return to the front garden empty-handed.

'Thank you for your time,' he muttered to Mrs Shelton at the gate, clearly unconvinced of her innocence. I stood with my back against the side of the house, fingers clawing at the bricks, watching.

'And thank you for yours, sir. You were more than thorough.' She unleashed a smile – similar to the one she had given me earlier.

The warden frowned and started towards the house, before concluding that there was no point in searching again. 'I'll be off, then,' he said curtly, tipping his hat in her direction as he made his way down the farm track to go back to the village.

Once he was out of sight, I came out of my hiding place, accidentally kicking over an empty pail on my way. Mrs Shelton turned towards me calmly, as if she had been aware of my presence all along.

'I suppose you want to know where it is,' she addressed me.

I nodded back at her eagerly, not quite believing that she might let me in on the secret.

'You mustn't tell anyone, do you hear?'

I shook my head. 'I won't breathe a word, Mrs Shelton, I promise.'

'Not even your father. He's a good man. But he can't know.'

'What about Pete?' I asked tentatively.

'The Archams' lad?'

'Yes.'

'That boy knows everything that goes on in this place as it is.' She smiled. 'He's Imber's spy.'

She led me through the hall and into the dining room where she proceeded to heave a large wooden dresser back on its haunches, causing it to take one cumbersome step across the floorboards. I smelt the meat before I saw it, running a finger over the seamless wall, confused. As I reached the centre of the space behind the dresser, the consistency of the wall changed from solid to soft, as if there were nothing behind the wallpaper but air. I breathed in.

'Give the paper a push,' said Mrs Shelton. 'We might as well break in. I promised the children a pork dinner. It was the only way to keep them quiet.'

She nodded towards the wallpaper, which was covered with thin navy blue stripes. I placed a palm on the wall again, feeling my way into the space where the paper became flimsy. Pushing harder, I made a puncture, then tore off the sheet cleanly in a strip. There was a cupboard-like alcove behind it and I could just make out the head of the pig, buried deep in a salt trough. The pork smelt almost foreign to me, I had gone without meat for so long.

'Ingenious!' I whispered.

'Join us for dinner next week and you can taste some yourself.' She smiled and placed a hand on the small of my back to guide me, like a sailboat, to the front door. I was already imagining a chop between my teeth and thanking her for it.

'You'd best be off. Or else folk will start wondering. And we wouldn't want that.'

'Are you sure about dinner?' I asked her.

'Certainly.' She smiled. 'Saturday next.'

I pushed the gate open and began the walk home.

'Violet!' she called after me. 'Why not invite the Archams' lad along?'

I stood still on the road. Did people think there was something between Pete and me? The idea bloomed. I loved speaking for him, receiving an invitation on his behalf.

It was a long run from the Sheltons' farm to Dog Kennel Lane, taking me through the entire length of the village. I passed along the ribbon of cottages to the north end of the valley and climbed the gradient of the lane, the houses vanishing one by one into the valley's bowl. The land on the surrounding hills was sparse and treeless; it did not try to compete with the sky. Here, the sky took prominence: it bullied the Plain with bulbous clouds and deep, heady blues, eschewing the neatness of the fields below with its boundlessness. I had become fixated by its depth – how, even on overcast days, it seemed colossal, unthinkable, a limitless expanse of blankness.

I arrived at the Archams' farm to find that Pete was still out on the Plain with the sheep. So I sat on the yard wall, scouring Rough Down for a sign of his flock. To sit like this was a luxury. The children from the farms hardly ever had a chance to enjoy the Plain for its own sake. And I felt I always had to find a practical reason to roam it so as not to appear as if I had too much time on my hands. Father didn't like me wandering around for the sake of it. He said it singled us out. Yet here I was, absorbing the whole scene as if it were a picture on a wall. Around Imber, there was no flat idleness – the Plain made us earn our presence in the fields. Unless you were from Imber Court, you had to be walking or working or else not there at all. Nothing was ever still up here, not on the surface; the air was always on the move, sifting through the grass in whispers before carrying on its way. Sitting on the wall, I felt like one of the Whistlers, surveying the view simply for its beauty, walking the hills for no reason other than my own leisure. I'd often hear them readying their cart from inside the school house, loading it up with blankets and hampers for a picnic. It was the one thing I was glad of after the evacuation: I was spared the thought of them eating strawberries in the long grass and knapweed while I was trapped indoors solving equations.

At last a dot appeared on the far side of Rough Down. It grew like a pool of ink, gaining detail gradually until I recognized it as Pete's flock. I ran up the hill to meet him, full to the brim with the news of Mrs Shelton's pig.

'Hello, Miss Violet!' Mr Archam shouted, when he was close enough to make out my figure. 'Lend us a hand, won't you?' This one's a little weary.' He passed me a lamb, which I took awkwardly, unfamiliar with the best way to hold it. 'Ah, she's no farmer's daughter, is she, Pete?' He chortled. 'Give her some grip, miss, or she'll bleat the houses down.'

I tried my best to cradle the animal, dropping behind Mr Archam in embarrassment when the lamb continued to flail in my arms.

'What brings you up Dog Kennel?' he asked.

'I wanted a word with Pete.'

'A word, eh? It'll be more than a word you'll give him, I'm sure of that.' He smiled. 'I'll be heading on now. That one you've got there is sickly.' He pointed to the lamb.

'Will she be all right?' I asked, passing the struggling animal to Mr Archam.

'Nothing that a cosy night by the hearth can't solve, Miss Violet. Don't you lose sleep over it.' He pulled the lamb close to his chest as he spoke and her legs became limp. She seemed calm all of a sudden; she knew her keeper. 'See you back at the house, Pete.' He tipped his cap at him and Pete nodded back. We watched him complete his journey to the bottom of the Down and turn into the farmyard. Mrs Archam would be happy to have a lamb by the fire for the evening: the flock was as precious to the pair of them as children.

'I discovered where the Sheltons were keeping their pig,' I told Pete, once Mr Archam was out of earshot. He kept quiet, eyes watching the flock. I caught myself craving his gaze – dark and unflinching – and tried to quell my disappointment when he didn't look up as I spoke. 'It was behind the dresser – they covered a hole in the wall with wallpaper, would you believe it?'

'You shouldn't tell me that, Vi. It's Mrs Shelton's business.'

'No, she showed me. And she said I could tell you.' I drew a breath. 'Actually, she invited both of us for a pork dinner on Saturday.'

Pete frowned. 'That's kind.'

A gust of wind caught my skirt and I rushed to pin it to my knees. 'I thought you'd be more pleased.'

'It's just that I'm busy.'

'But you will come, won't you?'

'No, Vi . . . I mean, it's difficult. I'm . . . Mr and Mrs Archam need me.'

As we reached the neck of the hill he busied himself with the flock so that they clung together more tightly. I tried to meet his eye but he would not look up from the field beneath his feet.

'It's all right,' I faltered. 'Annie will be just as pleased to come.'

At the crossroads, I turned in the opposite direction to the farmhouse, knowing he would not follow or call after me. Clouds blossomed and parted, and the light grew in intensity – the final swelling of the sun before dusk. The brightness – as sudden as a gasp – made me wish for shade but there were no trees for a mile, only the Downs. I felt exposed, as if the sky had witnessed everything. As soon as I had rounded the corner and was out of Pete's sight, I ran, red-faced, down into the valley.

The church was dark inside; I could sense the cool balm of the walls without touching them. All the light was shut out except for six shafts that fell in pillars across the nave. I settled myself in a side pew beneath the west window. The church was empty except for the dust that drew slow circles inside each line of light. In Imber, where every building had a dual purpose, where even houses doubled as barns for lambs, it felt rare to have a space so completely void of toil, movement and activity. And yet, somehow, I needed it, returning, as the other villagers did, to its quiet whenever I felt out of sorts. Only in the church could I still myself for long enough to feel as immutable as the vast expanse of the Plain outside.

From my place in the pew, I heard a shuffle in the base of the tower. I crossed to the back of the nave and found Father sorting a pile of bell ropes. He always punctuated his days with physical jobs like this one. Such was the pleasure he took in caring for the church that he refused to appoint a verger. It was only later, once we had left Imber and I came across other well-read men, that I realized how rare this was – to take as much trouble over fixing a bell as he would over writing a sermon.

'Hello, Violet.' My father did not need to look up from the ropes to know who had entered. He was familiar with my steps – my incapacity for stillness. 'Come and help me with these,' he gestured to the ropes, 'and tell me what's the bother.'

I crossed the floor of the tower and delved my hands into the pile, selecting a rope to untangle from the rest.

'Mrs Shelton offered Pete and me a pork dinner but Pete won't come with me,' I blurted, the problem shrinking even as I voiced it.

Father smiled to himself as he prised apart another knot. 'It takes a foolish boy to refuse a pork dinner in the midst of a war.' He laughed. Then he put down his completed rope and pulled me under his arm. 'Don't take it to heart, Vi. He'll be thinking of the lambs, that's all.'

Father knew exactly how to get me to let go of my worries – how to place them next to a simple task so that I could examine them from a distance and think, *There, it's only a matter of persisting until every knot is untangled, until every rope is smooth*. But I was not a girl who could let things rest. No matter how hard I tried to concentrate on the ropes, I returned to Pete's words again and again, knotting and unknotting them and not getting any nearer to the truth.

No sooner had I left Father in the church than I began to fret again. I went and found Annie, who was fetching kale from the bottom of her cottage garden.

'Something isn't right.' She frowned when I had told her everything – so much for keeping the pig a secret.

'I've ruined it, haven't I? Perhaps I was too keen.' I stood up from the wall where we were both sitting and paced up and down its length.

'Since when has your keenness stopped him?' she quipped.

'Oh, don't! I can't bear it! It's all right for you.'

'What do you mean?'

'You're the one he really likes, silly.'

She looked at me vacantly.

'Never mind.' I sighed.

'Maybe Mr Archam really does need him.'

'Do you think . . . ?'

'Your father's right. You know how it is with the lambing. Mr Archam will want an extra pair of hands at the ready.' We stayed silent for a moment, testing Annie's theory in the quiet between us.

'No, it's no use,' I began. 'You know how the Archams are. They're too afraid to make demands on him. And he's not the kind of boy to ever feel obliged, is he?'

'Apparently not,' said Annie, with a wry grin. She paused. Her expression softened. 'Vi . . . I don't quite know how to say it – and I really don't know whether it answers anything – but . . . there's another dance on at the military camp tomorrow night. An ATS girl told me about it.'

'What do you mean?'

'Well, do you think Pete might be going?'

'We both know he hates dancing,' I scoffed, with slightly too much fervour. I could feel myself whitening.

'That's what I thought.' Annie waved her suggestion away.

'You don't think he's taking someone, do you? I mean . . . a girl?'

She met my stare and I held hers. There was no need for a reply.

Chapter 5

Father enlisted on the day after I found Mrs Shelton's pig: it was 1942, the year before we were evacuated. His age and profession were enough to excuse him. But he felt duty-bound. As I listened to him discuss the matter with Mama, I found myself returning to our conversation in the bell tower: I had been so frivolous to worry over a pork dinner and a boy when, unbeknown to me, Father was contending with the prospect of war. *It's only a matter of persisting until every knot is untangled, until every rope is smooth.*

'It's *their* labour and *their* crops that are feeding us right now,' he protested to my mother, as they passed Mr Colton in his field on the way back from the church. He had a special solemn voice that he put on for this kind of comment, like the ones we heard on the radio whenever anyone discussed the war. 'And what am I doing that's useful?'

Freda and I listened in as best we could from behind.

'But they need you,' my mother countered. 'You're feeding them different things.'

'What good are my sermons at a time like this if I'm not out there pulling my weight? I'm a hypocrite, that's what I am.' He stopped in the middle of the path and turned to face her. At first, I tried out a smirk on Freda – he had talked in this manner on so many previous occasions and nothing had ever come of it – but she did not return it.

'What about us?' Mama waved towards Freda and me.

'I'll be going to protect you – protect what we have here.'

'They'll take you as a chaplain, Jack. You know that. How much help can you really be when they won't permit you to fire a gun?'

'It's my being there that counts.'

'You're not going anywhere. There's no need.'

Need or no need, he made himself known to the War Office and received his call-up within the week. The war had come to him so he might as well go to it. By then the army had arrived in the village – a scattering of Tommies occupied a deserted labourer's cottage, and three evacuees were sent to the Court to live with the Major and his wife. When I was certain the Major was out on his rounds, I would peer over the wall at the back of the house to look at the disused tennis lawn where Freda and I had wiled away so many hours. The net sank in the middle, sullen under a coat of ivy, and a troop of dandelions marched across the baseline. Nobody had time for tennis any more. It was the start of an unseen invasion, which crept so silently over the house and village and church that we barely noticed its presence until the war was in full bloom.

The military training on Salisbury Plain became more regular, and the explosions felt closer too, as if they were being detonated in the soil beneath us. Mama ran out to check the vegetables one night so convinced was she that a shell had landed in the garden. I joined her in my nightgown and we watched the sky stutter, like a frantic camera, between coal black and bleached white. The Downs were taut with mortars, each as prone to echoes as the skin of a drum.

Soon after the arrival of the evacuees, the real incendiaries started to fall. Before the war, we could come and go as we pleased, puffing up the chalk on the tracks at any time of day or night, even burning candles in the windows to guide the farmers home. But by the time Father decided to enlist, our shepherds were forced to navigate the fields unaided and nobody was to drive with headlights at night. The Plain became bathed in an unbroken darkness – and we feared that more than we feared the bombs. Mr Batch's lad Fred was the first to be lost; it was a death marked by its silence. The snow came down thick and fast in November, blanketing the entire Plain in the space of an evening. He had stayed up with the sheep to make sure none were lost but, with no light to help him, he could not find his way back to the village. The snow on Salisbury Plain had a way of cloaking the air in front of you so that north, south, east and west were obliterated; the only mercy it afforded you on nights like that was a glimpse of the space directly in front of your feet. Poor Fred must have found that no sooner had he laid a footprint in the snow than it was deleted. They discovered him two days later in a ditch, half a mile away from the door of his home.

It was hard to know which was preferable in those days – snow and fog masking the village, making farming impossible, or a night free of clouds in which we became a sitting target for the Gerries. When we heard German engines across the sky, we could do nothing but stow ourselves in the cellar and pray that there were no lights left on upstairs.

I hold myself responsible for the first raid. I was worried about Father, who had been kept out late visiting a colleague in Chitterne, so I left a single candle burning in the upstairs window to help bring him home across the tracks. I lit it out of habit without a thought for the blackout. Imber was distant from any town and folded away in a valley – the bombers wouldn't give it a second look. But I forgot about the light, leaving it burning long after Father arrived home. I was in my room when I heard the mechanical cackle of an approaching aeroplane. My mother came running upstairs with him to fetch me while Freda fumbled with the trap-door down to the cellar. There was no explosion, just a *bludge*-like thud on the parsonage roof.

'Don't move,' Father cautioned us. 'It's a delayed-release bomb. The Canadians at the camp warned me about them. It won't detonate until it's disturbed.'

'We must send word, give the others a warning!' cried Mama.

'We can't. It could be on the roof but it may have fallen onto the lawn. And I can't risk lighting a lantern to look. We must wait until morning.'

'We can't just sit here!' Freda protested. But Father told her we didn't have much choice.

When, finally, the night came to an end, he climbed the cellar steps gingerly and inspected the garden. The bomb was nowhere to be found. The thought of it nestling among the roof tiles, digging its heels in ready for the explosion, made my stomach curl. He sent for two soldiers from the army camp and they climbed up a ladder to disarm it. Just as they were about to make it safe, the bomb dislodged and rolled down the roof with a rumble reminiscent of the tanks on the Plain. We watched it drop – all of us – knowing that we had no time to run.

As it landed on the metal of the wheelbarrow it let out the murkiest of notes, like the mangled clank of a broken bell. There was no explosion, only an echo. I shut my eyes, expecting to be consumed by flying matter.

We waited, muscles clenched, but the bang never came. I thought of the Coronation party at Imber Court – how we had all stood around the bonfire and sung 'God Save The King' for George VI and watched, blithely, as a barrel of tar dislodged from the top and rolled – poker hot and flaming – into the crowd. As quick as a flash, Albie Nash grabbed a rug from a nearby table and threw it over the barrel. Then we all laughed, fear dissipating as quickly as the barrel's flames.

Perhaps if that first bomb had gone off, we would have grasped sooner what it was that was enveloping us. But the war remained in its cask – a threat but never quite an explosion. We found ourselves being eased into each new peril as if it were no more daunting than that single drum of flaming tar: a small, conquerable danger that simply required smothering.

Chapter 6

We are alone with our own thirst. The sight of the sea soon becomes too much: void of rescue and empty of anything drinkable. Everything is easier with your eyes shut.

We lie, like two wings of a butterfly, on top of his roof. I shake him once, to check he's still conscious, and he bats me away as he would a fly. The lines on his face seem as deep as the trough of our wave. They press together, then pull apart again as he breathes, and I think of the folds in an accordion. In my head I give him three children: two boys and a girl – the youngest. His house, before the wave hit, had ice-blue walls, a vegetable patch at the back, maybe, and a view of the ocean. Perhaps, if we survive, he'll move up the hill to a place where he can't see it, where he's high enough up to be out of its reach.

And there was no more sea. That's what it says at the end of the Bible when Heaven comes down from the sky as a city. When my grandmother died, Mum read it to me: I think she thought I'd like to know where Nana had gone. I was disappointed, though, to find out there was no sea in Heaven. To me, it smelt of Saturdays and Sundays and water so cold that it made me shriek with glee.

But now I see. Useless liquid is all it is. Liquid you can't even drink. A surface that's too changeable to inhabit, too fluid to be called home. A substance that can muscle into everything you build – wipe it out as if it were nothing more than chalk on a blackboard.

My grandmother wasn't like Mum; Mum kept her sadness buried in her face. But Nana told me things – things Mum only spoke about with her eyes. She would have liked James. James never ran out of things to say, stories to tell, questions to ask. Imber, the war, all the things that Mum had seen, I heard about them only from Nana. She'd talk and talk, stringing together whole generations, like lines of laundry. Endless lists of who married whom and who had which children. As soon as Nana began one of her stories, Mum's face would brighten, like a child's. It didn't matter how many times she had heard it, she'd hang on every detail as if it were new. But life for Mum stopped at Imber; she didn't listen to me like she did to Nana. She wasn't bothered about whom I would marry or what children I'd have. My stories – the ones from school or the park – would be greeted with a diluted smile, so weak it might almost have been a frown. The children she might have had in Imber – warless, naïve and grown from home – are what matter to her. They would have been as rooted and constant as trees: working the land, reading the weather, borrowing books from that grand old house and belonging to a man she really loved. A place she really loved.

Had I never known you, such selflessness would have left me aghast. Whatever my dad meant by his letter to her, he was foolish to think my mother selfless. If the war hadn't destroyed Imber, it would have crumbled under her love, so tight was her grip on it. And while she set about trying to preserve its memory, she lost sight of me – I, who was already adrift.

Ravindra sits bolt upright and shouts something – one word, over and over, flinching round to look over his shoulder. The roof groans under the shift in his weight. He's out of breath, sweating.

'It's okay,' I say. 'It's over.'

He looks at me, the tension in his face softening into sadness, as if he has suddenly remembered where we are. Then he lies down again on his stomach, his hands flat on the roof, wanting to be as close as possible to his home.

Most people think of a place when they think of home. But I think of the word – strewn all over the kitchen on cutesy little

57

knick-knacks. They sit on the fridge, hang on door handles and drape themselves over the window, spelling themselves out in sickly shades of pink. The first and only time Mum met James, I told him to buy her one as a joke. She made such a show of loving it, putting it in pride of place in the window above the sink, fearing all the while that he'd take me away to places she'd never been.

My step-dad tore one down once – a small cushion on a string with 'Home is where the heart is' embroidered on it. He threw it onto the floor beneath the sink where it bounced harmlessly on the lino and cosied up to his feet. He thought I hadn't seen him do it.

James was always too kind about my mother. He felt sorry for her, I suppose. Before we left for Istanbul, he drew up an itinerary for her, with the dates on which we were expecting to arrive in each town. Istanbul in early April, Tabriz two weeks later, Tehran the next day, Lahore at the beginning of May, Delhi in June, then again in August. I was furious with him when I found out.

'It's nothing, Alice. I can't see how it will do any harm.'

'I don't want her to know where I am.'

'It's not as if she's going to follow you out to Iran.' He laughed.

'I know. But it'll nag me – the fact she knows where I'm going and where I've been.'

'It's just for her peace of mind. You're her only daughter.'

'Yeah,' I scoffed. 'And don't I know it.'

I wish I could sleep like Ravindra. But there's so much sun and nothing solid to hide behind. It makes you crave darkness, dampness, a basement room with a floor and walls. I close my eyes and imagine our patch of the ocean evaporating, drop by drop, so that we are lowered into a vault of glassy columns and laid to rest on the seabed. The roof softens into a mattress and James is next to me. We're back to back, as we always are, curled away from each other like an x in algebra. Sleep comes just as the sea caves in on us. I fumble around frantically for him, knowing that, if we'd broken a habit, if we'd slept nose to nose, I could have caught a final glimpse of his face.

He gets angry when I don't look at him properly. But he's older. And, unlike me, he can hold a stare. I hoped my awkwardness would dissipate after I left school; Mum said that when I was older I would find it easy to talk to all sorts of people. But, to my dismay, it persisted through my adolescence and into my university years. Even after all our months together, I prefer the ground or the sky to the sight of James returning my gaze.

'What are you drawing?' he asked, when we first met. I was sketching the sea of tents that stretched over the fields ahead of us.

I turned the pad over. 'Nothing.'

He sat down on the starched grass next to me and I was aware, suddenly, of his skin and eyes and mess of hair – aware of them without even looking.

'I've seen your pictures – I've watched you work on them around the place.' I thought of the drawings, hidden in my tent, of ruined abbeys and palaces with their hollowed windows and ivy-riddled stone. I felt exposed: he had glimpsed something he shouldn't have.

'I'm sorry, I don't know your name,' I ventured.

Ignoring my question, he reached for the piece of paper in my hand. I snatched it into a ball just in time.

'I just wanted a closer look.' He smiled, unfazed.

'I was going to throw it away.'

'What was the point of drawing it, then?' He laughed, pulling out his Player's No. 6 instead and placing a cigarette between his teeth. He lit up with a match and cradled the flame with one hand. Then he took it from his lips and exhaled the smoke gradually, the wind carrying it off, like the carriages of a train. 'I'm James.'

I did not reply; instead, I tightened my grip on the screwed-up ball of paper as if to squeeze out the ink. I could hear the strum of a guitar muffling through the canvas of the tents and someone singing the Beatles' 'She's Leaving Home'. The song flurried in places and faded in others. It spoke of sacrifice, of how they had given her most of their lives.

'You're not making this very easy for me.' He sighed, wincing into his cigarette. I would soon learn that he had different ways of smoking for different ways of talking.

'What do you mean?'

'You know what I mean.' He raised a hand and tucked a stray lock of hair behind my ear. I tried not to shrink away. 'You're interesting. I'd like to take your photograph.' He patted a brown-leather case that hung on a strap over his shoulder, smoke unreeling in a river from between his two fingers.

'Why?' I murmured. The feel of his touch on my ear persisted long after he had removed it.

He took another drag and made no reply. I waved away the smoke as if I resented the intrusion. In truth, I enjoyed the smell – craved it, even, like a language I could understand but not yet speak.

I never fully grasped why he chose to spend time with me above everyone else in our cluster of tents. There were prettier girls. And girls who had plenty more to say. As was the way at the festival, we fell into a group, with a handful of Londoners and a Swiss couple. They were pleasant enough. But after a day or so I found myself slipping off to watch performances with James on our own; we sought each other out without even realizing we were doing it. I was taut, unsure of myself or my thoughts; he was full of ease. I kept my distance from him, careful not to brush against him in the crowds. I was aware of his movements always. After three days together, with Sly and the Family Stone on stage, he leant in close and kissed me. I knew then, with a flood of relief, that we were each other's.

*

When I open my eyes again, there's the heat of the roof on my belly, the bite of the sea on my hands and a faint drone, like a washing-machine, humming in the distance. I sit up to see a snag on the horizon. I've seen so many things over the last hours – pure water raining from the sky and falling into my open mouth, a pelican swooping down to pick us up in its beak and fly us back to the shore – that I can't tell what's real any more. But I'm sure I can see something. 'Wake up! Wake up! Quick!' I shout at Ravindra.

He snaps out of his sleep and sits up so suddenly that we have to freeze to make sure the roof stays stable. I jab at the shape on the horizon. The more we look at it, the more I'm sure of it.

'Start paddling!' I cry, rolling over onto my belly and digging my arm into the water. Ravindra mimics the movement he taught me, lying on his stomach on the other side of the roof. We move forward at a snail's pace. Don't go. Don't let the shape go. Then he stands up, the roof tipping like a set of scales beneath him. He waves his arms. Faster and faster he waves them.

'It's coming!' I yell. 'It's coming! It's coming!' I daren't stand up in case the weight of the two of us sinks the roof but I start to hear the engine, throbbing through the water, cutting it into submission. 'Help!'

The ship is a large tanker. A floating house. With a flat, solid deck that I want to spread myself out on and kiss. 'Over here! This way!'

At first we think it hasn't seen us. Our arms grow limp from waving. But when I shut my eyes for a while, then open them, it gets bigger. And bigger. Until the ship slides so close to us that its wake washes over our roof, sinking it an inch under the water. Someone throws a rope with a life-belt attached to it and shouts. Ravindra understands and calls back. He's grinning: a wide, unquenchable grin. He passes me the belt once he's fished it out of the water.

'No, you go first,' I tell him, handing it back. He gives it to me again.

'Alice,' he insists. 'Alice!' He thrusts it at me when I don't take it.

I give in and slip it over me, clutching the rope. Then they winch me up. I throw the belt to Ravindra as soon as I've set foot on the deck. 'Hold on!'

After hours of moving with the moods of the ocean, the surface of the tanker is deliciously solid beneath me. I flop down below the walls of the deck so that the sea is out of sight. A man in a boiler suit stoops to give me a cup of water; half the liquid misses my mouth.

There is a commotion among the crew. Ravindra is still in the water. He's clinging resolutely to the roof and the men on board are heckling and shouting in Tamil. He refuses to take the life-belt.

'It's his house,' I try to explain. 'It's the roof of his house.'

A huddle of men deliberate on the deck. They can't leave him. But he's staying on the water and won't be persuaded. I watch as three men are lowered in a dinghy onto the sea. He begins to flail and struggle and splash when they take hold of him.

'*Ithu yen veedu!*' His voice is pleading, almost a wail. He is inside the boat now, divorced from the roof. Just as the dinghy is winched off the water, the sea swells, overwhelming the sheet of metal. I wait, breath held, for it to reappear. But the water stays taciturn.

Ravindra sinks to the floor of the boat. The crew don't understand: it is only a sheet of rusting iron. Once the dinghy is level with the deck, I clamber inside and sit with him. He clasps my sleeve, like he did the roof, still holding on for dear life.

Chapter 7

Father's call-up date arrived from the War Office within the week, along with the name of his platoon. The letter sat unopened on the kitchen table – an unwanted turn of events folded inside its envelope.

My mother and sister ate their breakfast with it next to them and, putting to rest their knives and toast crusts, sat in silence for almost an hour. It was as if the letter were a lingering guest whose presence prevented them getting on with their day. I tried to distract them with talk of my dinner at Mrs Shelton's but it was no use. Not even the thought of pork could distract Freda. I bragged half-heartedly about it in front of her but she seemed indifferent to it. Every time I expressed excitement, a motherly look would spread across her face, as if she had long since thought better of craving such simple pleasures. I was sent after breakfast to fetch Father from the Plain. Mama did not send me with the letter: she wanted to be there when he opened it. I found him in Wadman's Coppice, accompanying Albie Nash on his early-morning shooting duties; Imber Court had given the blacksmith a gun and half a crown to keep the rabbit population in check. When I approached, Father was readying his aim with Albie's rifle at the far end of the woods. The blacksmith stood next to him; he held a dead hare strung by the feet in his left hand. I could see the mark on the animal's head where the bullet had entered, glistening like a third, knowing eye.

The hare dropped from Albie's hand with a thud when I told my father about the letter. Father himself remained unperturbed. If anything, he became more charged, more eager, during the walk back to the parsonage. When finally we were all together in the kitchen, he slit the envelope open, as though it were as commonplace as the electricity bill.

'It seems I'll be off within the month, Martha.'

'But when?'

'The twenty-eighth of April.'

Mama paused before collecting together the plates on the table, burying herself in the clatter of china. Freda stared at the floorboards.

It seems worthless now to look back on our fear of him going off to fight; I cannot imagine it or pity it even, superseded as it was by horrors far closer to home. He had given himself to a war that would not wait for him to make his journey across the sea before it reached over and claimed him.

The rest of the day was full of silence. Nobody dared mention Father's departure, but by four o'clock every soul in the village knew. I had only the pork dinner at Mrs Shelton's to distract me, and even that could not obliterate the thought of him leaving us.

After I had had dinner at the Sheltons' farmhouse I met Annie on the path home. She took my hand and delivered her news, breathless.

'Pete's gone to the dance . . . I saw Mr Archam on his doorstep, fixing a boot. And he told me straight.'

'Did you ask –'

'Yes, yes, of course. He came right out with it, as if it were no secret at all!'

A pause thickened between us.

'We've got to go to the camp,' I resolved eventually, landing my hand on Annie's shoulder.

'They won't let us in, Vi, we're too young.'

'We can find a way to spy . . .'

'But there's a war on. They're not about to let any Tom, Dick or Harry past the barriers.'

'Please, Annie, I'm begging you. Come with me. Or else I'm not afraid to go on my own.'

She let out a long sigh.

'Please . . .'

'We can't very well go there dressed as we are . . .' she began. I could see her thawing. 'If we go, we must play the part in case we're caught . . .'

I took hold of her arm before she could change her mind and set off to the parsonage.

'You're mad, Violet.' She sighed, all the while following me home.

Annie loitered in the dark of the garden while I crept upstairs in search of some clothes. I knocked on Freda's door and found her room empty. The crêpe dress I had wanted to borrow wasn't there – I assumed she had given it to Mrs Mitchell to have the hem fixed. It was probably for the best: I'd only have snagged it on something. I settled on an old red chiffon frock for me, a blue-velvet floor-length number for Annie and two fur stoles – one white and the other brown – to keep us warm. Freda's shoes didn't quite fit so I stuffed socks into the toes. Annie would have to make do with her school plimsolls; the blue dress was so long that they wouldn't be seen. We left our clothes in a bush at the far side of the churchyard, painting each other's mouths with a lipstick I had retrieved from the drawer of the dresser by the front door.

'Now all we need is a ride,' I whispered, as we joined the Warminster road.

'This is ridiculous,' moaned Annie, hitching up her skirt to avoid dusting the hem in chalk.

'Don't you dare back out on me, Annie.'

'But nobody's going to give us a ride – we look so silly! Besides, the road is always deserted at this time of night.'

'Nonsense. Somebody's bound to drive past and take pity on us.' I sat down abruptly on the lump of chalk that marked the edge of the track to Warminster. From there we could see all of Salisbury Plain; its contours curved in every direction from our point on the track so that it felt as if we were teetering precariously on an upturned basin. As the light began to leave us, the texture of the grass and the scars of the paths were soon smoothed into the surface of the land, like clay on a potter's wheel. I had grown to love the feel of this unbroken expanse on the eyes; the awareness it instilled in us of the distance between places. Imber was miles from any town, but at dusk it was as if it didn't exist. It stowed itself away in the base of the valley so as not to disrupt the Plain. If Annie and I were travellers – strangers to Wiltshire – we could have walked up to this point without ever knowing that there was a village beneath us.

Just then, the distant sound of an engine tapped its Morse code along the track.

'Can you hear that?' I asked Annie, standing up. She stepped up to the road and stooped into the darkness to see if she could make out an approaching vehicle.

'Dash these blackouts! I can't see a thing! It's probably not coming our way.'

'It must be! It's getting louder!' I said excitedly. 'We should stay by the road and make ourselves known.'

I joined her by the side of the track but Annie shrank back into the grass. It was only when the vehicle was nearly upon us that I realized it was a troop-carrier. By then, it was too late to hide ourselves, although Annie did her best by jumping behind the chalk rock.

I could think of no other course of action but to feign an attempt to walk to the dance so I turned as swiftly as I could and began to pace down the track towards Warminster. Soon the vehicle pulled up alongside me and the first of three officers leant out of the window.

'Where can you be off to at this time of night, Miss, and dressed like that?'

'I'm going to the dance, sir, as I'm sure you're quite aware.' My reply was curter than I would have wished.

'Walking? To Warminster Camp?' He smiled at me to let me know he had seen straight through my ruse. 'The dance will be all but over by the time you get there! Hop in, there's plenty of room in the back. Your friend can come too.' He nodded towards the rock. I was about to deny all knowledge of Annie when again I caught his eye and realized there was no point: he had definitely spotted her. Either I took the ride or missed the dance. And I wasn't about to turn him down for the sake of Annie's pride. She could jolly well look a fool.

'Annie!' I called, to little effect. She remained behind the lump of chalk.

'Annie! These gentlemen have offered us a ride to the dance . . . They know you're there. They saw you hiding.'

I waited for a few more seconds, relieved that my scarlet face was most likely masked by the darkness. Then she emerged, brushing dust from her clothes and holding her head a little too high to conceal her indignation at being caught. I watched as the gaze of the officer driving the van locked on Annie's dress and ran down its length, briefly pausing on the velvet that clung, like a second skin, to her hips. She looked beautiful, and I was glad.

One of the other officers swung open the door at the back of the van and offered us his hand, which I took first. Annie did her best to hide her plimsolls.

'You must be Imber girls,' the third officer said, once we were seated inside. I half nodded in reply, unsure how much to tell him. If Father were to find out where we were going . . . It did not bear thinking about.

'It can't be pleasant down there, what with all the artillery fire. A proper flap, I imagine.'

'Oh, we don't mind it, do we, Annie? It's home, after all.'

Annie nodded, not daring to lift her gaze from her lap.

'Well, I'm jolly glad you're coming out to the dance. The folk on the Plain are known for keeping themselves to themselves.'

The rest of the journey to Warminster was conducted in silence. I noticed the officer at the wheel of the vehicle steal more than one glance at Annie in his mirror. But she did not meet my eye when I tried to catch hers.

As the vehicle approached the barrier to the camp, I tugged at her arm and pointed at a string of women in high-heeled shoes and coats queuing at the entrance to a hall. 'Yours' and 'You'll Never Know' crescendoed, one after the other, through the windows and doors, making the air outside the hall feel warmer than it was. The women's dresses glittered like rivers at the edges of their coats. One of them balanced a cigarette pencil-like between her painted fingers.

'We can do it, Annie! We look just as good!' I whispered to her. But the sight of the women seemed only to make her more sullen.

'I'm afraid,' said the first officer, 'that I'll have to leave you by the barrier. I'm not off-duty for another hour or so. And the officers on the gate will want to admit you formally.'

My pulse quickened. I thought of Pete, already inside, asking somebody else to dance. After the officer had let us out of the troop-carrier, Annie seemed ready to turn back and walk home.

'Don't you dare leave me,' I said, taking her arm. 'It's too late to go back.' Before she could pull away, I marched her to the barrier, my heart thumping faster than the Glenn Miller song that was now playing. We joined the queue and waited our turn.

'We're here for the dance, please,' I told the officer at the barrier, making sure I met his eye with confidence. There was a younger soldier standing behind him – he stifled a giggle at the sight of us. He didn't look much older than Pete.

'What are you laughing at?' I turned on him, not knowing how else to react.

'Looks like you brought half the county with you, ma'am.' He laughed, pointing at our muddy hems.

'Indeed. Along with its wildlife,' the first officer added, gesturing towards the fur stoles. Annie looked as if she wanted to curl up in hers and hibernate.

'Hurry on in, then, or you'll catch a cold,' called a voice from behind us. It was the officer who had driven us to the barrier. Seeing Annie blush, he frowned at his colleagues as if to tell them off for upsetting us. Then he waved us through, lifting the barrier, his stare lingering on Annie.

He stopped me as we passed and whispered that if we required a ride home at the end of the evening we should come and find him at the gate.

'Lucky he took a shine to you,' I remarked to Annie, as we neared the hall.

'I'm going to be sick, Vi.' She put two hands on her stomach and grimaced at me. 'Please can we just watch from the outside? I can't bear being seen like this.'

'That officer back there thought you were beautiful,' I said, spelling it out as plainly as I could. 'You have nothing to worry about.'

'Please, Violet, I've come this far. We can look for Pete without going in. It won't be difficult.' Her hands had started to shake.

Swallowing my disappointment, I led her round the side of the hall. I had secretly been imagining the look on Pete's face when he saw me. I hadn't had much time to think of what he would say or what explanation I would give for being there. But I had hoped that I would be prettier than whoever he had brought with him and that, maybe, he might ask me to dance.

The windows were a foot higher than our heads but Annie found a barrel for us to stand on. I could taste the warmth inside the hall from the yellowness of the window panes, some of which had clouded slightly with the heat. It was difficult to make out the faces of the people on the dance-floor. The band had been taking a break when we first climbed onto the barrel but now they resumed their places, lifting trumpets and clarinets to their lips and starting a tune I had not heard before. I spent many an evening in the parsonage with my ear to Freda's door when it was her night to use the wireless. She'd sing of grey Decembers and faraway shores, of people leaving and then meeting again. I had learnt the words to a lot of the favourites. I didn't like to listen to her for too long. It made me think of Father going away. I knew that was why Freda liked the songs. Perhaps the singing made her feel better, as if rehearsing his departure might lessen the blow when it came.

We watched as more couples made their way into the centre of the hall, taking each other by the hand or arm and catching the cymbals' rhythm in the swish of their jackets and skirts.

It was then that I saw her. Dancing in her best dress, every step perfect, in Pete's arms. Annie gawped through the pane, raising her hands to her temples to get a better view.

'Is that . . . ?' She stopped herself. We both knew what we had seen.

The rain came from above, filthy and filmic, forcing us to leave the window. I was relieved to be away from the dance at first. But as we sheltered under a garage awning opposite the hall, I couldn't help but replay in my mind what I had seen through the window. It's all right, I told myself. They seemed so awkward together and that means he doesn't love her. But each time I revisited the scene, Pete looked at my sister a little more fondly and she took his hand a little more coyly until I could no longer bear it.

'Can we go now?' I murmured to Annie, who was poised patiently beside me, pawing at my elbow.

'We can't just leave,' she whispered. I had forgotten for a

moment that she was as mad about Pete as I was. 'Not after seeing that.'

'Father can't have given her permission to be here. He'd – he'd be so angry. I must tell him. And Mama.'

I took my weight off the post I had been leaning on and started into the rain towards the barrier.

'Violet, wait! What will he say when he hears that you've been here too? You'll get in so much trouble! And then your mother will tell mine . . .'

'I have to do something! I can't just stand here getting wet while my sister waltzes off with – with *him* in there!' I thrust a hand towards the hall. Then I trudged down the path to the barrier and waited for the scurry of her feet on the paving behind me.

'Don't ruin things just for the sake of it, Vi,' she called, catching up. 'She's your sister, after all.'

'What do you know?'

I pressed my lips together and took a breath but it was no use. My eyes filled and I hoped the rain would hide my tears from Annie.

'Oh, don't fret. It's just a daft crush,' she soothed, braving a hand on my shoulder. 'We'll grow out of it. Just you wait, when we're older and we've left Imber behind, we'll have so many boys to choose from. It'll be like one of those sweet shops they have in Wilton with so many jars it makes your eyes boggle. You'll see, Vi. You and me, we'll do perfectly well without him.'

We reached the barrier, me red-eyed and hobbling in my too-high heels and Annie hitching up her dress to keep it out of the puddles.

'Leaving so soon?' asked the officer who had driven us there.

'We've been jilted,' said Annie, with all the melodrama she could muster.

'Gosh, I'm sorry to hear it,' he replied, looking not in the least bit sorry. 'Our shift finishes in half an hour. If you wait a short while, I can take you home.' He was addressing Annie now; I had walked on ahead. 'There is one condition,' he added, with a lowered voice. 'You must do me the honour of a dance.'

'I can't,' I heard her whisper. 'I really ought to stay with my friend.'

'But how will you get back to Imber, miss?'

'You're quite right,' she said. 'We are in need of a ride. If you could wait there for one second.'

And with that, she skipped after me, gathering up her dress as she came. I could hear the two other officers at the barrier goading our new friend behind us.

'Violet, that nice officer back there is offering us a ride home. It'd be sensible to take it in this weather.'

'Will you dance with him?' I asked glumly.

'No, I shan't. I'll ask him to take us home directly.'

'But he asked you, didn't he?'

Annie stayed silent and, with a tug on my stole, persuaded me to retrace my steps to the barrier. True to her word, Annie refused the dance and asked to be taken home. The officer must have caught sight of my blotched face because he didn't question her and instead went to fetch the troop-carrier. Soon, we were negotiating our way back up Sack Hill in the military truck and riding along the potholed track to Imber. The rain had cleared to reveal a crowded sky – stars scattered across it like dropped sprockets. Just this once, I willed the enemy planes to come. I wanted them to tear open the Plain with craters to match the one Pete had inflicted on me. But the air above us remained blank and beautiful.

'You're dressed for bed already. Good girl,' my mother remarked, putting down her book as I entered the kitchen in my nightgown. I had had to wait in the bedroom for at least half an hour so that my rain-soaked hair could dry off. I had hidden Freda's dress under my bed, quelling the urge to cut it into a million pieces with Mama's sewing scissors.

'How was dinner at Mrs Shelton's?' Father asked.

'Delicious,' I murmured.

'It was so kind of her to have you,' mused my mother. 'I'd like to call and thank her, but clearly I can't.'

'Don't worry, Mama. I did tell her how grateful you'd both be.' My voice sounded flat but I couldn't lift it, no matter how hard I tried.

'Is everything all right? You seem a little out of sorts,' remarked my father, who was laying a pair of his socks on the hearth to dry.

'I'm fine . . . thank you, Father.' I tried to unearth a way of telling him but the words shrivelled inside me. It was as if, by giving it air, I would make it more real.

'Off to bed, then. We shan't keep you up any longer.' My mother nodded towards the hallway, leant back in her chair and relocated her place on the page with a finger. She always read in the kitchen, hauling in one of the comfy chairs from the study and thumping it down next to the stove. There was hardly any point in us having the other rooms because we spent most of our time in there.

'Good night. Sleep well,' I said to them both, walking towards my mother's chair.

'Sleep tight, my darling,' she replied, pulling me towards her for a kiss. I glanced at the volume of poetry in her right hand and thought again of Pete. There would be no more letters. Perhaps he had been writing to Freda as well as me. I rummaged around for a memory of her opening an envelope with the same texture and shade of cream as the ones Pete sent to me. Unable to recall one, I set about inventing one: a morning when I arrived at the breakfast table to find Freda's head bowed over a sheet of familiar handwriting. Then, in my mind's eye, I burnt the letter in the fire, right in front of her nose, watching the edges curl and vanish.

Father kissed me on the forehead. I left the kitchen and

climbed the stairs. Rather than returning to my room, I slipped through Freda's door and sank down on her bed. She had made an eiderdown quilt with the same pattern of pink roses as the wallpaper she had selected from the shop in Wilton. I ignored my reflection in the mirror above her dressing-table; the rain had brought out all the scarlet in my cheeks and the crying had left small sacs of skin under my eyes. I thought of Freda's face – the notion of it marking me in a way it had not done before. Her conker-brown curls. Her button nose. Her doll-like skin. I couldn't believe how naïve I'd been, worrying all this time about Annie when the real threat was my own flesh and blood. Freda and I were not at all alike; if there had been a resemblance, perhaps I could have forgiven him more easily.

I lay awake in bed, the inside of me a cave, listening for her return. I tried to predict which door she would come in through and what excuse she would give Father and Mama. Maybe she, too, had had a change of clothes hidden in the churchyard. When, at last, I heard the latch, I crept onto the landing. I heard my mother's voice, as composed as a cantata, in the hall.

'Hello, my darling, did you enjoy yourself?'

Freda's reply was lost in the folds of the coat she was taking off. I watched her hang it on the stand.

'Oh, I am glad. I expect the NAAFI girls were good company. So kind of them to invite you.'

'Yes, Marie's a good sport. I wish you'd been there, Mama. The hall was full to bursting.'

'Your father never did like to dance in public. He gets so bashful – you should see him!' She seemed lost for a moment in recollection. Then she looked up again at Freda. 'Hurry on up to bed now. Father and Violet are already fast asleep . . .' She paused. 'And, Freda, I must ask that you don't tell your sister about the dance,' she instructed, in a whisper. 'If she discovers your whereabouts this evening, she'll only want to go along to the next one. Heaven knows, Pete has probably tried to take her already. He's harmless enough right now but we wouldn't want it to . . . develop. And these dances have a way of fostering . . . Do you understand?'

'Perfectly, Mama. Pete's a farm boy. Violet is the parson's daughter.'

'Well, I wouldn't put it –'

'We may as well call a spade a spade.'

A faint look of surprise drifted across Mama's face. I wanted to call down from the banisters and tell her everything – how she was wasting her concern on me. Freda was right: he was a farm boy. Just a farm boy, for pity's sake. And two years her junior. So why him? Of all people, why him?

It was a redundant question. As Freda turned from the coat stand, her eyes rose to the banisters and fell on my shadow. A smile ghosted across her lips – so ethereal that only a sister could have seen it. She had danced with him because, of all people, he was mine.

Chapter 8

I lie down in the hull of the dinghy and try to delete the sound of the sea from my ears. The water clenches and unclenches beneath me. If it wasn't for the thought of finding James, I would be wishing I was back on the tanker. An hour or so later, Ravindra tugs at my shirt, thinking that I'm asleep. I sit up to see the ocean brimming with cars, bits of buildings and snaking cables. The wreckage gets denser the closer we sail to the shore.

It is then that we see the first body – face down in the water, limbs splayed in a star, as if in awe of something on the seabed. It's a man. I'm sure of it. A white man. 'Stop! Please stop!'

The driver cuts the engine and we drift sideways towards the body. Both men cover their noses. I want to back away as much as they do. But I can't. Not without knowing if it's him. Ravindra sees what I'm thinking of doing before I do it. '*Illay!*' He tries to pull me back.

I lean over the rim. My hands lock on the body's fingers, which have turned to putty from having spent so long in the water. Then the smell arrives in full: putrid rot for which there is no word that fits – the opposite of blossom. Holding onto my nausea, I roll the man over and he starts to sink. His face is blank, descending. There is nothing left of his features, the wave having plundered the eyes, nose and lips and, with them, any trace of a name or even a race.

They weren't James's clothes. He was wearing a striped shirt: blue and green. I want to sigh, feel relieved, but when I slump down on the deck and shut my eyes, the face appears again, refusing to be drowned. How many more will I have to search? What right do I have even to be looking for him? When he married me,

I felt too flimsy for what had occurred – as if 'marriage' were too heavy a word for what existed between us; as if I would sink beneath it. It's the kind of word that takes years to own, more suited to my mother than to me. But James and I – we married as a way of introducing ourselves to each other: an act of childish curiosity that, to others, is the crest of something full-bodied and substantial. And now his whereabouts is in my hands. Eleven months. That's all we had together before he asked me. And I'm left searching for him, rooting him out from among the dead, convincing myself that if I'd said no, losing him would not have meant so much.

'Marry me.' He'd said it as if it were a dare. We were leaving Delhi at the time, pressed together on the top bunk of a sleeper train with a fan whirring bird-like above our heads. His fingers had laced into the gaps between mine as we hurtled towards the southern tip of India. This closeness felt new to me – as if I were emerging from a deep sleep and had forgotten everything that occurred before. I had missed him: the day – our argument – had left me raw with longing. But now we were acting like one and the same person again, and I had thrown myself into him, not knowing how long it would last.

'You don't mean it,' I replied.

'You're barely giving it a second thought.'

'You're being facetious, that's why!'

'I'm serious.'

'Where?'

'I don't know. Somewhere in the south. On the tip of India.'

'But what about Delhi – everything that happened?'

'But you love me?'

I paused. I couldn't remember the last time I'd told Mum, even, that I loved her. And here was James, who made the word feel effortless. 'You know I do.'

'Then you can marry me.' He was closer now – our knees and noses were touching.

'You're not serious.'

'So it's a definite no?' He smiled, putting a hand on the small of my back and pulling me towards him.

'Not definite. No.' Mum would kill me. She'd only met him once.

We try to start the boat but the throttle chews laboriously at the water and, with one last gulp, the engine dies. We are just a few hundred yards from the shore. The thought of lowering my legs into that open tomb, swimming through everything that was loved and lost, makes my throat contract. Other bodies, numberless, must be hidden under the water, fingers flowering upwards towards my soon-to-be-kicking feet. The man at the wheel reaches into a compartment and pulls out two life jackets. Ravindra throws one to me and puts on his own before climbing over the rim of the boat. Doesn't he care what's in the water? The driver drops his anchor and Ravindra calls for me to follow. I stay rigid.

'Husband!' Ravindra shouts, treading the sea and waiting for me to join him. For a second, there is understanding between us. James. I must find my husband. And Ravindra must get back to his wife.

He might be drowned or buried. Or, worse, he's seen through our spontaneity – the haste of it all – and left me in the wave's wake. How unswerving he was, saying that he'd known from the start we'd be together. But my father saw Mum for what she was and gave up. It can happen to me too: I can be left. *I can't recover what I ruined any more than I can rebuild Imber*, was what Dad said to her in the letter. Perhaps, after all this, James and I will suffer the same fate.

I only came close to Dad once. It was summer and I was on the verge of my thirteenth birthday. Mum and Tim were out when the doorbell rang. Through the spy-hole, I could see a woman with a thick, bleached bob and a paste of makeup on her face, which, instead of covering her skin, settled in the contour of each wrinkle. I'd heard her heels on the paving before she rang the bell. Mum didn't wear heels. I slipped the chain into its rivet before opening up.

'Hello there . . . Are you Alice?' she asked. I nodded and narrowed the gap in the door.

'Don't be frightened . . . please . . . I'm . . . I've come about Peter Statton – or Archam, as you might have known him.' She seemed to be testing the name on me, to see if I would recognize it. In my childishness, I frowned.

'You know who he is, don't you?'

My head bowed in an uncertain nod.

'I'm wondering. Is Violet at home?'

'No,' I murmured. 'Mum's out.'

The woman faltered slightly on the doorstep. For a moment, I thought she was going to make her excuses and leave. Instead, she turned to her handbag – a big cream thing on her arm, whose lacquer caught the sunlight like the enamel of a car. She fished out a photograph and handed it to me. The man in the picture, who was my father, was much changed from the portrait my mother kept of him. There were so many things that were unfamiliar; it was hard to decide what to look at first. He was dressed in jeans and a chequered workman's shirt, not a uniform like in Mum's frame. A muddy stubble had spread itself over his jawline and his hands were rough – not like Tim's, which tapped at a typewriter all day. He had my eyes, and I wanted to take them back.

'You know my dad?' I whispered.

'No . . . Well, yes . . . I've known him.'

'Why are you here?'

'I won't trouble you for long . . . Alice.' My name clunked uncomfortably on her tongue. 'I thought you and your mother might like to see the photo. That's all.'

'Does my mum know you?' I asked. She returned to her

handbag again without answering and brought out another photograph. It was of a girl, sitting on a stool, with a stone-hard face that seemed to resist the camera. I took hold of the photo. Again, I saw my eyes staring back at me.

Was this a test? If I got the right answer, would there be other pictures? I wasn't sure I wanted more; I wanted her gone. 'Who's this?'

'It was taken a long time ago . . . It's me . . . as a girl.' She paused. 'I'm Peter's sister.'

The woman stared expectantly at me. *Don't you know your own family, Alice Fielding?* I scanned the picture again for a clue as to what to say.

'Did your mum tell you he had a sister?' she asked.

I didn't answer.

'We were quite a complicated family,' she added. 'It wasn't easy for my mother – to do what she did . . .'

I frowned. The woman caught my confusion and stepped away from the door uneasily. 'I'm sorry . . . I thought . . .' There was another pause. Again she seemed to be weighing up whether to stay or go. After a moment's thought, she reached into her handbag again and handed me a card hesitantly. 'This is my number. If you ever have any questions, you only have to call. Do you understand?' I nodded. Sadness reared momentarily from under her makeup, but before I could ask her anything else, she twisted on her shoes and walked back down the drive. Before long she was hidden from sight by the rhododendron and all I could hear was the slick clop of her heels on the road.

I tried to tell Mum, but the words never came. Every time I saw her looking at the uniformed photograph of my father, something caught in my throat and I felt unable to supplant this framed, fixed, knowable version of him with the one the woman had given me. It was an anchor to which Mum had tethered everything, and I wasn't going to be the one to cut the rope.

*

The engine has failed us completely. There is no choice but to try to wade to shore. I roll over the rim and drop down into the water to join Ravindra. I can feel the debris close in on me, melding me into its ill-fitting jigsaw. Eyes shut, I start to swim.

Every few seconds, waves roll under us, like fists under blankets. The shore inches nearer. Ravindra is ahead by a good few strokes, needling through the patchwork of wreckage. I'm floundering in the same segment of water, paddling through it again and again, urging the beach to arrive. After a while, I find I can't keep a steady rhythm, stopping between each stroke to take a breath. Ravindra lets out a shout. He is standing, two feet rooted on the seabed. We've reached the shallows. I lower my legs timidly, not quite believing that I can step on actual ground. Just as I gain my balance, a wave picks me up from nowhere – along with my panic – and sets me down. I swallow the urge to scream. It could drag me out again in seconds if it wanted to. I push as quickly as I can through the water, dreading the next swell. The sea drops to my waist, then to my thighs and finally to below my knees. Here, the water rushes through the gaps between my toes. I'm aware, suddenly, of its warmth. It regains the texture of my childhood – those days spent darting into the shallows, surrendering gleefully to the water's grip. Mum used to get so worried about me going swimming. She wouldn't sunbathe: instead she would stand like a watchman on the shore's lip, fixing her eyes to the crest of my head as I leapt into the smother of another wave. I thought her silly for believing the sea could be anything other than benign.

Her first letter had arrived when we were in Istanbul. James had picked it up from the post office, expecting that she'd write. I'd refused to read it at first, but eventually he persuaded me to open the envelope. Her handwriting, unlike mine, was compact and efficient: it stretched in impeccable lines across the blue airmail paper, filling every inch of the page.

Dear Alice,

I hope you'll forgive me for writing. I couldn't bear the thought of us parting ways on such bad terms.

What a time you must be having. Tim says Istanbul is a fascinating place; the gateway to the East. Already you are doing things that I never dreamt of doing and you are not even in India yet. I won't pretend it doesn't worry me, but I am proud. You are bolder than I ever was.

Tim and I are well. He is about to start his new job for the electricity board in Oxford. It's quite a task he'll have, with the workers proposing yet another strike: power cuts are already two a penny in the south. The board seems to be happy with his plans to continue living in Salisbury. It's quite a drive for him and we did consider moving but, well, you know what a hassle it would be. Besides, Tim understands that you grew up here – and we both want you to have a home to return to, should you choose to come back.

I'm thinking of you, darling, all those miles away. Take care of yourself and send my regards to James.

With love from
Mum

Her meanderings seemed different on paper. I could see her holding back, attempting to phrase things in ways that I would understand. I had been so angry with her for so long, and for no good reason. Yet she didn't retreat: she continued to move, vulnerably, towards me, in the hope that I would give in. *That's what mothers do*, I thought: they love out of reflex – like moths returning blindly to a flame. Except she was different: it seemed more conscious, her decision to persist and be burnt.

Chapter 9

On the morning after the dance, the words I'd planned to say to my sister at the breakfast table emptied from my head when she entered the dining room. It was as simple and sudden as the pouring away of water. She yawned, took a seat and began speaking to me but I could not muster a reply.

'Violet?'

I watched the roses claw up the trellis on the other side of the window. We had knocked together the frame last summer, using Father's hammer and nails. Freda and I had grown the roses for Mama's birthday. It had been my idea and it was my fingernails that had carried a crescent of soil beneath them for weeks on end. My sister had joined in just as the roses had budded.

'Violet, I asked if you could pass the toast.'

I withdrew my eyes from the window and handed my sister the rack.

She frowned at me. 'You look awful. Trouble sleeping?'

Mama carried in a pot of honey and took a seat next to us. Father's steps were heard on the stairs and he joined us at the head of the table.

'Pass me the toast, Freda, that's a good girl. I want to hear all about the dance. I gather there was quite a turn-out.'

'Jack,' hissed Mama, drawing his eyes towards my place at the table.

Father looked down at his toast.

'It's all right, really . . . I don't mind.' I tried to sound sincere but, catching sight of Freda's face, I lowered my eyes to my plate.

'You're a good sport, Vi. I knew you'd be fine with it,' she cooed.

'Violet, forgive me for keeping it from you,' said my mother, placing a hand on my arm. 'I thought it would be less trying for you if you didn't know. You can go too when you're older.'

'It's only two months until your sixteenth birthday,' chipped in Father. 'Perhaps Pete will take you then.' Under the table, I tightened my grip on a fold in my skirt and twisted it into a knot. Freda picked up her knife, which was lying on the table opposite me, and shaved off a sliver of butter from the dish next to her. She caught my eye as she withdrew the knife to her plate and smiled as if the butter were our secret.

'Mama,' I murmured, which caused my mother to look up from her toast.

'Freda, what do you think you're doing bringing the butter out from the larder?' came her remonstration. 'I shan't tell you again – it's not to be wasted on toast. Put it back this instant.'

Later, on the way to church, I crossed the field with the rest of my family and prayed Pete would have a reason to miss the service. Enduring my sister was one thing; seeing him was quite another. Noticing that I had fallen behind, Freda slackened her pace, drew level with me and took my arm. 'Chin up, Vi. Don't be down-hearted. I promise you, as soon as Ma and Pa let you, we'll go to a dance together.'

I detached my arm from hers and bent down to attend to my shoelace, which was already well tied.

'I'm more than happy to take you for your birthday,' she continued. 'After all, I wouldn't want you to count on Pete. He may not ask you, you know, and then who will you go with?'

I stood up from my shoe and met her stare. 'Freda . . .' The sentence fossilized inside me, and before I knew quite what my feet were doing, I was walking away from her back towards the house.

'Violet!' she called. 'Violet, you can't miss church – Father . . .'

Nobody followed. They could not afford to be late for the service.

Letting myself in through the back gate, I went up the length of the lawn to the house. I could hear tanks moaning, like overgrown flies, on the Plain and, every now and again, the guttural stutter of an unknown gun. These sounds, previously alien, had imbued themselves slowly on my consciousness so that now they seemed as natural as the wind and the birdsong. I reached the terrace at the end of the lawn and looked up at the parsonage. It had two triangle-roofed wings that jutted onto the terrace from the main body of the house. I loved its red brick, which glistened in the rain and gave off a rasping scarlet dust in the summer – perhaps one always feels this way towards a home once it is gone, but I would not have laid a single brick differently. I flopped down on the bench next to the roses and breathed in the scent. I had deliberately chosen to plant them there because it was sheltered from the wind by the west wing of the house. Here, in this small pocket of still air, the scent could mill and linger. Mama had thanked Freda and me equally for the roses when we presented the bed to her on her birthday. I suppose, in their fully grown form, the flowers suited my sister more than they did me so it was easy for Mama to think of them as Freda's idea. She forgot the boyish hours of digging, training and watering that had given birth to them, and saw only the stems and petals before her, as feminine and effortless as her elder daughter.

Annie would have no trouble guessing why I wasn't at church. I only hoped she wouldn't give me away to Freda. The notion that Pete might also be aware of my absence rose briefly before I dismissed it as pure fancy. The realization – there, in the garden – that I would not be the one in his thoughts made me retreat into the house. I removed my shoes and went into Father's study. I liked being with the books: they reminded me of how many ways of thinking existed outside my own – how small and fleeting my pulse was when set alongside those ageing spines. The headiness I had experienced since waking up that morning seemed to disperse beside them. On the shelves by the door, I found the ship in the bottle that Father had kept since he was a boy. His own father, my grandfather, had left it to him. As a child, I used to puzzle over the bottle, pondering ways of extracting the ship without breaking the glass. Freda had different concerns: she was always asking Father how the ship had got into the bottle in the first place. But at fifteen, alone in the study, I was caught not by these questions but by the thought that the ship would outlive both Freda and me and, most likely, our children; sealed inside the bottle, the only storms it would ever face would be imaginary. When I think of what came later, of how ill prepared I was for everything that occurred, that hour in the study seems absurd – as isolated as the ship I held in my hand. The shallow hurt that I felt towards my sister for something as small as a dance seems illusory now: I can never retrieve it, or imagine, even, how it came to feel so deep.

Chapter 10

When I saw where it had seeded itself, I thought of a rose, dark as soil, flowering from the mouth. Or maybe the rose came later – to cover something I did not want to see.

Major Whistler had been enthusing about the Salisbury Plain demonstration for weeks, telling Father how he would hear up close a Hurricane's throbbing song and witness the effect of live ammunition. *Live ammunition, Mr Fielding*. There would be no other opportunity like it before he went to war. My father needed little persuasion.

I begged him to take me too – anything to distract me from Freda and the dance – but he refused. In a crowd of over a thousand, all jostling for their own piece of sky, I would only be a nuisance. I did not protest. I knew Pete would find a way of getting us there, whether my father approved or not.

I did not talk to Pete about Freda. When, two days after the dance, he appeared at the parsonage door, asking for me and not my sister, I convinced myself that maybe he was sorry or had thought better of his actions. So hungry was I for things to go back to how they had been that I fed this notion of his repentance until it gained flesh and bones and had a life of its own. I did not have to worry about him broaching the subject. He talked of nothing but the demonstration, concocting plans about how we would get into the audience.

When the day of the exercise arrived, a thick mist pasted itself across the Plain. Father stared glumly at the sky from the dining-room window with a piece of toast in hand and bemoaned the fact that it would be tricky to see the planes. Major Whistler soon called at the door for him and they set off on foot. Pete had agreed to meet me at the back of the school so that we could follow them at a distance. I waited at home for a few minutes, then told Mama that I was going to the Archams' farm to play 'kick the can'.

'With Pete?' Freda cut in. 'Isn't he a little old for games?'

'We'll go for a walk as well. See the sheep,' I murmured, fumbling around for my boots on the hall floor. I avoided my sister's stare, which I knew had settled on me from where she stood in the kitchen doorway. Ever since the dance, I had tried to limit our exchanges to as few as possible – a knot of anxiety tied itself inside me every time I was forced to address her. I finished lacing my boots and listened with dread to her approaching steps.

'If I were you, Violet, I would steer clear of him. He'll only upset you,' she whispered, standing over me.

'I don't know what you mean. He's my friend,' I replied, rising to return her gaze. It was the first time I had met her stare directly since the dance. She was the first to look away, searching the coat rack behind me with her eyes.

'There are things you don't know about Pete . . .' she added, putting a hand on my forearm and meeting my eye again. 'Things he won't tell you.'

'And you're the expert?' I replied, shrugging off her touch and letting myself out of the house.

I followed my father and Major Whistler with Pete along the Imber road towards Warminster, careful to keep a distance.

As we climbed a gully wall, we were met by the tiered terraces of Battlesbury Fort sunk in the haze ahead of us, like the pleats in poured cream. Pete drew me behind a tumulus while my father and Mr Whistler exchanged greetings with an officer on the track ahead. With his eyes focused on my father, Pete kept his hand on my arm as we crouched and watched them. I tried desperately to quell the quickening beat in my chest. Perhaps he simply forgot to let go of me. I wondered what it was that Freda knew and why he hadn't told me. Dancing was one thing; secrets were quite another. Once my father and Major Whistler had set off again, we skimmed the edge of Bowls Barrow and immersed ourselves in the cover of the swelling crowd. Our youth drew a few stares but I whispered to Pete that, once the fighter planes arrived, everybody's eyes would be pinned to the sky; we would soon be forgotten.

At first, stories of air raids minnowed among us, darting from person to person until the excitement was such that I could not make myself heard. *I spotted a Hurricane over Chipping Norton the other week, I'm sure of it. You're in for a treat, old chap.* A moustached old man in a waistcoat with a pipe between his teeth angled his head towards the sky and cried, *Well, if it teaches those dirty Jerries a lesson, I'm all for it.* A low chuckle rippled through the bellies of those around him. As the wait increased, the talk diminished, with more and more heads tilting towards the sky in search of the planes.

About five hundred yards from us there was a convoy of dummy soldiers and battered lorries, flanked by two tanks, whose wrinkled armour cast jagged shadows on the grass. Someone had painted a moustache on the face of one of the dummies so that it matched the man in the waistcoat in front of us. *That one's got it coming to him!* He chortled, pointing towards the dummy with his pipe. The crowd inched over the dotted line of tape in front of them, eager to get as close to the firing zone as possible. Tapping his watch, an officer crossed the boundary and turned to address the crowd with a megaphone. We were about to witness two affronts, he told us. The first was to be a dry run in which no ammunition would be fired.

'Move, Vi, you're treading on my foot!' hissed Pete, as he bent in to get a better view of the officer.

During the second affront, he continued, the convoy ahead of us would be shelled and shot at to demonstrate the damage that fighter aircraft equipped with cannon and machine guns could do to soldiers on the march.

The officer stepped back behind the dotted line, lowered his megaphone and adjusted his cap for a better view of the sky. No sooner had he positioned himself in the safety zone than the shudder of an engine could be heard gaining volume, like growing applause. The crowd jostled. Heads were raised. I spotted Father near the front in his dog collar, beaming boyishly up at the sky.

The nine Hurricanes dipped one by one through the haze above us, sketching the swoop of a valley with their smoke. The crowd stilled their lungs. We watched them loop back over to Battlesbury.

'Here we go,' breathed Pete, clutching the sleeve of my blouse. 'The dummy run's over.' I could feel the nearness of his fingers, as thrilling as the closeness of the aeroplane's underbelly, which broke into the body of air above our heads.

The sky let out another growl, engines rising up their octaves, like a gathering wave. A stutter of bullets could be heard breaching the haze, eliciting the same gasp from the crowd as a firework's crackle. All eyes were fixed on the convoy. Just then I heard the sound of a seam ripping in front of me. A hole caused by I-don't-know-what opened below the ear of the man in the waistcoat. He dropped his pipe and slipped to his knees, liquid no thicker than a pencil mark carving a path from his head to the nape of his neck.

'Pete!' I screamed, grabbing hold of the man as he fell backwards onto my calves. 'Pete!'

The bullets were hailing down on us now, slipping as easily as a kitchen knife into the pith of the crowd. I felt a weight push me to the ground and, at the sight of Pete's shirt, thought, with horror, that he'd been hit. But he yelled, 'Stay where you are!' So I cowered underneath Pete, eyes drawn to the pupil of the man in the waistcoat in front of me – bullet black. To my horror, Pete reached for the man's body and hauled it across us to shield us from the bullets, while the rest of the crowd buckled and scattered and flailed.

The air fell silent. There was a shudder. The ground beneath gave way.

I let go of Pete and was propelled upwards. My stomach folded in on itself, like it had on the Waltzer at the Warminster fair. I clawed around for something to hold but felt only air. The ground arrived again with a punch, stealing my breath and leaving me sprawled on my back. Then the dust came, in rain, and sealed my eyes shut. I could feel it lining my throat and painting my skin. I blinked. And blinked again. A man in uniform to the right of me stumbled, dazed, through the dust cloud. His left arm was missing and blood, dark as tar, was seeping through the chevrons on his uniform. I opened my mouth to tell him but there was no sound. Then Pete came running, his skin as painted as my own. He pulled me to my feet, took me by the hand and began to tug me out of the crowd. My head pounded and throbbed, pounded and throbbed, until I thought I would drop into sleep and be done with running for ever.

Trampling over stained grass after Pete, I saw a man my father's age receive a river of bullets across his chest – the holes following each other like a scattering of stones from his hip to his shoulder.

An officer with a leg wound was waving a red flag at the planes overhead, upon which their metal hailstorm thinned and evaporated. The dust parted. Sound came back in snatches. All around us were bodies and debris and earth. The ordered rows of spectators were no more. It was as if the Plain itself had reared up like a sea and sent its inhabitants flailing. There were no screams. Only faint raspings and the slow movement of limbs through smoke.

I wish I could say that I thought of Father straight away. That he was my first concern. I screamed at Pete to find him. He must have been somewhere near the front. When Pete kept on running, I turned, let go of his hand, and ran back in the direction from which we had come. Ahead of me, emerging silently beyond the smoke, was the untouched convoy, the dummies in the trucks wearing the same nowhere stare as they had done before the planes arrived.

I found him face down in the grass, set apart from the rest of the crowd – a red shadow underneath him. I bent to see to his wounds but Pete, who had run after me, put a hand out to stop me.

'Don't, Violet.'

'You don't know!' I cried, breaking free of his hold. I took Father by the shoulder and turned him.

A bullet was seeded

dark as soil

in the flower of his

mouth.

Chapter 11

The stiffer and colder his body became, the more quickly they moved on to those whose breath still lingered in them. I kept pleading with the ambulances to take him but we were one of the last to be seen to. A nurse helped me lift him onto a stretcher. She threw open a sheet as if to make a bed and laid it across the entire length of him, even his face. I thought of Fred Batch, buried in the snow. Perhaps then I knew. Whatever knowing means. Do you ever know? Because it seemed as if he had just left something behind, something he would return for later. I climbed into the back of the ambulance where he had been placed, along with two others, and we trundled, with none of the urgency I had anticipated, down the Imber road. A blue more delicate than a harebell threaded itself through the outer layer of skin on his hand. I let go. And have spent years trying to let go again.

It was just him and me; no Mama; no Freda. Pete ran from the Plain to fetch them from the parsonage. So there was no Pete either. They put Father on a hospital bed in a room of his own. There were no nurses or doctors. The curtains were drawn. I sat with him for an hour, thinking of the lump of lead that had yet to be removed from his throat. I told him that he couldn't go to war any more, that he was to stay with us for good.

They arrived at the hospital, Freda coughing tears and Mama bleached white with fear. We stood by his bed, as distant from each other as milestones, none of us able to surmount the yards between us.

It was two days before we were allowed to take him home. A full investigation into the demonstration was launched and a post-mortem conducted. *A combat pilot . . . only his third ever flight . . . in the glaring sun . . . Canadian*; rumours ripened in every corner of the hospital. Mrs Whistler, who sent flowers by mistake when she heard that Father was still alive, arrived and sat with us long enough to watch them wilt.

Pete cut down one of the ash trees at the end of the parsonage garden and had a coffin made from it. The gap that it left was far from large, but it was enough for us to feel more keenly than ever the cut of the wind come wintertime. A memorial service was held in the church. They rang the bell for him – the one with the deepest knell. The noise moaned hopelessly across the Plain, dwindling in the hollows of the Downs, limping across the expanses of grass that lay between Chitterne and Lavington. There was not a soul outside Imber who would hear it.

He was buried in the churchyard, in a freshly dug grave. The headstone, which was clean and pure compared to the weathered ones around it, has now grown its own lichen skin and is hidden under a thick knot of goose grass. Like the other graves, it is hemmed in by barbed wire and an eight-foot fence – as if a fence alone were enough to keep the shells at bay. *And the old order of things will pass away* was the scripture engraved under his name.

Freda became quieter and quieter in those days. None of us spoke; inhaling the air was enough to contend with. But my sister's silence was of a different, more strangled, kind. She no longer joined Mama and me for meals. Yet the food in the larder and even the pile of coupons in the dresser kept being depleted. The sourer the food, the more likely it was to disappear. I once found an empty pickled-onions jar discarded at the back of the house; raw runner beans, tomatoes short of their blush and tins of peas soon followed. Mama said nothing. Some days I wondered whether she even noticed.

Freda didn't take the wireless up to her room any more. There was no more singing. Sometimes, from outside her bedroom door, I heard her crying. She wouldn't let me in when I knocked.

She disappeared in July, some months after Father was buried. I woke in the night to the sound of an engine on Church Lane only to lapse back into a thin sleep shortly afterwards. In the morning I knocked on Freda's door with a cup of tea. Silence was nothing out of the ordinary in the parsonage now so, on not receiving a response, I went into the room. Her bed had been stripped and the wardrobe was open.

Things were missing. Her nightgown. Her shoes, the ones that she used to change into at the last gate along the track to Warminster. *Town shoes*, she called them, if ever there was such a thing. Her coat was gone too. Not the rough waxed one that she wore on our farm visits, but her Sunday best. I crossed the room and opened the top drawer of the dressing-table. Her hairbrush was not in its usual place and the small medley of makeup that she had eked out of her pocket money over the years had vanished.

I ran across the landing to find my mother, still in her bed, with one arm cast protectively over the pond of space where my father would have slept.

'Mama, it's Freda,' I mouthed, almost inaudibly. She didn't stir. 'Mama, please, wake up.'

She opened her eyes and, seeing me at the door, sat up and whispered, 'Come in, my darling.'

'No, Mama, listen, it's Freda . . . She's . . . Her things are gone.'

'Violet –'

'Her town shoes are missing, and her coat, her hairbrush and toothbrush. I think she's run away.'

'But . . . She's probably just gone out for a stroll, darling.'

'No, I went into her room, you see, to take her some tea. If you don't believe me, go and look for yourself.'

Mama rose from her bed and, sliding on a loose dressing-gown, glided across the landing to Freda's room. She emerged again a minute or so later, her dressing-gown pulled more tightly around her ribs. She hastened down the stairs and I followed.

'Get your boots on,' she ordered sharply, rummaging around on the coat stand. 'I'm going to the Court to see if Mrs Whistler will lend us a car. And don't you go anywhere without me, Violet. One daughter's enough to be worrying about.' The door slammed behind her and I was left alone in the hallway, Father's old boots next to mine.

It wasn't long before I heard the rasp of a car outside. I pulled on my shoes and an overcoat and opened the door onto the dawn. Mist moved in barrels along the lawn. I stowed myself in the back of the car; Mama was at the wheel. Noting that I had left the front seat empty, she turned her head for a moment towards the space where Father might have sat. Then, with one swift press of her foot on the pedal, we sped away.

'Blast this mist,' she gasped, as she pulled out onto the road. 'Where do we even start?'

'Pete,' I whispered. 'We start with Pete.'

At the end of Dog Kennel Lane, the mist began to lift. The birch trees outside the Archams' farmyard glimmered like ornaments; palm-sized cobwebs crocheted the spaces between the branches and caught the dew in beads.

'I don't understand. Why are we looking for her here?' my mother protested, as we switched off the engine and entered the yard on foot.

'Pete might know something. It's just a . . . I'll explain afterwards.'

Mrs Archam looked up from inside the farmhouse kitchen, her face filling with the same clash of dread and pity that met us everywhere we went in the village, these days.

'You know what he's like, Miss Violet,' she told me, when I asked to see him at the door, 'always disappearing off here, there and everywhere.'

'You mean he's not here?' I asked.

'We've not seen him since dinner yesterday.'

'He's with her,' I muttered to Mama. 'You have to trust me.'

Mama only frowned.

'He did say something about meeting a friend at the station,' continued Mrs Archam. 'When I pressed him, that is. I didn't like to trouble him too much – it upsets him when I interfere.'

I thanked her and took my mother's arm. We strode over the yard back to Mrs Whistler's old Crossley. The journey to the station began in silence. There was something about the fog – the way it deleted the folds and creases and divides of the Plain – that insisted on no noise. I felt that if I were to speak my words would be swallowed instantly and reduced to a mere shape on my lips. The whites of Mama's knuckles became more and more pronounced the closer we got to the edge of the Plain, forming a line of moons as she tightened her grip on the steering-wheel.

'Vi, I know you know something,' she asserted, once we had crossed the Plain.

I faltered at first. But, inch by inch, the explanation came to me. I told her about the dance, how I had seen Freda with him, how I didn't know whether they had gone together or simply met there, but that it had been clear he felt something for her.

'They've *eloped*?' she asked, aghast.

'I don't know, Mama. I've given up trying to make sense of it.' My voice did not lose its steadiness, as my mother's had, but instead slipped into flat resignation. Father's death had eclipsed everything. Any recollection of the hurt my sister had inflicted elicited nothing from me but guilt – regret at having spent my worry on something so slight.

'Why on earth didn't you tell me about what you saw at the dance? I could have put a stop to it! Your father – he – your father would . . .'

Mama's resolve seemed to fold in on itself at the mention of

97

him. I shrank into the back seat as the car picked up speed. The road dipped and rose beneath us with a haste to which I was not accustomed. I held my stomach and thought of them, tucked away in the corner of a carriage, her head on his shoulder, city-bound. Flower. Bullet. Mouth. That was why I hadn't told her.

We arrived at the station to find the platform deserted. I stared down the tracks, willing a train to arrive and carry me towards them. I made compromises in my head. If only they would both come back, I could live. I wouldn't care that they were together: it would be enough just to have them here. I thought of the bombs – as common as rain – in the cities. They needed to come home, the pair of them. It was no use losing them as well as Father. I turned round to see my mother opening the door to the waiting room and walking up to a bundle stretched along one of the benches. A pair of shoes coated in chalk dust was pressed together on the floor below and I recognized them instantly as Pete's. There was a time, before the accident, when I would have cried at the sight of him still there and not far away on a train with my sister. Mama shook his shoulder and woke him.

'Pete,' she began coldly, before he had had a chance to rub the sleep from his eyes. 'For Heaven's sake, wake up.'

He sat up, momentarily unsure of his whereabouts.

'Where's Freda?'

He fumbled around for his hat, stood up and placed it on his head. Why he felt the need to put his hat on, I do not know. Perhaps he was buying time. He locked his hands behind his back. 'I'm sorry, Mrs Fielding . . .'

'An apology is not going to achieve anything, young man. Where is my daughter?' Her tone hardened.

'In London. She's gone to London.'

'Why didn't you go with her?' I blurted. Pete frowned at me briefly before returning his gaze to the floor.

'I was never going to take the train myself,' he replied. 'She asked for help. Said she couldn't make it to the station on her own.' He rubbed at the patch of skin under his nose and looked past us towards the door.

'And to think we counted you as a neighbour, Pete – all of us,' exclaimed my mother.

'You wouldn't have behaved so despicably had my father been around,' I added.

'If a person's fed up with a place, you should let them go,' Pete retorted. 'There's no point trying to keep them when they don't want to be kept . . . Mrs Fielding.' He added my mother's name as an afterthought, all the while glaring at me.

'She's lived here all her life, Pete,' I cried. 'She wouldn't just pack up and leave without a good reason. Father's gone and she doesn't know what to do.'

'Look here,' my mother intervened. 'This isn't solving anything. You must tell us which train she caught – it's the very least you can do.'

'The last one to London yesterday. It left at midnight.'

'And what will she . . . ? Where will she stay?' I asked.

'I swear to you, Mrs Fielding,' he said, ignoring my questions, 'I've told you everything I know.'

Mama checked her watch, turned her back on him and took me by the arm. 'Listen here, Violet. We can make enquiries from Imber. I'll telephone Aunt Dorothy in Battersea. But there's little point in trying to fetch her back ourselves. She'll only dig her heels in. Once we're sure that she's safe, we must let her be. Do you understand?'

I nodded and followed her out of the waiting room back towards the car. To my disgust, Mama paused, turned back to Pete and said, 'You'd better come with us in the Crossley. I don't see how else you're going to get home.'

By the time we reached the Imber road, the mist on the Plain had dissipated into a mute sky. I kept my eyes on the window the whole way into the village, only releasing them when Pete had been deposited at the Archams'. Like me, Mama did not see fit to shed tears. We had nothing left to give Freda but wide-eyed fright.

In the days that followed, evidence of my sister's getaway began to surface. Mrs Taylor was the first to call on the evening after our drive to the station. My mother bowed her head over the kettle, bleary-eyed, as her visitor began to speak.

'I did wonder why the girl wanted so much laundry done at once. I was cross with her, you see. We're overrun with all the uniforms as it is, and I told her she'd have to wait her turn.'

'Oh, Kathy, why did you not think to tell me? I should have known straight away what she was up to.' Mama put her head into her hands and sighed.

'Fancy running away without leaving so much as a note! She was brought up better than that, Martha, don't blame yourself,' our guest responded. Mama raised her head again and Mrs Taylor, whose fingers were so creased from the wash-house that they had started to resemble a wrung-out cloth, put a palm on my mother's shoulder and took my hand in hers.

'Do you think she's gone for good?' I murmured.

She telephoned from London a week later, leaving a number with Mrs Carter and a time at which we could ring. Mama wasted no time in arranging for a trunk call at the post office but we were forced to wait several days before the call could be made. When the moment finally arrived, and Mrs Carter held out the earpiece, Mama's courage failed and she gestured for me to take it instead. Mrs Carter thrust it into my hand before I could refuse; the call had already connected. Mama came near to the earpiece so that she could hear. But it wasn't my sister who answered.

'May I speak to Freda Fielding, please?' I put on my best telephone voice, elongating my vowels and clipping my consonants.

'What's the name?'

'Oh, um, Violet. I'm her sister.'

'Sister? She ain't mentioned a sister.'

'Sorry, no, of course . . . I have papers?'

'Whatcha gonna do? Read them to me? We're on the bloody telephone, darling!'

My mother, who was straining to hear the other half of the conversation, took the receiver from me.

'Look here, this is Freda's mother. Please fetch my daughter this instant. I'm telephoning on urgent business.'

'Urgent business, eh? All right, missus. I'll call her down.'

There was a pause. The line muttered softly to itself.

'Hello?'

'Freda! Thank God!' cried Mama.

'Hello, Mama,' she replied matter-of-factly.

'Freda! Are you all right?' I interrupted.

'I'm perfectly fine.'

'We were worried sick!' my mother exclaimed, the weight of her voice landing on the last word.

'And you left no note!' I chimed in.

'What were we to think, my darling? Anything could have happened.'

'Well, I'm fine. I've enlisted. As a nurse.'

'Darling, why didn't you tell me? I could have telephoned Aunt Dorothy, made arrangements.'

'I want to do this my own way, Mama. No one else's.' The muffled sound of a siren began to sing in the background.

'What's that? Freda? What's going on?' Mama's voice started to fray.

'I've got to go, Mama. I'll write and explain.'

'Write?' The word came out of Mama's mouth as high as opera while the siren grew louder at the other end of the line. The noise went blank, suddenly, and my mother dropped the earpiece. I said nothing, watching it pirouette on its cord.

Chapter 12

Three nights. That was all we'd spent in Kanyakumari before the wave came. But I find that I'm hunting around for surviving buildings – fragments of places that he took me to. We never had a home together and neither did we plan to make one; instead we littered the East with pieces of ourselves – a row in Zahedan, a kiss in Quetta. We'd plant minuscule roots without realizing it. And yet there was so much more to discover.

'What did you buy that for?' I said to him in a Frankfurt flea market, when the giddiness of our first months together had begun to wane. He had picked up a postcard of a seafront, the colours of the houses almost neon against the cliff. A blonde girl posed in a bikini on the front, her curves superimposed on the coastline with '*Ich denke an dir*' scrawled across her breasts. 'You're not thinking of sending it?'

'I don't know,' he quipped. 'I thought your mum might appreciate the thought.' I laughed and watched him slip it, when he thought I wasn't looking, into his camera bag.

A month later, when we had reached Pakistan, I came across an entire pile of postcards bound together with an elastic band in his luggage; they were from Belgium, France, Austria, even Istanbul, always the most lurid and hackneyed images he could find. Afterwards, I couldn't help but notice how, in every town we travelled through, he rifled through markets on the sly – the kind that were stuffed with plastic knick-knacks, flip-flops and *faux*-gold jewellery. Whenever I scarpered off to find a toilet or scout out a place to stay, I'd return to find him in the shade of a new stall, thumbing his way through boxes of photographs and cards. I refrained from asking him what the point of it was, other than to stockpile junk in a loft he was yet to own; but three months into the overland trail, once we had reached Kashmir, I formed my own theory.

'It's strange, isn't it, how you can't ever piece together a place once you're away from it?' He nosed into the Kashmiri heat with his camera lens and pressed the button. 'It doesn't matter how many pictures you take.' We were sitting on the edge of the Dal lake, warming the backs of our calves on the boards of the houseboat, and I murmured something about the trip being unforgettable with or without the photographs. It was only afterwards that I thought properly about what he had said and remembered the postcards. He liked to examine every crevice of a city, absorb its layers, without exchanging a word about why it was made that way or how it differed from home. A visitor couldn't grasp what it was like to breathe the air of a place for thirty or forty consecutive years, how it changed your understanding of the city. The postcards were talismans, telling him of how he had only skimmed the surface and, once he had departed, how much he would leave behind.

As time went on, I did this more and more – created a theory about him and then bound him to it, so that it started to suit him and then *was* him. It mattered to me immensely why he behaved as he did – I wanted to know the origin of every habit. I was envious, I suppose, of him having a past that existed outside my own. But now, in India, with the beachfront in ruins, I feel only that first sting of seeing him stare at another girl's breasts.

Ravindra is the first to leave the sea. He shakes it from his feet and does not look back. He doesn't stop to take in what I see – the town pushed down flat. Instead he walks with purpose towards the ruins, not even pausing for breath. I bend down, with my hands on my knees, and lap up the air. The sea pushes its plunder onto the sand behind me and returns, seconds later, to reclaim it.

There is a pool of green to my right. A woman's sari, half unravelled from her body, lies in a coil beside her on the sand. A sling, empty, is still in her grasp – the kind she would have used to carry a baby. I look around for the child. It seems important, somehow, that she should hold it in her sling, that the two should lie together. Of all the things the wave has carried off, this is the smallest, the most precious, no heavier than a small sack of rice. And yet I still search, as if somehow the wave might have mustered the kindness to return what it so coldly took away.

Ravindra looks back and sees the woman. He points at her body and twirls his finger around as if he were stirring something in a bowl. I know what he is asking me to do. So I approach her, quietly, not wanting to wake her up. The sea has decked her in its ugliest perfume. I choke, burying my mouth and nose in the damp cuff of James's shirt. Taking hold of her sari, I unravel it. She is not heavy to lift. I roll her slowly along the stretch of cloth until she is folded inside, embalmed in green.

Had a Tamil woman found her, she would have been able to dress her properly. I try to picture the sari I wore for our wedding but I can't settle on which shoulder I should drape the end of the cloth over. Ravindra motions towards the left so I roll her one more time, tucking the fabric underneath her as if closing a book.

We stand for a moment, not moving. Neither of us lifts our eyes from the woman. There are more bodies nearby, washed up like shells, half buried in the sand. Some are curled in on themselves limply, trying to hide. There are so many. We can't see to them all.

At the nape of the beach, we walk across together to the place where the town once began. From here the wreckage continues all the way to the foot of the hills. Hardly hills, more like raised plains. I hadn't noticed them before. But now my eyes latch onto any kind of high ground they can find, making note of it – for next time.

The line of palm trees that used to break the ocean winds has been deleted. Five clay huts at the head of the beach have been hollowed inside – barren without their fruit and hot snacks and the women who used to sit, hands on knees, watching the day. The third hut along is where James went to buy breakfast. There are no bodies, no shopkeeper, no girl ladling *dosa* batter into the pan outside the door. And no James. Shashi Kapoor's wave-rippled face rests on a billboard blocking the entrance. I have to duck under it to get inside. Behind the counter is the girl who makes the *dosa*. She is lying, arms close to her sides, her ladle a few metres away – its inner curve licked clean by the sea. There is no one else. I search between pots and jars and tubs of near-fluorescent spices for a sign of James: a piece of fabric, an English coin – my mind fumbles for the memory of what might have been in his pockets.

Behind the counter is a wooden till – drawers gaping and empty. Either the sea looted it or someone has come since the wave. Next to it is a metal prong where the paper orders for each hot snack are impaled. Lifting the wet mass off the spike, I try to separate the scraps from each other. James's breakfast order must be here somewhere. But the Tamil lettering is nothing but a string of pictures to me. I can't decipher it. Even if it is only a pencil mark confirming that he was there, it's something at least. A beginning.

Chapter 13

Father's name was at the top of the evacuation letter, along with Freda's, Mama's and my own. Mama was angry with the War Office for not consulting their records: they of all people should have known that he was gone. We wrote to tell Freda of our removal to Wilton and she might have replied, but we had no forwarding address to give her: we received word of a vacant town house on 15 December, just two days prior to the departure deadline; there was no time to send word.

Mama had not tampered with Father's belongings since he had died – no new vicar had been appointed so she had not needed to do so. If a letter arrived for him in the post, she would continue to place it on his study desk as if we were expecting him to return any day now to open it. She could not bring herself to load his things into boxes so, when the evacuation order came, I was left to dismantle his study alone. I packed all the books but kept back the ship, which I determined to hold on my lap in the lorry.

We had been informed of the evacuation only a week earlier. The army subsequently called a meeting in the school. Not everyone was invited but my mother insisted on attending on my father's behalf. The Archams had wind of a rumour that they were going to announce the construction of a military road through the village. But Mama returned from the meeting as white as a sheet. It was a day before she could bring herself to tell me what had been said. I heard the news, along with others, through Mrs Carter, the post mistress. Rumours gathered pace that they were to use the village as a training ground for the Yanks. *To prepare the troops for inland assaults on urban settlements.* Allies, they called them. We were to be invaded by our own friends.

On our moving day, Annie called in to say goodbye. Her mother and father had found accommodation in Devizes; we would be living twenty miles apart.

'You will write?' she asked, with a note of uncertainty.

'Of course.'

'I can't imagine us not being friends, Vi. I know there's a war on but we must stay in touch.'

I told her we would arrange to meet up soon, but we both knew it was a lie; since Father had died, Mama and I could ill afford to travel. Annie and I hugged tightly and she scampered back to her cottage. There were so many goodbyes to be said that we kept them brief. Everything seemed bearable when completed with as little fuss as possible.

An ATS girl arrived with the lorry to collect our belongings and we tried our best to load Father's desk into the back of the vehicle. But, between us, we could not lift it, not even with a third pair of hands. There were few men left in the village who could offer help and those that remained had their own homes to see to. I feared for a moment that Mama might ask me to send for Pete. Instead, she extracted the drawers like organs from the desk. As we drove away, she clenched her fists and tried with all her might not to look back at the oak frame which stood, as firm as a custodian, in front of the house.

We were taken to a terraced cottage in Wilton whose owner – a widower – had recently passed away. His relations had no need of the house and were prepared to let it to us for a modest sum. Since they had not been to visit the place, they could not vouch for its upkeep, but we were not about to refuse a roof over our heads, offered on such reasonable terms.

'There we are, Mama. It's not so bad,' I remarked, as we drew up outside our new lodgings. The cottage had a sandstone front with arched windows that looked as if they had been borrowed from a church. 'Quite cosy, really.'

The ATS girl helped us unload the lorry into the front garden but Mama insisted on sending her back to Imber directly to assist other households who were yet to move. We were left alone to shepherd our belongings, one box at a time, into the cottage. Mama let herself in with a key and carried the first through the hallway. Upon entering the kitchen at the far end of the house, I heard the box of crockery drop clean onto the tiles. I followed into the room to find her staring up at the clouds, our teacups in fragments at her feet. The walls had been reduced to rubble and there was little left of the roof. Surveying the damage from the lawn, we saw that the entire back of the house had been blown open by a bomb. The kitchen, the bedrooms and the landing were all exposed to the open air as if someone had unhinged a doll's house and rifled through the rooms.

The War Department's Estate Office was alerted to the situation but the clerk informed us that accommodation could not be found on our behalf with so little notice. Mama appealed to the landlords in writing that same afternoon but the letter would take two days to arrive. I doubted they would be able to afford the repairs.

We had no other option but to leave our belongings in the ruined cottage and seek a room at a guesthouse. An elderly lady living at number ten directed us to the Pembroke Inn, just a street away. We entered to find it brimming with men in uniform, some stooped over the bar in the corner, others immersed in newspapers spread wide in the leather chairs by the fire. I tried not to think about the warmth of the flames.

The landlady at the desk was sympathetic but said it would not be appropriate to house two lone women in a makeshift officers' mess, even if she did have rooms available. 'It's been nothing but trouble since they took over Wilton House,' she explained. 'Air raids every week.'

She arranged for a small supper of bread and broth to be brought to us before regretfully sending us on our way. We retraced our steps along King Street.

'What would he do,' Mama asked, 'if he were with us?'

The air had sharpened with the light's departure and I dreaded arriving back at the cottage. 'He'd say that things are bound to seem better in the morning,' I replied.

'Warmer, yes, but I don't know about better.'

Inside the cottage, we retrieved as many blankets as we could find from our luggage and pulled my parents' mattress into the space next to the hearth. The living room was the only part of the house with its ceiling still intact. As we crawled into our nightgowns and hid our shivers in the blankets, I heard Mama's laughter filter through the cold.

'I'm just thinking of Freda,' she whispered. 'She'd be wall-papering the place in no time.'

'Wallpapering what?' I smiled. 'It's not as if we're spoilt for walls.'

Then, side by side in the quiet, we waited for our laughter to melt underneath the ache of everything – his death, our depar-ture, this poor excuse for a home.

We spent three nights – cold and awful – in that blitzed shell before we were offered a vacant cottage on Russell Street. Mama and I were in no fit state to spend another night in the freezing air without a fire so we accepted the property, regard-less of its reputed disrepair. Damp and lack of electricity were nothing to contend with compared to the near-open air of Hor-ton Cottage, King Street.

Once we had installed ourselves, we spread our saucepans across the loft to collect the rain and resolved to fix the holes as soon as we could gather together the funds.

Upstairs, the damp had drawn maps – strange, expanding con-tinents – over the walls of the bedrooms. Mama kept telling me that we would be able to find something better as soon as the war was over. She was talking as if we would never be allowed back home and I told her as much. But she had no reply to give me.

Father's belongings stayed in their boxes. There was no room for shelving. Mama removed one volume at a time, working her way religiously through them in the evenings. *The Observer's Book of British Birds*, *Peake's Commentary on the Bible*, Spenser's *Faerie Queene* – no matter how dense the book, she would press on through it until it could be returned to its box with a deeper crease in its spine. She'd read with such vigour that it seemed as if she were searching for something, some clue as to why he was still gone.

I found a window-sill in our bedroom for the bottled ship. I surrounded it with some of the shells he used to collect and display on the window-sills of his study. Their shapes always seemed so foreign under the landlocked parsonage windows, surrounded on every side, not by a sea, but by a vast plain. But to Father, the Plain was a kind of ocean; it behaved in mysterious ways. He always said he would not be surprised if it had claimed as many lives as our nearest stretch of sea. Mama used to complain about how the shells collected dust but he was resolute about keeping them there. I would catch him from time to time, standing by the window with a shell pressed to his ear, listening for the breath of a wave.

We spent our first month mending the roof with whatever money we could spare, all the while fearing that the parsonage was gathering the very holes that we were patching up in Wilton. Civilian men were scarce in the town and there was nobody we could ask to do the work. In the end, I took shifts in the old carpet factory, making camouflage and tarpaulin for the troops. Whenever a sheet of fabric was found to be faulty, I would smuggle it home at the end of the day to rig up over one of the holes.

Pete called round on one of those hole-patching Sundays. My mother was working on the back wall while I was up in the loft. We had been informed by the Major that Pete had gone to work as a farmhand less than a mile away near Coombe Bissett, parting ways with the Archams, who had been rehoused in Lavington. I did not know how he had come by our address. He told us in the doorway that, as it was his day off, he had thought to bring some meat from the farm. He had to jam his foot against the door to prevent my mother slamming it in his face.

'You've got some nerve showing your face here.'

'Mrs Fielding, I shan't come in if you don't want to see me but please let me speak to Violet.'

I shied back up the stairs at the sound of my name, unsure of what he might say.

My mother bristled. 'That depends on whether she wants to speak to you.'

I wanted to dissolve into the wall with the damp and be gone.

'Vi?' He leant past my mother and caught my eye.

'I'm sorry. There's a lot of work to do,' I replied, glancing up towards the roof.

'Let me help,' he offered. 'You'll be finished in half the time.'

I shook my head but my mother accepted his offer, rather more quickly than I was expecting. She was so fed up with rain-soaked carpets and damp beds that she was not about to turn down an offer of help, particularly from a competent pair of hands like Pete's.

'I suppose it's the least you can do,' she muttered, standing aside for him in the hall.

Pete followed me up to the loft and watched as I tried to tack a square of tarpaulin to the back of the first hole. 'That's useless, that is.' He sighed. 'The rain will pour straight back through. You need to get a man up onto the roof to fix the tiles.'

'Oh, and they're two a penny right now, are they?'

'I have a friend who could help.'

'How kind,' I replied, not sounding as if I meant it.

Pete came up close and held a second piece down while I fumbled with the tape. I had missed his smell – fields and chalk dust and smoking fires – as much as I had missed Imber.

'I heard you've found work in the factory,' he said.

I nodded.

'I hope you didn't avoid the Land Army because of me, Vi. The girls on the farm say the factory's tough as anything.'

'A girl's entitled to a change of scene,' I said coldly. 'And there would be no one around for Mama if I chose farm work. My sister isn't here any more, remember?'

He dropped his hands and stood back from me. 'I wanted to talk to you about Freda.'

I reddened at her name and hoped the light in the loft was dim enough to hide it.

'She asked a favour of me, that's all. I can't be blamed for her going to London.'

'You knew how much it would upset us.'

'But – she hadn't been herself, not since your father . . . I thought it would help if she got away for a while.'

His voice had softened. There was an intimacy in it that alarmed me.

'I saw you dancing with her, Pete.'

He cocked his head, slowly grasping my meaning.

'At Warminster Camp. I was outside. Looking in.'

He did not fidget, as I expected him to. He held my gaze.

'Mr Archam told Annie,' I continued. 'So we caught a lift to Warminster to see for ourselves.'

'A lad can dance with a girl. It doesn't have to mean anything,' said Pete. 'People set too much store by these things.'

He took a step towards me but I backed away. 'Nothing *happened*, Violet.'

'You're talking as if you owe me an explanation and you don't. There's nothing . . . We're not –'

Pete raised a hand to the hole in the roof, dropping his stare. 'I didn't mean to hurt you.'

'I'm not hurt,' I retorted. 'There's nothing to be hurt about.' My voice had wavered so I bit my lip and paused. 'I'm only sorry,' I ventured, 'that you felt you could tell her things that you couldn't tell me.'

'Whatever Freda's said . . .' He paused. And swallowed, Adam's apple kneading the length of his throat. 'Your sister likes you to believe she has secrets. Because they make her feel better about herself.'

Then he put down the piece of tarpaulin he was holding and walked over to the loft ladder. 'I'm at Welham Farm near Coombe, if you or your mother needs help . . . a roofer . . .' He trailed off and stepped down through the gap in the loft floor. A minute or so later, I heard the front door open and close. Through the holes in the roof, I could hear his steps on the road.

Chapter 14

One man shouts into the face of the rubble. He puts his ear to the heap and waits. There's no answer. He tries again. This time, the other people on the pile begin to murmur and jostle and pick off bricks. Someone must be underneath. I get close enough to the front to hear the trapped voice, barely louder than the buzz of a fly. A woman digging on the opposite side of the pile lets out a shout and we all scramble over. She has grabbed hold of some dust-caked fingers that flex and cement their grip on her hand. I swallow back the thought of the body at sea – fingers like clay in mine. It's James – or at least the hope of him.

Ravindra has lost interest in the rescue. He is walking vaguely away across the wreckage. I shout after him, his name still not fitting on my tongue. He doesn't turn, even though I know he heard me, fed up – I can tell – with being unable to make himself understood. I try again.

He calls back in Tamil, and points wearily towards the fringe of the town. Nothing more. I nod as if I understand. But beyond that we've run out of the words we never had. Pressing his hands together in an upright prayer towards me, he says one last thing. There's little point in a proper goodbye. I lift my hand, vaguely, and he's gone.

The voice under the bricks grows into a moan. More and more debris is removed. The fingers become ecstatic, grasping at the sun until all the veins are taut and purple. Soon, we have made a large enough hole to pull at both arms. The crown of a head emerges, then eyelids sealed shut by the dust. It's a boy – barely ten or eleven years old – reborn from the rubble. His lips are parted slightly as if he were in the midst of speaking when the walls fell. The man who first called for help buries his head in the boy's chest. A woman pours water over his mouth, holding it high above him and letting it bounce and splash off his face. He barely has enough energy to drink, mouth opening and shutting, like the gill of a fish.

Everybody wants to be close to him and hold him as if he were their own. Hands clutch at the warmth of his skin, and I find I am reaching towards him too. I grasp at his heart – feeling for myself its frantic, living beat.

The sun burns. There is no shade, only ruins. A few buildings remain standing – frozen ghosts whose hollow windows gawp inwards, in awe of their own survival. I tread on old doors and iron roofs and tell myself he isn't under them. Even the dead are in hiding. It was easier to search for him on the beach where the wave had laid out the debris for all to see. Here, it has been more covert, hiding its victims under slabs and beams and mountains of dust.

The paper orders from the *dosa* stall are still in my grasp. Moving from the rubble where the boy was found, I cut a path towards the centre of the town. I need to find someone who speaks English.

In the part of the village that is furthest from the sea, more men and women emerge, each lifting hands to heads at how little has been left behind. One woman stops beside a pile of dust and, sinking into the silt, starts to weep. Another man digs beside her. I want to tell him to stop: he'll only unearth the worst. James would know what to do if he was here. He would have begun to peel back the town's layers in search of survivors. If only it was him looking for me: he'd root me out like one of his postcards and maybe we'd stand a chance of making it, the two of us. But things fall apart in my hands.

It started a month ago in June, Near Kerman, halfway through the overland trail. But sometimes, looking back, I wonder if it had been going on for longer. We had picked up eight passengers in Istanbul: two New Yorkers called Jeannie and Curt, an Australian named Rob, then David, Clara and Sue, who were all from the Home Counties, Erik from Sweden and Marc from New Zealand. Marc paid the least for his seat: he was on his way home and, after burning all his cash in Europe, bargained his way into the van with smiling ruthlessness. The final price was barely enough to cover his share of the petrol. James took an instant dislike to him. He wore his hair short and dressed anonymously in black and navy blue, even in the desert heat. Once on board, he was warm and affable and seemed able to sway the trip in any direction he pleased. It was his influence – his insistence on so many detours – that James grew to despise. James – eager to reach Kashmir – was cajoled into making a three-hundred-kilometre diversion to Shiraz so that Marc, and the rest of the van, could see the ruins at Persepolis. Secretly, I was grateful: there was a whole treasure trove of drawings to be made from the slim pillars that led to nothing and the walls that held millennia-old etchings in their stone. It was a must-see on the overland trail, as significant as Arafat, claimed Marc.

'We can't keep diverting. We have a route we're trying to get through,' James told him flatly. We were driving to Kerman at the time and the Pakistani border remained open only for short periods. The nearest town to the border, Zahedan, was nine hours away, and we were yet to stock up on supplies. It was a desert drive, which required two days' worth of food and water. Up to this point, we had meandered off the route whenever the name of a town took our fancy. Guesthouses had been easy to find in the cities and we had camped in tents near villages in between. We'd grown a taste for spontaneity, which, James feared, would stop us reaching Pakistan.

'You came here for an adventure, didn't you? Nobody cares how long it takes,'

'We were very open about the itinerary. If you were so desperate to go there you should have joined another group.' I had not heard James use that tone before. We had treated everyone on board as friends so far, not as paying customers. He was usually so laid-back.

'Alice,' Marc said, turning to me. This was his first mistake – to draw me into it. 'You want to see the ruins. You told me so yourself. Tell James you want to go.'

James shot me a glance from the steering-wheel. I hurried to read what was in it – anger that I liked the idea of Persepolis, hurt that I had talked about it to Marc.

'She's an artist.' Marc turned to James. 'I've seen her sketches. Think of the drawings she'll make of the ruins.'

James kept his eyes on the road. 'There are eight other people to consider.'

'We all want to go,' persisted Marc. 'Jeannie, Curt and Erik agree. So do the others.'

'It does sound like an impressive place,' added Clara, from the second row of seats.

By the time we reached the turning to Shiraz, James had relented and accepted the diversion. We stopped in a village for water and Tabrizi bread, which the others coated with Spam and mayonnaise they took from the back of the van. James pulled me to the far side of the vehicle while the others ate so that we were out of earshot.

'What were you playing at back there?'

'I – We don't have to go to Persepolis, not if it's too much.'

'We do now, thanks to you. I should have known you'd take his side.'

'What do you mean by that?'

He sighed and looked past me across the sand – as bleak as a sea ahead of us.

'James . . . what do you mean?'

'You don't realize how important this is – for me.'

'That's unfair. I want to finish the route too. We all do. But we always agreed it was about seeing what there was along the way, rather than reaching the end.'

'Sometimes I wish the van would just break down so that they'd all leave. You, me, on a train – it would be so much simpler . . .'

He put a hand on my waist and I softened. 'I'm sorry I said what I did to Marc. You know what he's like. It was a way of shutting him up for a bit.'

'It's not that.'

'What's wrong, then?'

'He said he'd seen your drawings.'

'He asked to see them. We had hours to kill on the Turkish border, remember? Why does it matter, anyway? The whole van has probably seen them by now.'

'I've been trying to persuade you to keep hold of them for months and suddenly, since the border, you've been keeping them.'

'I was always worried Mum would find them if I kept them at home . . . but here, it's different.'

'As if it would have mattered, Alice.'

I fell silent. Even I couldn't explain what I was hiding from her. 'I know it doesn't make sense,' I said eventually.

He leant back on the side of the van next to me. We felt the heat from the enamel seep through our T-shirts.

'Marc asked if we were an item.'

I looked at him, saying nothing.

'Back in Istanbul. He said you were pretty.'

'He's with Clara, isn't he?'

'Not like I'm with you.'

'I would never –'

'I know, I know. It's just . . . It's been on my mind, that's all.'

I knew what I should do: I should tell him I loved him, that he was the reason I had come away. The others were just a means to an end – he and I together in India. But the words stalled and became trapped.

'If I just knew where we stood . . .' he continued.

'Then what?' I asked, eyes on the sand. I thought of Alexander the Great throwing his burning torch into the palace at Persepolis: the city dying in his mind before the fire even gathered pace. James didn't have to hem me in like that. He should have known that I, too, had a torch I could throw – something precious to burn.

With Kanyakumari in rubble around me, I clench the wodge of orders from the *dosa* stall. James's must be in there somewhere. It won't help me find him but at least I can trace his last movements – where he was when the wave hit.

'Do you speak any English?' A man lifts his head from the debris and doesn't reply. I show the orders to him and he frowns. Another man parrots, *How are you I am fine*, then drifts on his way.

A third woman reads the first order. 'It is food, sister,' she explains. '*Dosa.*'

'How many *dosa*?' I ask, holding up my fingers one by one until I reach five.

'Sister, look.' She casts a hand towards the wreckage, the bangles on her wrist chiming together. 'There is no time.' Then she presses the water-logged order back into my palm and, with full eyes, walks on.

'Please!' I shout after her. 'Please help me! It's my husband – he's gone.'

She turns and tilts her head at me, pointing again to the flattened houses beneath her feet and joining a group of men and women who are trying to roll a car off the top of a collapsed building. The under-carriage clasps the concrete stubbornly. I watch as she places her palms on the silver metal above the bumper and heaves herself forward with the rest of them. As if it will make a difference.

I scrunch up the order in my hand. He was always so curious, wanting to try everything and learn everything – fitting together the nuts and bolts of how a place worked. I would have settled for a packet of biscuits for breakfast but James wanted to search for something authentic.

'You're not going to lie there all day, are you?' he'd asked me, half an hour before the wave came. He stood fully clothed in the doorway of our guesthouse room, rucksack slung over his shoulder.

I lay on the bed, not replying, even though I was awake.

'Come on, Alice!' He crossed to the mattress and planted a kiss on my forehead. Then he took hold of the sheet and pulled it from me.

'Let me sleep.' I groaned, pulling my legs up to my stomach.

'It's a beautiful day outside.'

'It's always beautiful. And hot,' I mumble.

'You're acting like a teenager!'

I batted him away with a hand. He'd smelt of smoke and old banknotes before we'd arrived here. But once we reached the coast, he went swimming so much that the sea sank into his skin and clothes so that now he smelt of saltwater too.

'What do you fancy for breakfast?'

'Whatever you're having.' I spoke into the pillow.

'I'll get us a few *dosa*. The landlord was telling me about them. Indian pancakes. South Indian. Can you manage three? Then we can go swimming. A swim'll wake you up.'

I sat up and stretched the night from my arms and legs. 'I'm sorry, nothing changes,' I laughed, 'not even on the other side of the world. You go ahead. I'll catch up.'

'Meet you at the beach in half an hour, then?' And, with that unanswered question, he closed the door.

I think of him walking up to the *dosa* stall on the beachfront, ordering our breakfast and then waiting. Maybe he stepped onto the sand, like others, to stare at the mass of grey building and building in the distance. Perhaps he saw the sea being sucked out and drained, like I did from the hotel window, as if someone had pulled a plug from the seabed. I should have known then and gone to fetch him. But instead I was pleased, *pleased*, at not having to go for a swim. I didn't know what it meant. Nobody did. I saw some of the locals running out and picking up fish, huge uncatchable things with purple markings, that had been left to flip themselves to death in the sand.

Then the first person started to run. And another. Maybe James stood his ground, took out his camera. Maybe he ran too.

Chapter 15

The factory made me half deaf. It was lonely work – impossible to raise your voice over the hammer of a hundred sewing-machines. I knew the names of the girls on my bench but little else; conversation was impossible. At night, I dreamt of the motions I performed during the day – the pinning of a hem, the feel of the tarpaulin between my fingers. There was a rhythm for everything: folding, cutting, stitching. I tried to break free from the work of the others, do things in a different order or manner, but it did not last: soon I had fallen into line again.

The larger equipment moved so quickly and with such sharpness that I feared for my fingers. One girl, Lucy, lost her thumb on her first day and couldn't work after that. Others got pregnant – the only way you could get out of your job. After three weeks, I was half tempted to push my hand under one of the levers and injure myself deliberately but the blot of blood under the chair where Lucy used to sit did away with my courage; the stain remained there as a warning to us all.

The day was split into three shifts: six until two, two until ten, and then the night session. Once you were allocated your shifts for the week, there was little opportunity for manoeuvring them. My mother – who had started work as a volunteer in the officers' canteen at Wilton House – hardly ever saw me. On Tuesdays, at six in the morning, we'd pass in the road, she on the way to her work, me on the way back from mine.

I began to wish it had been me, not Freda, who had run away to London and become a nurse. Anything but the bang, bang of metal hitting metal, of machine talking to machine.

Sometimes, when the noise grew too tiresome, I thought of

Imber's winds. I pictured myself back in the parsonage cellar, listening to the bursts and flashes, beautifully irregular and erratic above us. But the factory noise was too harsh and fast to forget for long; even the most militant of Imber's storms could not have drowned it out.

I didn't let on to Mama how difficult the work at the factory had proved. She had been set against me taking up a job there from the beginning, saying it was beneath me. I was still the parson's daughter and the factory was unbecoming. But with Father gone, I had little choice but to work. The colourlessness in my face soon gave away my discomfort and she begged me to hand in my notice.

'Your father would not approve, Violet. You know he wouldn't. He'd much rather you were on a farm in the fresh air than cooped up in a factory all day.'

'If I worked on a farm, I'd have to leave you, Mama. And I'm not prepared to do that, not while Freda is away. And, besides, the wages –'

'I will not have you thinking of the roof! They pay you a pittance! They'll wear you down until there's not a scrap left of you. Mark my words, they will.'

Even if Mama had persuaded me otherwise, I didn't want Pete to be proved right. He didn't approve of women in the factory any more than he did of the land girls and I wanted to show him that we, too, could pull our weight in a war. Whenever I saw him about town, I'd pinch my cheeks into a healthy glow and find someone to chat to, hoping he wouldn't notice that I was out of sorts.

In Imber, I could never track him down. He had always been off on errands – prising lambs from fences or mending a hedge beyond the Barrow. And he had had a knack for vanishing onto the Plain whenever I needed to find him. But in Wilton – now that I wanted him gone – he became impossible to avoid.

I hated him for helping Freda, for putting his hands on her

waist before I had let him near mine. I hated him for being there when Father died, for bearing witness to the one thing I wanted to forget. But the town kept knitting us together, as if we were a pair of terraced houses, irrevocably joined at the wall. The only way to ensure that I never saw or heard of him was to lock myself away in our fraying cottage. There I would stare for hours on end at the maps drawn by the damp across the walls of my bedroom. With my feet propped against the skirting-board, I would sit and read my makeshift atlas until its hills and valleys took on the shape of the ones I used to call home.

Pete often came into town to pick up supplies for the farm. I frequently saw him queuing for sugar or tea with one of the land girls on my way back from the factory – always the same one. On the few occasions that he caught me looking, I buried myself in an errand until it was complete. Yet the more I came across him, the less I could channel myself into an attitude of indifference. *He can't have cared much for Freda if he let her run off to London without him.* I began to concoct excuses for him, rehearsing them over and over until they resembled the truth. Mama told me to let him be. She didn't trust him. But there was something in the rhythm of the factory machines that caused thoughts to turn over in the mind. Sally used to say the place wasn't made for broken hearts. Her fiancé had been killed in action and the machines would not let her forget it. I resolved to call on Pete after my Thursday-night shift.

I left the factory at sunrise and wove my way along the shuttered row of shops that lined North Street. As I reached the fringes of the town, the houses started to take on a different shape, the roofs slowly softening from tile to thatch. I could feel the rhythm of the factory lagging behind me as I walked, the whirr of the machines dissipating finally, like an ache in the head.

Only in Coombe could I be free of the factory's thud. It was a place with no rhythm: houses half gathered themselves into a hamlet yet maintained their distance from each other. It had no valley to hem its people in, no sudden dip in which journeys could be halted and forgotten, like in Imber. Instead, it clung loosely to the curve of a river where the water never paused. It was a place that people passed through in order to reach somewhere else – never a destination, always a turn in the road. If Pete were to make anywhere his home, it would be here.

'He's out milking,' one of the girls shouted across the yard when, arriving at the farm, I knocked on the door of the farmhouse. I crossed to the milking parlour and stooped inside: it smelt of cud and cowpat and wet earth – the same smell that coated the floor of the valley back home. I could see his silhouette at the far end, hunched over a stool, arms working an udder. The sun had not yet fully come up.

'What do you want, Violet?' he asked, without turning round. He must have heard me in the yard, and I was caught for a moment by the thought that perhaps he recognized my gait.

'To talk to you.'

'What's changed?' He removed his hands from the cow and swivelled on his stool to face me. His hair and eyes – as dark as each other – caused something to dislodge inside me. I hated the way I was drawn to them. I felt as if I had been tricked, like the other girls, into losing my composure and settling my gaze on him.

'I see you've been keeping an eye on that sugar queue,' he continued. I could just make out his smirk through the darkness.

'I don't know what you mean,' I retorted.

'Bea's a good girl.'

'Oh, Pete, don't start.'

'You're angry with me, aren't you?'

'No.'

He stood up from the seat and waited for me to reach his end of the parlour.

'I didn't come here to . . . You can't have expected things to stay the same after Fa–' My eyes started to prickle so I turned away and walked back towards the entrance to the milking parlour. The light had entered the yard, pouring itself into the far corner and then spreading, slowly, like spilt milk.

The cattle shifted and groaned. I could hear his steps behind me. I dreaded the feel of his hand on my arm, then wished for it when it didn't come. 'Look, I'm almost done here,' he called. 'We'll take a walk up Throope Hill. You'd like that.'

'Don't tell me what I'd like.' I stooped back into the light. He drew level with me.

'Come on,' he said, finally taking my arm.

The grass on the hill was still blurred with dew but the sun would make quick work of it; the sky had all the makings of a hot day. We cut our own wet trail up to the peak. I breached the silence by telling him how much I missed Salisbury Plain and how this landscape, with its wide-brimmed rivers and steep peaks, felt like a different country.

Pete thrashed at a bush with a stick. 'It won't achieve anything thinking about it, Violet.'

'That's all very well for you to say.'

'What do you want me to tell you? That I miss the place?'

I only just caught his question, tangled as it was in a gust pushing at us from across the hill. 'You must . . .'

'I'm sorry, Vi, but I don't miss it.' He was face to face with me now. 'I wasn't like you. I couldn't just sit around in the parsonage all day and go into town whenever I liked. The lambing was hard – the Archams worked me hard. I was fond of them. But I don't miss it. Not a bit.'

'But you had Annie and me,' I murmured quietly, unsure of whether I would be heard.

'I still have you,' he replied, slowing his pace and reaching for my hand. He had never held it before, not properly. Our fingers had touched once, unconsciously, up on the Plain. We were keeping an eye on his flock, grazing up near Brouncker's Well, and he had put his hand down flat, thinking there was grass beneath it, his smallest finger overlapping onto my thumb. And he didn't move it. Not even when he must have realized his mistake.

'Yes.' I smiled, giving him my hand and letting him pull me up the path. 'But I miss home . . .' I added.

'Do you miss Freda?' he asked.

'No.' I released my hand from his.

'But she's your sister.'

'What does it matter, now Father's gone for good?'

'It's difficult. I mean, I know how difficult . . .' He trailed off. 'I know how you feel.'

'Do you?' I asked, but the directness of my question seemed to silence him. It was a full minute before either of us spoke again. There was a lull in the wind as we reached the top of Throope Hill. A stillness seemed to fall on everything so that even the grass ceased to sing. 'You spent six years there, Pete. Surely you must have thought of it as home.'

'I went there for work – 's all there is to it.'

'But –'

He let out the breath in his lungs and began walking again. I broke into a run to catch up with him. 'If Imber's not your home, then where is?' We were descending the other side of the hill now. 'You must come from somewhere.' I drew alongside him and tried to take his hand again but his palm lay slack in mine as we walked. I wondered later, if I had been gentler, whether he might have told me more. But the fissure in our conversation made me fearful and I thought of how much I dreaded people bringing up Father when they talked of Imber. Whatever had happened before Pete had come to us, he had assigned it the same closeted silence as I had my father's death.

'Freda will be back,' he said, after a while. I was so grateful to him for saying something that it took me a moment to register the mention of my sister.

'Will she?' I answered vaguely. There was nothing to lose in asking my next question. 'Do you miss –'

'Do I what?'

'Do you miss Freda?'

He paused, taking up the slack in his grip on my hand. 'I danced with her because she looked pretty . . .' Then he watched as I swallowed my disgust. 'But she's not my friend,' he added.

'Friend?' I echoed, the word coming out clipped and prickling. I found, however, that I could not let go of his hand.

'I didn't mean . . . What I wanted to say . . .' A surge of scarlet invaded his cheeks mid-sentence. I had never seen his face burn like that. We reached the middle of the Down – a bed for sleeping bombs. I could already see a few, nesting in the grass.

'Look!' I wanted to save him the embarrassment of actually having to say it. It was enough for me to know he had been on the cusp. I pointed at one of the bombs – the biggest we had ever seen.

'What a shocker!' yelled Pete, as we ran towards it. I stopped ten yards short of its metal casing, suddenly scared. Pete kept running. 'Come on, Violet!'

'What if it goes off?' I called.

'Don't be silly. None of the others have.'

'But this one's bigger.'

Ignoring my protests, he bent down and tugged at the grass around it. Then he ran a hand across its skin, tracing the number etched on it with a finger.

'It's a Satan! I've never seen a Satan!'

'You've probably felt its blast, though, that's for certain. Please, Pete, it's not safe.'

'All right, all right.' He backed away from the bomb slowly until he was level with me. We froze for a moment, fearful of disturbing it any further. Then he took my hand and marched back towards it, dragging me along behind. I dug my feet in.

'Pete! No!'

'There's nothing to be scared of!'

He stopped so close to it that I could reach out and touch the rusting metal. But he wasn't looking at the bomb like I was. I felt his arm around my waist, his stare on my neck. Then he pulled me downwards, suddenly, so that we were sitting on the casing. He kissed me – a barely there kiss – but it felt perilous, as if we could be blown apart at any moment.

Chapter 16

The 3rd Armoured Division of the US Army arrived in Wilton two months after we did, in 1944. They brought telephone lines, and noise.

My mother had been volunteering at Wilton House for a month now, serving tea in the NAAFI to the soldiers and bringing the homesick ones back to our cottage for a home-cooked meal. Their American accents cantered around Wilton in a way our English ones never could, like a saxophone outdoing a cello. Pete couldn't stand them; whenever he caught sight of their uniform in town he'd mutter, 'Yank,' under his breath and spit out something about how late to the game they were. The rest of the town, however, was enamoured; he was forced to watch open-mouthed as they showered these transatlantic curiosities with their best tea and meat.

On one of my trips to Wilton House with Mama, I picked up an American serviceman's manual, which had been discarded on the floor of the dining room. *On a small crowded island where forty-five million people live*, I read, *each man learns to guard his privacy carefully.* Privacy did not abound here: I learnt the hard way that Wilton wasn't built for secrets. Yet when confronted by a clamour of GI Joes coming towards me on the stairwell, I thought of that manual more than once – that you were better off keeping your distance on an island as small as ours. I tried to stay away from them, for Pete's sanity more than my own. But any reserve on my part only strengthened the resolve of the infantry to advance across the gap I had left between us.

They came home for dinner in groups – two or three at a time, most of them four years my senior. When my mother was out of the room, they would lean across the table and ask if I was *going steady* with anyone. I would say yes, not entirely sure of what they meant, but thinking all the while of Pete.

'Mrs Fielding, you cook like a dream!' they'd coo, when my mother re-entered the kitchen, clattering their cutlery around their plates as if they were playing percussion. The accents soon got the better of me, each word sugar-coated and easy on the tongue. And when they laughed, they'd rock right back in their chairs and throw their heads back, letting themselves go in a way I had never seen anybody else do.

It wasn't just their homesickness that my mother was trying to cure: it was her own loneliness. Freda's absence and my shifts at the factory meant that she often ate by herself. When the Americans were in the house, we could almost forget about the missing fractions of our family who used to occupy the chairs around the table. They were easier to befriend than the British soldiers: far away from home without their mothers and sisters, fathers and brothers. A whole ocean away from their wives.

Sam – short for Samson – came home with her on a Tuesday. I remember the day because I was supposed to be working. Sally had begged me to swap shifts with her so that she could see her brother, who was home on leave.

After letting myself into the house, I was met by the sound of that peculiarly American laughter pealing through the hallway from the kitchen.

'You shoulda tasted it, Martie! I never tasted something so darn awful in my whole life!'

Martie? I nudged the kitchen door open.

'Hello,' I interrupted.

'Violet!' She scraped her chair back over the tiles and tucked her hair behind her ears. 'You're back early! Don't you have a shift, my darling?'

'I swapped with Sally.'

I walked over to the American – an officer, I noticed, from his chevrons, not a boy – and offered my hand. 'I'm Martha's daughter.'

'Samson,' he replied, taking my hand and shaking it with vigour. 'Most folk here call me Sam. I take it you're the famous Vi-vi?'

I informed him that, given the freshness of our acquaintance, I would prefer it if he called me Violet.

'Violet, darling!' my mother intervened, smiling fixedly at me. 'Come and have some food with us.' She got up from her chair and ladled some stew onto a plate. I watched as a generous hunk of bread was placed in the centre of the table. Sam winked at me. The loaf was clearly his doing.

'The chef at Wilton House likes to spoil him,' explained my mother.

'It's worth a few greenbacks over here, I'll guess,' Sam added. 'There you are, take a slice. I brought it for you.' He reached over and pushed the bread towards me.

'You didn't know I'd be here,' I muttered, glaring down at the loaf.

'We would have kept some.' Mama waved away my comment as she spoke.

'She's a tough cookie!' laughed Sam, clapping a palm on my shoulder from all the way across the table. 'I have a feeling we're going to get along just fine.'

He was right. It pains me to think of it, but he was. To begin with, I hated everything about him – the big movements he made with his big hands; the way he did everything far too vigorously. Sometimes he'd rip whole sections of the newspaper just by turning a page. And when he talked, he'd fling his arms about and knock ornaments or crockery from their places, getting carried away with some story or other. Doors were slammed rather than closed, in spite of his constant good mood. But the house had noise in it again. And that in itself was enough to make me thaw.

The frequency of his visits increased until barely three days would pass without him coming home for dinner. I tried to arrange my shifts so that I would be there on the days that Sam came. I even stopped meeting Pete at the factory gate on Thursdays. At first I convinced myself that I was merely protecting Mama; we both knew how the town could talk. But when I arrived home to find him absent, I would feel the disappointment of it so keenly that I could no longer ignore my fondness for him. On the days he did come, he would take me down to the bomb shelter at the bottom of the garden after dinner and tell ghost stories with a torch while my mother washed up. I protested – tried to look bored, but then he would coax out a twist when I was least expecting it, causing me to jump or wince or put a hand to my mouth and give myself away. When Mama had finished at the sink, she would join us in the shelter with hot cups of Horlicks. Sometimes I wished the sirens would sound just so I could stay there with the two of them all night, swallowing story after story with each sip of my drink.

Mama did not like to talk about the past. And Sam learnt not to ask. As far as he was concerned, we had lived in Wilton all our lives. He guessed what he could about my father but Mama never spoke of Imber or the accident. Despite her guardedness, I became greedy for details about Sam – what he had done before the war and what he would do after; what the cities in America were like and how much he missed home. Mama loved to listen to him talk and, while she refrained from asking him questions, she was secretly glad of mine.

After a while, she started to do her hair differently. She bought pins and a net from town. It puzzled me for weeks – the neat bun at the back of her head. Among Imber's farmers, she had never fussed over her looks for fear of being accused of having too much time on her hands: her hair had roamed free in strands across her face and she had had no qualms about letting the sun brown her skin. Father had liked it that way. Yet she had taken to wearing wide-brimmed hats of late while tending the vegetables in the garden. And, despite the soil, her fingernails were always kept filed and clean.

I caught Sam once, removing one of the pins from her hair. He backed away calmly when I entered the room, as if he didn't mind the disturbance. 'It was giving her a headache,' was his placid excuse. My mother was more flustered, swivelling towards the sink and turning on the tap, as if the sound could blot out the memory of what I had just seen.

One night in March, when the sirens wailed across the town, I was on a night shift in the factory. The supervisors were stubborn with their evacuation orders, ordering us out of the building only when they could see the bellies of the planes opening above them and the baskets beginning to fall. Quotas, it seemed, were more important than limbs. I watched Sally's eyes widen with fear opposite me as she restarted her sewing-machine under the whine of the sirens. We all knew we'd go up in flames as fast as a box of kindling, were anything to land on us.

I was about to return to my work when I spotted Sam at the door, out of breath and arguing with the supervisor. I couldn't hear what he was saying: the noise of the machines stamped out their discussion. But he caught my eye from across the factory floor.

Before he could be stopped, he strode over to me and took my hand. 'Martha sent me. We've got to get into a shelter, they're aiming for the factory and you'll be done for if you stay here!'

'I can't leave the girls!' I yelled, over the hammer of the machinery, glancing across at Sally, who had stood up, bemused.

'Violet, I'm serious,' he urged. 'We have to get you out!'

Before I could stop him, his hand had locked itself onto one of mine and he dragged me through a door at the far end of the floor, swearing loudly when he found himself in the supply cupboard. He pulled his jacket sleeve over a clenched fist and smashed through the window at the back, lifting me up and pushing me through the gap as if he were posting a parcel. I cut my leg on the glass and the blood trickled down the back of my calf, like the stocking lines I'd once drawn on myself to impress Pete. Sam followed me.

We ran as fast as we could down three blacked-out streets to my front door, the sirens still cawing dizzily over our heads. Mama was already inside the shelter, peering out of the opening. 'I thought you'd never come!' she shrilled, as we climbed down inside with her. I assumed she was talking to Sam but it was me she pulled into her chest, so close that I could feel the breath shuddering up from her lungs.

We couldn't see the sky from the shelter. We didn't need to, though, to know when an incendiary was on its way. The inside of the shelter would glow orange so that, for a few seconds, you could see everyone's face. It was as if somebody had struck a match and held it up to find their way. The illuminations happened five or six times as each bomb fell. We watched in shock as one landed in the garden, near to our timber-framed porch. Before Mama could protest, Sam jumped out of the shelter and emptied rainwater from the wheelbarrow over it, my mother all the while screaming for him to get back inside.

'I'm not having you risk your life over that shabby excuse for a house,' she chastised him, in the darkness. I listened to her words dissolve without an echo into the dirt walls and floor.

'Don't think they'll find you another, Martie, if you get hit,' Sam warned. 'If you're not careful, there won't be a home for him to come back to.'

I could feel my mother's horror, hooking darkly onto his words.

'You know full well he's not coming back,' Mama replied, as another basket inflamed the sky. 'You don't need me to tell you he's dead. Did you think I would – What kind of wife do you think I am?'

I had to bite back the urge to exit the shelter and run. Sam, for once, stayed silent.

While we waited for more incendiaries to fall, I tried to turn my mind to the girls spilling through the factory door. The shelters were at least two hundred yards away. At least. The quick ones might have made it. It depended on how much time they were given. But even if they did reach them, they were far from safe: the shelters were full to bursting with rolled carpets and folded tarpaulin stacked like tapers waiting to be lit; nobody within a stone's throw would stand a chance.

A fire of that size, they said, would be seen as far away as Lavington. I thought of the Archams, asleep in their makeshift cottage. The sky outside their bedroom would gain an orange tint; a new sun would ink its way into the east. And Mrs Archam would sit up and wonder, without knowing for certain, whether it was morning.

Chapter 17

A man in a white *lungi* is the first to notice a quiver in the wreckage. By the time he gets my attention, everything around us is shifting from left to right. I crouch on my knees and ride the movements as best I can, hands pressed on the stones. There is nothing firm to hold on to. People stumble, lowering themselves to the ground, clamping hands on loose beams, running from the shade of shaking walls. I ride each sideways swing until the debris settles and breathes out powder. The dust brings to mind those frigid Wiltshire mornings where it was cold enough to watch our own breath – steam seeping from our lips, like the clouds from the cracks beneath me. I can't quite grasp how I've been flung so quickly from one to the other.

The land quietens. And I can walk again.

There's a tug on my shoulder. Someone points to the sea. Two women on the same patch of rubble have stood up to examine the horizon. With a shout to the crowd, they hurry in the opposite direction to the beach. The man in the *lungi* beside me mutters a few words, then scarpers after the women, a lick of fear on his face.

'Sister. They say another wave is coming,' says a voice to my right. It is the woman who deciphered my *dosa* orders.

'But how do they know?'

She holds up a hand and shakes her head. 'No truth.'

I stare at the tide of people leaving. Then I glance back at her; she steadies herself and placidly attends to her silt-covered *dupatta*, which has lost its pins and come loose. There has already been one wave. How can I rule out another? The water didn't just come and go, after all. It arrived and kept on coming.

I head for the hills, walking at first and then, as the fear takes hold and I remember how little time it gave me, I break into a run.

Further up the hill, the wreckage thins. For the first time, I see trees whose roots have held them steady. The town shrinks into a dizzy map beneath me: the wave has left vague traces of streets and half-drawn walls but everything seems blurred and unfinished. I begin to wish I knew the place better. Perhaps then I could piece it together in my mind. Everything that was built by human hands – the huts, the streets, the temples – has vanished. Only the Vivekananda Rock remains, knuckle-stubborn, next to the shore. It was the first object in the path of the wave; it took the brunt of its punch and yet there it is, wet and glistening, as if it has received nothing more than a ritual washing.

The climb quickens my breath and I think suddenly of Mum, dragging me up that ridge in Westbury to see the White Horse. When I was younger, I wanted to know why they had carved a horse of all creatures into the chalk of the ridge. I didn't ask Mum; I just let the question simmer inside me, hoping she'd give away the answer one day. She never told me useful things, only that, as a girl, she used to dream that the horse had galloped away. I pictured it freeing itself from the surface of the hill, shaking the chalk from its mane and cantering to Warminster.

'Dad might have liked it up here,' I said to her, as we neared the crest of the ridge. I would do this all the time when I was younger – make up statements about him and test them on her in the hope that they were true. Mum would either let out a cooped-up laugh or nod silently. I learnt from an early age that she could talk about my dad only when we were up high – able to see everything in its context. 'Why did he go away?'

She stopped still, just short of the horse's front hoof. 'He didn't know you when he left. You weren't born yet.'

'Would he have stayed if he did?'

The fields knitted themselves together in a quilt beneath the haze. Mum kept quiet.

'Did he like it up here?' I tried again.

'I don't know, Alice. There are so many things I don't know.'

I have never searched for him. Not like I'm searching for James now. With James, I have the smell of his skin, encrypted with years of smoke, and the colour and texture of his shirt. With my father, I have nothing. No place to start except a worn-out photograph and a conversation with his sister. Like Mum, I kept the thought of him buried, afraid of what I might unearth. When I got older, my questions dried up. I stopped climbing the hill with her because I no longer wanted to know. She never lied to me but, in my own way, I had grown tired of her circumventing the truth.

The debris beneath the hill loses detail in the distance and I wonder if I am high enough now to escape another wave. At the roadside, a woman is serving tea from a makeshift stall. She ferries pans of steaming water from the house behind her and pours the tea into whatever container she can find. All around the house, people are drinking out of pans and bowls and empty turmeric jars tinged yellow from the spice.

'Thank you,' I whisper, as she passes me a bowl with tea in it.

'Where do you live? USA?' she asks. I'm surprised to hear fluent English.

'No, I'm from England. Is this your house?'

'Yes, it is my husband's house. London?'

'Yes. But I've only just moved there.'

'Sure, sure,' she says, nodding. 'My daughter. She lives in London. And we visit. You're staying in India only you, sister?'

'I – No, I came with . . .' I find myself clutching my ring, 'But I don't know where he is.'

'Don't worry.' She smiled, taking hold of my ringed hand from the other side of the stall. I step back. 'Your husband is here. Outside,' she continues, once she has caught my eye.

'James?' I ask, incredulous.

She tips her head from right to left. 'Come.'

I cup a hand to my mouth, trying to stop the hope hopscotching inside me. She leads me into the garden of the house and approaches a figure stooped over a cup of tea with his back to us. He looks broader than James. But the hope won't be quelled.

'Here,' she says, tapping him on the shoulder. 'Your husband.'

He turns to face us. 'Can I help?' he asks, in a European accent.

I want to cry. 'I'm sorry, there's been a mistake.' I turn back to the woman.

She creases her eyes into a narrow frown, unsettled at the thought of not being able to match us up. Taking my hand again, she leads me inside the house. I'm glad of it. I can't bear to stay and make conversation.

We enter an echoing room with a cool, terracotta floor and I listen to the peel and clip of her flip-flops on the tiles. She stops at the centre, pulling me in towards her with a soft tug on my shirt. 'I call my brother in London, sister, and they know nothing. They hear about the wave only yesterday,' she murmurs.

'You have a telephone?'

She raises a finger to her lips. 'No, but my husband – he has a booth. Very bad line, sister.'

'I'll pay you. Please. I mean, I just need to get through to home.'

'For oversea telephone you have to make a booking,' she says, 'and the line is coming and going. But we help,' she continues. 'I will finish with the tea and then I will take you.' She turns towards the kitchen and bats me away gently with her hand.

The muscles in my chest stiffen. They know about the wave back home. Mum and Tim have no idea that I'm in Kanyakumari. We told them that Delhi was the furthest south we would go. *A wave came . . .* Nothing seems adequate. *We heard about it on the news*, they'll say, as if that counts as having seen it. There is no way of explaining and no one at home who will understand about James – too much to squeeze through a crackling handset.

I wait for around an hour; the time is full-bodied and exhaustingly slow. Seeing the tea queue diminish, I make my approach, hoping the sight of me will remind her about the telephone.

'Sister?'

'I'm sorry to disturb you again. You said you could take me to the telephone booth?'

'Yes, yes.' She picks up the edge of her sari, grasps my hand and slips on her sandals at the door of the house.

We walk halfway down the hill to a line of concrete units just short of where the wave died. I follow her into a cupboard-sized room with a narrow slit of light at the top of the wall. The heat here has fermented into a furious temperature and it is difficult to breathe. I look up at the fan that lies dormant above a well-organized desk. In the corner, a telephone is drilled to the wall between two screens, which are largely redundant as the booth is in full view of the desk. A man emerges through the door – presumably her husband. She talks to him and he frowns at me.

'What can you give him, sister? He won't take rupees.'

I look down at myself. I have nothing on me except James's shirt, my mother's coral skirt and my wedding ring – the last thing I have left of James.

'Please, I will pay him when I am home. Whatever he wants.'

They launch into another discussion. The husband sighs and raises his hands, his words speeding up. She interjects, taking me by the hand again and smiling at him as if to make my case. She turns back to me. 'No problem, sister. He says he will book a call. What is the destination?' She pulls across a blank sheet of paper from the far side of the desk and hands me a pen.

Her husband crosses his arms. He looks far from happy.

'Are you sure?' I ask. 'What did you offer him?'

'Masala dosa and chapatti.' She smiles.

'Thank you. I don't know what to say.'

'You will send my wishes to your mother. You must tell her that her daughter is well.' Her eyes soften for a moment, and sadness graces her face. She turns to her husband again and gestures at the log book on the table, the one he must use to record the bookings. He runs a finger along a line on the page, then goes to the booth to make a call.

'Tomorrow, sister, at twelve,' says the woman, after he has replaced the receiver. She ushers me out of the office. 'It's dark already. Will you stay with us?'

'Thank you, but I have to keep searching.'

'With no light?'

I shrug my shoulders vaguely. Sleep seems such an impossibility that there doesn't seem any point in trying to rest.

'Okay. Twelve o'clock, my husband will be here to meet you.'

Outside, the earth turns from the sun as if it were any other day. Night arrives in quick increments. In Wiltshire, the sunset was always shifting with the winters and summers, but here the light departs on cue: an inbuilt clock. The town, which would usually have glittered at night, is as dark as the sea. Noises seep disembodied from the hillside: a foot dislodging rubble or a rat scratching through a pipe. I try in vain to find my way back to the wreckage. The woman was right. I'll have to wait until morning. Back outside the office, I try my best to sleep. But I think only of home – of Mum staring into the cavern of the bath as she wipes it clean. Over and over she would wipe it until she could see her own eyes blinking back at her. It was not so much the cleanliness that she enjoyed but the feel of the enamel sliding under the cloth. It was small tasks, like that one, which absorbed her; she never cleaned the entire house, only minor parts of it – afraid, perhaps, of leaving things incomplete.

After reading her letter in Istanbul, I had visited the post office in Quetta to check for more post. But she had not written again. It puzzled me, that silence, and I found I thought of her more often. When we arrived in Lahore, James picked up an aerogramme, which had been there for more than a week.

Dear Alice,

I hope this finds you safe in Lahore. You would have been very proud of me: last week, I took a trip up to London on my own to the British Library to look at some paintings and photographs of Pakistan. I had to put in a request for the photographs before I arrived. I thought it would help me – to be able to picture where you are. I couldn't quite imagine Pakistan before, let alone Lahore; it seemed to blur with India and Afghanistan in my mind. But now I can envisage perfectly that dusty red stone which they use in the buildings and the flatness of it all. The train was diverted awfully on the way back from the library. I was glad your father couldn't see me; I have never been good with journeys, not in the way that he was.

I often wonder if you ever think of him on your travels. I'm sure you do. You had plenty of questions when you were younger. But I couldn't furnish you with many answers and I suppose that's why you stopped asking. The truth is, there is so much that I should have told you. I know you will think I am writing out of desperation – inventing reasons to see you. But there are things I would like to tell you, Alice, if you will give me a chance.

Your trip has been good for both of us. It has given me clarity – and I know now what should be done. I can only hope that all these miles you have put between us will help you see that, despite my failings – of which there are many – I do love you. Perhaps more than a mother should.

She ran out of space at the bottom of the page, pushing the words into a concertina in order to fit them in. I didn't give a moment's thought to what she wanted to tell me, not until she wrote to me again in Delhi. I just assumed it was another memory that she mistakenly thought might compensate for Dad's absence. I travelled, oblivious, from Lahore, feeling my stubbornness towards her thaw. In Delhi, everything changed – between her and me, between myself and James. I trailed my anger through Tamil Nadu until it settled into numb shock. She had held onto things that long since ought to have been mine.

In my dreams, the debris evaporates with the night and the streets are as smooth as the enamel in my mother's bath. But the heat soon bleeds into the morning and the smell – which pervaded even my sleep – returns more strongly than before. I wake up to find the ruins as real as ever.

Outside the office, I have no way of telling the time, except to watch the sun arc up to the top of the sky. It reaches its summit but there is no sign of the husband or his wife.

In my mind I run through the digits I will have to dial. Each number attaches itself to a body – the man at sea, the woman in the sari. Sometimes I wonder if a person can see too much – that if what they see outweighs what they say, something inside them will tip and sink irreversibly downwards.

Twelve noon is seven thirty a.m. British time. There's every chance that they'll be at home when I ring. Even if Tim has gone to work early, Mum will be in. When has she ever been out? Now she and Tim are married she doesn't have to work.

If she doesn't answer, I won't have to give it words – this thing that I've seen. My step-dad will launch into a flurry of reassurance: he'll plan for a million and one contingencies – ways of not really making things better. But Mum is the one whose voice I dread hearing on the end of the phone, and the one that I want to hear most.

Finally the woman from the hill arrives with her husband. Inside the office, he picks up the receiver and frowns at the tone of the line. He tilts his hand in the air at me: it isn't good but at least it's working. He passes me the phone and stands next to his wife. I dial the operator, wishing they'd leave me to it, but they watch me closely from the opposite side of the desk. Finger pausing for a moment, I hold my breath, release the dial and wait to be connected. I'm answered, and give the number in Wiltshire. There are faint voices at each telephone exchange – I am transferred to three separate operators. The final ring is long and low, a single tone followed by a dragging silence. Then a click.

'Hello, Tim Richards speaking,' says my step-dad. His answer is so well worn that he almost sings it each time he picks up the phone. 'Alice, is that you?'

I can't reply, but I know he can hear my breathing – heavy and irregular. 'Are you all right?'

'Please . . . get Mum. I'm in Kanyakumari,' is all I can manage.

'What?'

'The wave . . .'

'But – you can't be.' Tim's voice becomes muffled for a moment. He is calling Mum's name. There is a clunk as he rests the receiver on the table. Then I hear him thumping urgently across the house. She can't be out. Please don't let her be out.

'Alice,' he cuts in, as he picks up the receiver again, 'I can't find her. Are you hurt?'

'I – But . . . James is missing . . . Has he telephoned or got in touch? Maybe he left a message . . .' I feel my face relaxing into tears for the first time since it happened. 'It took him.'

'Don't panic – don't, whatever you do, panic. We'll find a way to get you home.'

'I can't leave without him.' The line splits our voices into echoes.

'Everything will be all right, Alice. I'm sure he's all right.' His voice roughens and trails off.

'You're talking as if –'

There's another click, the slow moan of a dead line, then silence.

Chapter 18

As soon as the raid was over, I ran back with my mother and Sam to the factory. I stopped at the gate to see it completely intact, the girls emerging one by one from the shelter. The supervisor came striding up to us, stooping as she walked to brush the dirt from her skirt.

'I'll have you know that you can't just run away at the whiff of a siren! This is important work.' She stabbed her finger in the direction of the factory behind her.

'She didn't have a choice.' Sam stepped forward. 'I made her come with me.'

'A Yank, of all people.' The supervisor looked him up and down. He was twice as broad as her and at least a foot taller. 'You should know better than anyone how vital it is for us to keep on top of our quotas.' She stopped short of prodding him in the chest.

'You can't just coop them up like chickens while there's an air raid going on,' he retorted.

'You try telling that to the War Office.' She turned on her heels and strode towards the girls, who had lined up in order of their workbenches, ready to file back into the factory.

'It's a miracle you weren't hit,' I whispered to Sally, taking my place in the line.

'He must care about you and your ma an awful lot, Vi, to come and rescue you like that.' She nodded across to where my mother and Sam were standing.

'Not really,' I murmured, seeing the flower again in my father's mouth.

*

It was Pete, not Sam, who had rescued us that day, albeit unwittingly. Earlier that morning, soon after he had started milking the cows, he was met by a private in uniform who took him to some buildings at the far end of the farm.

'You're to stand guard here,' the soldier said, pointing at the barns.

'Why? What's inside?'

'It's better if you don't ask questions. If you see them flying over, the Luftwaffe, I mean, I want you to light these and throw them into the nearest barn.' The soldier pointed to a pile of hand-made torches – sticks with rags at the ends that reeked of meths.

'But –'

'Don't worry, we've doused the entire place in petroleum. She should get going in no time at all.'

'Good,' nodded Pete – never one to admit when he didn't know what was going on.

'One more thing,' said the soldier, matter-of-factly. 'It would be advisable to get away as quickly as you can as soon as the barn is lit. We've built a shelter to the west, two fields away – that should be far enough.'

On the evening of the raid, Pete had heard engines approaching and dutifully set light to the barns. From the safety of his shelter, he had watched as the Luftwaffe peppered the barn with bombs, stoking the fire to a monstrous height until it looked as if a whole town had been set alight.

'It was a decoy!' he exclaimed, after I explained about the suspected raid on the factory. 'I made the Jerries think the farm was the factory!' Then he started to brag to others about his involvement in *the great decoy*, as if he had known about the plot all along and played his part valiantly.

I was in two minds about whether to tell Pete about Sam. In the end, the decision was not mine to make. Towards the end of April, when the Americans had been with us for nearly three months, he met me after my Thursday shift and I walked with him back to the farm at Coombe. Our strolls had allowed me to steal time with him between his work and mine without being seen to be too keen. There wasn't anywhere to go other than the dances at Salisbury and Warminster and I wasn't about to show my face with him there any time soon. Not after Freda.

This regular jaunt of ours had petered out of late; Sam was almost guaranteed to be our guest at dinner on a Thursday and so, week after week, I had made my excuses to Pete and went home to help Mama prepare the meal.

As we skirted the edge of the American barracks at Fugglestone, he seemed aloof, displeased with me, somehow, walking two steps ahead of me no matter how much I picked up my pace. The air was full of those dark, pregnant clouds typical of April. To begin with, it felt acceptable to leave the unremarkable weather unremarked upon. But as our walk went on, I feared he was imposing his silence on me, withholding words so that I would feel their absence. On previous strolls – usually to take our mind off the rain or the cold – we had told stories: mine from the factory, his from the farm. I had exaggerated the injuries some of the girls had incurred, multiplying the volume of blood and the strictness of the supervisor. He had done the same with the farm, laughing at the ineptitude of the land girls under his watch. I would try to contradict him, telling him that I had met the girls and felt their hardened hands in my own. I'd seen them fell trees and shear sheep single-handedly, and knew what they were capable of. But he would always find another way of discrediting them – broken eggs, sloppy hedge work, a cow that had been left to wander more than two miles from its field. Today there were no stories to tell. He did not speak a word to me until we reached the final stile before the farm.

On the other side of the fence, he stopped me walking on and turned to face me. 'Violet, there's something I have to tell you, but you won't like it. Not a bit.'

I kept quiet, thinking through the possibilities of what it might be: another girl, farm work in a different county. I tried to prepare myself for either.

'It's about your ma,' he explained.

I frowned at him.

'I know it's tough for you to hear – what with your father . . . Only, I've seen her . . . with someone.'

'I beg your pardon?' Mama would never deliberately hurt Sam, I thought. Then I worried that I had thought of Sam before Father.

'He's an American based at Fugglestone. Big stocky fellow. I saw them walking together by the Nadder.'

I caught Pete's eye.

'You know about him?'

'He's a friend. He's been very good to us.'

'It didn't look like that to me,' he replied.

I asked curtly what he meant by 'it'.

'I saw how they were walking together –'

'It's nothing,' I interrupted. 'And why is it your business anyway?'

'You can't pretend he's just a friend of your ma's.'

'He's looking after us. Doing his duty. I don't understand why it bothers you so much.'

''Cause the town's talking. Your pa's not been gone that long, Violet –'

'I'll not have you speak of him in that way!'

'The Yank or your pa?'

I paused, chest tightening. 'My mother doesn't need a lesson in what's proper – least of all from you.'

'I only thought you should know that people are talking.'

I came to a standstill by the riverbank and watched the water draw patterns in the silt. It couldn't stop. It had to keep going, following its course from source to sea

'What will happen after the war, Violet?' began Pete again.

'D'you think the American will come back to Imber with you, live in the parsonage and preach sermons like your pa in St Giles?'

'Stop it!' I marched back in the direction from which we'd come.

'Fine!' he shouted, behind me. 'But you'll want to go back after the war. I know it. And Imber's not a life that a Yank can share. He can't ever be your pa.'

'What do you take me for?' I turned towards him. 'He's dead and buried. I can't change that any more than I can wish us home again.'

Pete sighed and walked towards the farm, leaving me faltering on the path behind him. *You'll want to go back after the war.* I should have known that, even if we were allowed back, Pete would not come with us. I had lost all hope of life resuming its original course – so much so that I was prepared to sit and watch while my mother, the wife of a parson whose fresh grave went untended at home, fell in love with another man.

I caught up with Pete just before the gate into the farmyard, out of breath, crimson-faced. 'What should I do?' I asked, planting myself between him and the farm.

He pushed past me and clamped the gate shut behind him, his eyes entreating me not to follow. 'Speak to your ma, not me.'

Ever since the bombing raid, Mama had been shy around Sam and, at times, even short with him. She rebuked him when he offered to peel the vegetables and cut himself with the knife; she asked him to leave the house one evening when he suggested that the Allies couldn't win the war without the Yanks. Yet he continued to come to the cottage. If anything, he approached my mother with renewed confidence since he had broached the subject of my father's death. My mother could no longer hide his attentions from me or herself. She relented, slowly, with the unease of someone who knew what she had held and how difficult it would be to make room for something more. We should have hated Sam for muscling in on our home, for touching my mother's hair, for stirring up her feelings when he didn't understand how much she had lost.

He arrived late for dinner one evening, brimming with stories of his latest exercise. He pulled back a chair from the table. The hind legs jittered over the tiles. By the time he sat down, he was already in full flow.

'Violet, you would have loved this place! So quaint and English.'

I took the pot out of the oven and smiled weakly at him, not properly hearing his words.

'It's a darn shame they let us train there, really. We try to be careful with the ammo – the genuine stuff, I mean – but you can barely see it. It's tucked up in a valley. And the fog's so thick in the mornings that we can't even see the church tower.'

The pot in my hands thudded onto the table.

My mother spun round from the sink. 'Salisbury Plain – you're training on Salisbury Plain?'

'Yes.' Sam frowned. I blinked down at the steam coming off the dish.

'This village – have you been into it?' asked my mother, with urgency.

'Oh, yeah, hundreds of times. Nobody lives there now, though. It's like a ghost town. Some folk left their groceries there, though, and the hymn books are still in the church. It's like they all just vanished. Creepy, if you ask me.'

'They let you *inside* the houses?'

'Yeah, we pretend it's a German village. Half of us invade, half of us defend. It's kinda fun.'

'Fun?' cried my mother, eyes as full as inkwells. 'Anyone would think you weren't in a war!' Mama flicked her hands free of tap water as she spoke, mopping the remaining damp vigorously on her apron. 'You're just playing soldiers and playing in places that you've no right to be in!'

After drying her hands, she left the room, the food still steaming in the space between Sam and me.

'The village,' I murmured to him, after a pause. 'What is it called?'

'I don't think it has a name,' he replied, frowning at the door through which my mother had just left. 'If it does, I've never heard it spoken.'

Chapter 19

A single-limbed doll; a watch whose face has filled with water; one gold chain. A plastic urn, fluorescent green – the kind that would float; a number plate; two non-matching flip-flops; an empty suitcase. When I ask where the suitcase was found, the woman from the hill bends down to read the chalk letters in front of it. 'In a car, sister.'

We have walked to the marketplace together from the telephone booth. The line went dead after my call home. Mum wasn't in. The one time I call. She's always in first thing in the morning. I try hard to feel relieved but I'm craving her concern, her fear, even if it means breaching months of silence.

A space has been cleared where the market stalls used to be. Unclaimed belongings are laid out in rows, like clues, replacing the mangoes, tomatoes and ladies' fingers that were illuminated in green under sun-soaked tarpaulins before the wave came. The women who used to draw chalk flowers on their doorsteps now etch facts about each object into the dirt of the market square. A house name, a street, a stretch of beach; the place where each item was found. James dragged me to the market on our first day here so that I could copy the women's drawings. But instead of the patterns on the doorsteps, I sketched the women themselves: the way they squatted for hours next to their work, gently teasing a new breed of geometry out of the stick of chalk in their hands. Once I had finished we bought food in the market from a man cooking *sambar*. He spooned the contents of the pan into see-through bags – our own portions of sunlight, hot and bright in our hands. I think of the pan upturned by the wave, the *sambar* painting the waters yellow.

On the fringes of the ruined square, I can see the fruit from the stalls, pulped amid beams and bricks and roofs. Doorsteps are washed blank. The women, like their patterns, are gone.

I bend to the suitcase on the ground in front of me and unzip the pocket on the back of the lid. Inside there is a pencil, a coin and a photograph. The photo is of an older woman with a bent spine and toothy grin, her purple sari folded around her impeccably. A sentence is scrawled on the back in Tamil. I show it to the woman. 'It's for her son Adesh,' she tells me, pointing to the woman in the photo. 'So he will remember her.' I think of her searching for him, as I am searching for James.

A bicycle – royal blue with no spokes; a fishing net. We were told on our first day here that each fisherman has a different way of making his net: some string long diamond-shaped holes together; others have trademark knots. This net's owner will be identified by the weave of the thread. I wish James's traits could be woven into a net like that of a fisherman. I might stand a chance, then, of having something left to hold.

An orange *dupatta*; a kitchen knife; three glass bangles, blue and intact. It stripped the breath from hundreds of lungs, the roofs from so many homes, yet it leaves these glass rings untouched. A woman in front of me bends over them in silence. She takes them in her hands and lifts them to her cheeks, her lips. Were they a gift? She slips them over her wrists, where they clink and collide and mingle with one another, like old friends. Then she kneels, hands blossoming from fists to open palms, and sends up a prayer.

Next in line is a rucksack: the shape and colour are unrecognizable under the silt. I unzip it, forcing myself to assume it's not his, fingers oscillating. I rummage at first, and then, out of frustration, I tip the bag upside-down, the contents scattering and settling in the dust. My gaze falls on a dark blue cover: it is hunchbacked by the water. The gold crest on the front has lost its glint, mud gathering in the grooves where the colour has peeled away. Staring down at the other objects from the bag – five *dosa*s, a few coins, a towel and a bottle of sun cream, I already know the face that I am going to find in the passport. I know, and yet I'm hesitating, scrambling around for a reason not to look. My fingers turn, before I'm ready, to the front pages. He's paler in the photograph than in real life. His hair – a sandy mess in the mornings – has been tamed into place. I remember the way he took out the passport at each of the borders along the overland trail, pushing it wearily across the table towards the official. He always said that a border check was worse than a job interview: the number of questions, the hours of waiting.

Every border check had gone smoothly until we reached the edge of Pakistan. All of us passed through to India unscathed, apart from Marc who was detained. Three hours became six and James was impatient. I thought him irrational at the time for suggesting what he did – and perhaps he was. But if he had followed his impulses, things would not have kicked off so terribly in Delhi, we would not have married so hastily, and I would not be here, in the wake, without him.

'We should order Marc a driver and press on ahead.' He sighed. 'It's not as if he's paid his way.'

'We can't just leave him,' protested Sue. The others in the back of the van agreed.

'It's been six hours. That's practically a day of driving we've lost. What if he doesn't make it through?'

'They've got no valid reason for keeping him,' I murmured. 'They'll get fed up soon enough.'

'What makes you so sure?' he asked, looking me straight in the eye.

'We can't leave him, James. You know we can't. It wouldn't be kind.'

'Well, that's just great, isn't it?' He threw up his hands and brought them down onto the steering-wheel. 'A real vote of confidence.'

'Don't be –'

He started the engine and was about to pull away when there was a rap on the window. 'Sorry, mate, I thought I was going to be in there all night.' Marc grinned. He threw open the door and stooped inside. James rolled his eyes. I felt a pang of relief, and swallowed it.

'It's spelt with a *c* not a *k*,' he told me, when we finally reached Delhi. I wrote down 'Marc Rawson' in my address book, above his Auckland address. The *c* at the end of his name seemed incomplete somehow. A *k* would have been closed, finished, unquestionable.

The van had failed us twenty miles from the city centre; the gearbox had eaten its fill of desert sand. James stayed with the van, hoping to flog it to a passing driver for a few thousand rupees. I wanted to stay with him and let the others go on ahead but he said he needed space.

'I'm happy to sit with you,' I offered.

'Go on with the others. We said we'd get them to Delhi. I don't want to leave the job undone.'

'You'll be all right?'

'Yes.' Our eyes met. I sensed distrust in his.

The rest of us caught auto-rickshaws to the railway station and camped in the grounds of a nearby hotel. The girls stared enviously up at the balconies on the first floor, imagining fresh towels and boxes of tissues. It was our last night as a group. After four months together, we were to part ways in the morning. Marc was following Rob, Sue and Clara to Kathmandu. The others were making their own way to Thailand while I would wait for James in Delhi.

The symmetry of the hotel gardens felt contrived, awkward even, after miles of unruly sand. The grass was ornamental – roped off, luridly green and prickly. A shock to the eyes after the sand-blurred roads of Iran and Pakistan.

'And what's your address?' asked Marc, as we sat by the fountain. He handed me a notebook and gestured for me to write mine in return. Without thinking, I scribbled 'Alice Fielding, 8 Magnolia Way, Salisbury, Wiltshire, England'. I could have put my London address but this was the one that came to mind. It was a strange ritual to go through, when we knew neither of us had any intention of keeping in touch. I flicked through the pages of his notebook after I had finished writing and dislodged a folded sheet, which had been pressed into the spine. It fell open on the paving – one of my drawings.

'Where did you get this?' I took a closer look. It was the one I had drawn of a collapsed arch in southern Turkey – the symmetry broken into two uneven columns.

Marc didn't answer immediately. He clasped his hands between his knees and tapped his foot up and down. It was the first time I had seen him visibly unsettled. 'You threw it away . . . in Lyallpur.'

'You should have asked before taking it.' I tried to harden my voice but the words came out porous and pleading.

'It was . . . I just . . . It was something to remember you by . . .' Catching my frown, he added, 'This whole trip, I mean.'

I sighed and planted my hands on the hot paving behind me. He hung his head over his knees. 'You must think I'm an idiot.'

'I'm thinking we've all been shut up in that van for too long.'

'Yeah, too right.' He laughed.

I thought of Mum and the Wiltshire address I had written in his notebook. 'It's funny, isn't it, how journeys can make you feel things that you wouldn't normally –'

He looked up suddenly, as if I had given something away. 'Alice . . .'

He was leaning in. I should have backed off. It was a startling rush of attraction, one that caught you momentarily and then let go of you as quickly as it had arrived. I already knew it was madness.

He put his lips to mine and I didn't move away, not at first.

'I've got to go,' I said, eventually pulling back.

'Where?'

'To James.' I reached over and took the drawing from under his knees. Then I stood up, put it in my pocket, and walked away. He left in the morning. There was no need for a goodbye.

Each time I think of that kiss, I can remember only the fringes: what came before and after. I have forgotten completely its texture, the swell of feeling that must have brought it about – as if, by forgetting it, I can pretend it never really occurred.

James's passport is still in my hand. I want it to tell me something more than I already know, give me a clue as to where I can find him. Even touching something he has touched makes me feel closer to knowing his fate, if only by a fragment. He could have left the rucksack behind in an effort to get away more quickly; or someone could have removed it from him, from his . . . and brought it here. I put the passport down and run my fingers around the inner seams of the rucksack, checking I haven't missed anything.

His wallet isn't here. He must have taken it with him when he ran. Surely. Out of instinct. Did he get away in time? I gather up the objects. They carry the same dank, out-of-date smell as the rest of this place. Any smell that he might have left has been superseded by the water. I try to recall it but it is covered by burnt rubber mixed with trapped sewage and rot. There is no escaping it in the heat. It follows you everywhere, permeating your clothing and then your skin, until you, too, are its carrier.

Before the wave, the town was filled with smells that reminded us of being somewhere other than home. Tamarind and turmeric lingered on the shirt cuffs of store owners. And pollen – thicker than you've ever smelt it – dangled blearily in the air around the market. Sometimes the air was so pregnant with scent that it tasted overripe. Even before the wave, it felt as if something were about to burst.

A place like this would frighten Mum. The heat would make her giddy. The food would not sit still inside her. *Everybody is busy and yet nothing is done*, she would say, in the exasperated voice she puts on when she knows she is out of her depth.

When I made the mistake of bringing James home to meet her, she was in a state about Tim wanting to sell the house. He'd got a job for the electricity board in Didcot, or something like that. The agent called round to put a sign up in the garden without checking first with Mum. Tim must have known that she would be reluctant to move. But we had only been there for the six years since they'd married and she'd never really liked the house anyway. To her it was just walls; it was Wiltshire she couldn't leave.

She tried her best to ignore the for-sale sign while James was there, storing the thought of it under a pursed lip. But I saw her glance out of the window at it every time we entered the kitchen. She couldn't help but linger on its shadow, as dark as a ghost on the front lawn.

When I was a child, I used to beg her to take me to London, not knowing how the thought of it alone made her fearful. She gave in when I was eleven and we took the train together to Paddington. By the end of the day, I was wishing I had never made her come. I felt responsible, as if I'd taken her on a rollercoaster and made her sick. The city dizzied her with its blur of trains and buses and glass-fronted towers. She couldn't seem to feed off its frenzy in the way I did. I watched in horror as she stuttered on the sides of roads, waiting until I picked the gaps that were big enough to allow us to cross. Instead of persevering through the crowds on the pavements, she would retreat periodically into shops, only to find herself shoulder to shoulder with thicker, noisier crowds.

We caught the tube to St Paul's from Paddington; it was the only name she recognized on the map. I was disappointed, hoping she'd choose Piccadilly Circus or Elephant & Castle or

Angel, any of the stops that sounded as if they might unleash an adventure. The heat in the Underground made her skin sticky and her breath heavy, and she winced as a man in a black coat stood close enough for her to breathe the breath that he had just exhaled. We whizzed through the tube's concrete veins and emerged at the other side, climbing the steps to the cathedral and hiding ourselves in the quiet of its nave. Away from the pulse of the traffic, the muscles in her face relaxed and she loosened her grip on my hand. Finally, I was allowed to roam, albeit in silence. Meeting again in the dome, we looked up. She seemed transfixed for a moment by its shape.

'Did you know, Alice . . .' she began, trailing off as a string of tourists clustered nearby briefly, then departed.

'What, Mummy?' I asked, tugging on her hand, pleased to hear her speaking.

'When they bombed London . . . when London was bombed in the Blitz . . . this dome here managed to survive. Everything around it was destroyed. But this,' she gestured up to the light-filled arches above us, 'this lived on.'

'Can we go somewhere else now?' I asked, swinging her arm with my hand. For a moment I thought that the day might be saved, that she might even bring me to the city again.

But, as we walked outside and made our way around the perimeter of the cathedral, I felt her hand tighten on mine. In front of us was another church. Only, this one was ruined. In place of the nave there was an overgrown garden, which had been allowed to roam over the remaining stone. It was as if, a long time ago, in a fairytale, a wave like mine had passed over it, taking with it the walls and windows and bells and doors, leaving only ruins.

Chapter 20

In April, Mama stopped reading my father's books. I returned home from the factory one evening to find the boxes taped up and the shells I had placed on the window-sills back inside their crate. The ship was nowhere to be seen. She seemed to avoid the front room completely now, as if the books could spy on her from their boxes.

Undoing the tape, I fished around for a volume of Eliot's *Four Quartets*, one of her favourites, and placed it carefully on her pillow upstairs.

> *In my beginning is my end. In succession*
> *Houses rise and fall, crumble . . .*
> *. . . in their place*
> *Is an open field, or a factory, or a by-pass.*
> *. . . old timber to new fires,*
> *Old fires to ashes, and ashes to the earth . . .*

I found the ship tossed into a box on top of Father's dictionaries – a small fissure had appeared on the bottle's neck. I thought about the sails inside the glass, filling with air for the first time.

Returning from the canteen, she came and joined me in bed. She picked the book up from her pillow before lying down and stared, bewildered, at its cover.

'I thought you might like to read it.'

She held it out to me. 'Put it back where you found it.'

'Mama . . .' I paused, leaving the book loitering in her hand.

'It doesn't belong here any more. It never did.' She thrust it towards me again, and when I still didn't take it, she left the bed and carried it downstairs herself.

The following day, I found the book back inside one of the boxes. I left it there but took one of his shells when she wasn't looking and kept it in my underwear drawer. I came home from my shift to find Mama and Sam ferrying the boxes into the cellar. Sam was whistling, oblivious, as he lugged one box after another down into the darkness. Mama avoided my stare. I wanted to stop her but the words clotted in my throat. Instead, I ran upstairs and did not come down until I was sure they had seen to the last box. Something changed that day. It was as if a part of me had been taken down to the cellar to dwell with the books in the dark and the damp. Something that I couldn't recover. I wasn't aware of what it was until the trip to the beach.

Sam had use of an old army van for the week and talked of taking us to the seaside. It was against the rules but he wanted to show Mama the 'ocean'. She told him that she had never seen the sea and I knew why she lied: I, too, had thought of our day with Father in Bournemouth. On our first night in Wilton – the night we had slept in the blitzed cottage – we laughed about that trip, the only time we had seen the sea. Father had bought Freda and me ice-creams that painted big, clown-like grins around our mouths. Mama had taken particular delight in the sand, which slithered into the space between her toes, like thick, dry water.

I remember standing under the legs of Bournemouth pier and squealing at the arrival of each wave on my shins. I stood for a full hour, puzzled at the feeling of being tugged backwards as the waves retreated, only to be told by Father that I had in fact not moved an inch.

Mama lied to Sam about never having seen the sea because she couldn't let him have any share in that day: it felt perfidious. She had placed the memory of it high on a shelf, so high that she could no longer retrieve it or tamper with it or bear to see it replaced. He could not understand her reluctance to take the trip so she persuaded him that she had heard poor reports of Bournemouth. He suggested the Purbecks as an alternative and she could think of no other way out, except to suggest bringing me, which did not deter him.

I should not have told Pete about the trip to the beach but the thought of it welled up inside me so often that I could not let it rest. I felt uneasy, as if I ought to seek out his anger before I had even committed the offence. He did not say much. Only that he would not be meeting me at the factory that day.

When Mama and I heard the sound of the horn outside the cottage, we gathered our towels and a modest picnic we had assembled from our rations and clambered into the back of Sam's van. I watched as the thick-set trunks of the ash and oak trees thinned into pine, fern and bracken. Wiltshire's plains melted into Dorset's heaths and the colours became more lucid. As I opened the window of the van, I found I no longer had to pitch my face against the wind. Rather, I basked in its sand-flecked warmth. It felt like he was taking us home with him – to somewhere across the sea.

'Are we expecting an invasion?' my mother asked, as we stepped onto the dunes at Studland.

'Not exactly,' Sam replied, casting an eye back towards the dozing soldier inside the military booth we had just passed.

We picked our way across the reed beds and over a dune to the beach. Large concrete blocks had been placed in the gaps between the dunes to prevent tanks from journeying inland. Rings of concertina wire reared up from the sand sporadically like sculpted waves. I shut my eyes and tried not to think of what they might have done to Imber.

'Who's coming in?' grinned Sam, pulling his shirt over his head as he spoke. Eyes glued to the shore's new armour, I hardly registered what he was saying.

'Oh, I'm all right, Sam, not today. You'll catch your death.' My mother laughed, lowering herself to the sand.

'Vi?' He looked across at me hopefully. I shook my head and sat down next to Mama.

'What's got into you both this morning?' He laughed, striding towards us. He stooped and picked Mama up, tipping her over his shoulder in a fireman's lift.

'Put me down this instant!' she shrieked, pulling at her skirt so that it didn't ruck up and reveal her petticoat. I wanted to stop him, tell him to let her go. It didn't seem right. Not amid the barbed wire and the concrete. Soon he was holding her over the shallows. She clasped his neck and begged him to let her go, but the more she protested, the deeper he waded. Eventually, she wriggled free. I expected her to come straight back out again and demand to be taken home. But, to my surprise, I heard her laughter blurting skittishly across the sands.

I brushed the beach from my pinafore and hurried along the dunes. A bay lay just around the corner of the headland: I would be hidden from them there. All along the shoreline, patches of shells clung together in schools. I could feel them sink into the sand under my feet as I forged a path along the wet part of the beach. I bent down and picked one up. A bivalve. My father knew all the proper names. I preferred to give them my own names. 'Helter-skelter' for the spiral, cone-shaped ones; 'Freda fans' for the ones that resembled ladies' fans; and 'swords' for the ones my father called scaphopods, or tusk shells.

The shells here were as numerous as the flowers on the Plain: visitors to Imber would bring armfuls of its flora back to their lodgings to make bouquets, marvelling over the number of species that could be found in a single patch of meadow; they carried the words 'bird's foot trefoil', 'bellflower' and 'ox-eye daisy' so carefully on the tongue, as if an incorrect pronunciation might cause the flowers to wilt. Locals, however, could brush past a thousand such blooms in the most perfunctory manner – as I'm sure Studland's sailors and fishermen glossed over the shells. My father would not have been half as interested in shells had he lived near the sea: each new specimen was as fascinating to him as an unexplored island, full of foreign markings and structures and smells.

'Found you!' called Mama, as she reached the centre of the bay with Sam.

I was holding a Freda fan. 'Father would have liked this one, don't you think?' I held it out to my mother. 'I might put it in his crate.'

She returned my stare for a moment, the water dripping from her clothes and darkening the sand beneath her feet.

'I'm sure he would have loved it,' Sam chipped in.

'How do you know?' I turned from them and cut a stiff path across the sand. It became drier and thicker near the dunes and I couldn't get my feet to move as fast as I wanted them to.

'You go, Martie, I'll only anger her,' instructed Sam behind me.

'Martha!' I shouted back to them, not dropping my pace. 'Her name is Martha.'

I returned home from my shift the next day to find my mother, alone, in the kitchen. She was peeling potatoes in the sink – enough to feed three.

'Are we expecting Sam again?'

'Darling! You're home late,' she remarked, ignoring my question. She flicked up her wrist to check the time and turned to face me. 'Did they make you overrun?'

I nodded. 'Is it all right if I talk to you about something, Mama?'

'Of course, my love.' She smiled, placing her knife on the table. Then, clocking my frown, she took a seat.

'It's about Sam, you see,' I said quickly. I watched the minuscule muscles under her eyes tense slightly.

'What about him?'

'You're good friends . . . That's all you are, isn't it?'

'What are you asking, Violet?' Her eyes widened with something close to fear.

'Nothing. I'm not asking . . . only, you know how people talk.'

'Vi-vi, remember what Father used to tell you about gossip?' she began. 'It betrays more about the individuals who indulge in it than the people it purports to be about.' Her voice was firm but even the most cursory mention of my father seemed to cause her face to melt. *She raised the subject, not me.* Putting a hand on her forehead, she stood up and turned back to the sink. 'I can't keep doing it, Vi.'

'You don't have to. If you choose to put an end to it, Sam will understand.'

I crossed the kitchen and drew level with her, only to discern from the look on her face that she was not talking about Sam.

'I can't keep waiting, thinking we'll go back to him, back home, when there's nothing to go back to.'

I told her not to be silly, that of course we'd go home. It was what Father would have wanted.

'Am I always to live my life in this way? In the shadow of what he would have wanted?'

I stared at her in disbelief. She hung her head over the sink, a hand planted on each side of it, gazing into its hollow.

'You're talking nonsense. Listen to yourself!' I cried, my voice fracturing. 'He loved us. He was prepared to go to war for us. And this is how we repay him?' I was pointing at the cutlery on the table – the place laid for Sam at the head of it. She refused to turn and face me.

'None of this would have happened if Freda was still around,' she whispered – so quietly that I could barely make out what she was saying.

'Are you saying I'm to blame?'

'No, that isn't what I said.'

'How can it be my fault? I wasn't the one bringing home the

soldiers . . .' I would never have dared to speak to my mother in this manner in Imber, no matter what her offence. But Father's death – the war – had made me numb enough to say what I felt.

Mama's voice faltered. 'I wouldn't have given in so easily if you hadn't taken to him so well. Don't tell me you didn't think him charming. I know you did. You still do.'

I stood in the quiet of the kitchen and tried to blot out what I was hearing. My mother should have known that, still seventeen, I was too young to bear any share of the blame, whatever the true extent of my culpability. But she couldn't have guessed how her words would play on me for years, decades afterwards, how they would alter us permanently – more than Sam ever could.

I begged Mama to telephone Sam at Fugglestone and postpone dinner, but she thought it would seem impolite at such short notice. He arrived with a bunch of daisies, which my mother tried her best to coo over, fumbling around the kitchen to find a vase. It was clear to him from the start of the evening that something was amiss. I saw it in the way he quietened his voice and diminished his gestures, asking for the salt rather than reaching across me genially to take it, like he usually did.

'The greens are just so, Martha.'

Mama acknowledged him with a nod.

'There'll be carrots and other things in the garden at Wilton House in July. The cook's growing a jungle of them out the back. I'll ask her to keep some for you.'

'It's all right,' I intervened. 'There's a few on the way in our garden, aren't there, Mama?'

She shot me a terse smile.

'I'm serious. It'd be no trouble.'

'We wouldn't want to put you out,' she told him, seeing that he was not going to give up.

Sam frowned.

'How is your training going?' my mother enquired, swiftly changing the subject.

'Oh, swell. The boys are settling down. They miss home. But there's a war to fight . . .' He carried on in this vague manner, desperate to fill the silence that he knew we would have left had he stopped speaking. As soon as we had finished our food, he stood up to excuse himself, saying he had an exercise scheduled early tomorrow for which he needed his sleep. I attended to the dishes in the sink.

'Sam, before you go, there's something we – I . . . must talk to you about.'

I dropped the plate I was washing and it sank with a gulp into the water.

'Vi, will you excuse us?' continued Mama.

'I'll see to the dishes, Mama. You go into the garden.'

My mother seemed pleased with this suggestion: it bought her more time. Sam followed her outside. The kitchen window looked down the length of the lawn and I could just about make out their two figures by the rockery at the far end. My mother said something, taking a step back from Sam as she spoke. She put a palm to her mouth and I could tell she was crying. He moved to comfort her but she raised a hand to stop him coming any nearer. He leant in slowly and kissed her on the cheek before lumbering back to the house.

'Goodbye, Violet,' he said, as he passed the entrance to the kitchen. I couldn't bring myself to turn from the sink. 'I never meant you any harm.'

I heard the front door close – softly for once – behind him. My mother was still standing at the end of the lawn, wrapped tightly in her cardigan, her eyes fixed on the rockery.

Chapter 21

May arrived. Everybody sensed that the forces were preparing for something significant. In the factory, the camouflage we produced had turned from earthy green to beige – the colour of sand. More American troops arrived; Wilton House was swarming with them.

My mother no longer visited to serve tea. She began to bring lunch to the girls in the factory instead. There was something different in the way she carried herself these days. She had gone back to wearing her hair in a loose plait and her hands were reassuringly unkempt. She didn't exhibit the frantic happiness she had shown with Sam. But the hidden doubt that had marked even her most heightened moments in the last few months seemed finally to be dissipating. We couldn't know for certain whether we would ever return to be with Father in Imber but, if it came to it, we would be here waiting; Mama would be here, waiting.

One afternoon I was walking home from my shift when a girl whose face I could not place approached me on the high street.

'Violet!' she called, crossing from the grocer's to meet me on the other side of the road. As she approached, her saucer-shaped eyes registered in my mind.

'Annie! Gosh, is that really you?' She had grown taller, helped along by a pair of open-toe high-heeled shoes. Her face was neatly made-up – a far cry from the lipstick I had smudged over it two years ago on our way to the dance – and there was a ring on her finger, her fourth finger. 'You're engaged!' I cried, grabbing her hand and staring into the opal.

'Oh it's not much.' She giggled, keeping her hand in mine. 'David's promised me a proper ring once this silly war's over.'

'Annie, I'm thrilled for you! So thrilled! . . . And how is Devizes treating you?'

'Do you know? I'm rather enjoying it, Vi. Except you're not there, of course!'

'Well, I did write!' I laughed.

'Oh, you know how pathetic I am with my letters. I could barely keep up with you when we wrote to Pete, remember? And how is Pete?'

'He's keeping well. He's found himself some work on a farm near Coombe Bissett, not too far away.'

'Do you . . . Are you . . . After that nasty business with Freda . . .' She couldn't finish her question but I knew what she wanted to ask.

'Sort of . . .' I said. 'You never know with Pete.'

'Good for you, Vi.' She smiled, taking me by the arm and suggesting a place on North Street, which was rumoured to have in stock a large batch of tea. 'I have coupons – do let's have a cup together. It's been too long!'

I don't quite know why but I told Annie about Sam. She leant over the tablecloth towards me with the same wide-eyed disbelief as when I'd told her she was beautiful all those years ago.

'But, Violet, it's not two years since . . . They could just be good friends.'

'Yes, that's all very well, but I couldn't just stand and watch in the hope that she didn't develop feelings, could I?' I held the cup of tea to my lips and, on finding it was still too hot, blew gently at the steam.

'No, you couldn't. You did the right thing, Vi. I know it.' She leant back in her chair and stirred a spoon vaguely through her tea, as if imagining the absent sugar. She had started crossing her legs, I noticed, sitting slightly sideways on her chair to make room for them.

'I feel such a fool to have let it get this far,' I told her. 'Freda would be furious if she knew.'

Annie laid a hand on mine and looked at me earnestly. 'He's gone, Violet. Nobody is to blame . . . However raw things might feel, your mother hasn't done anything wrong.'

Flower. Bullet. Mouth. I stayed silent, thinking only of him.

'Chin up. You stepped in as soon as you could.'

'Tell me about David,' I said, after a pause, leaning in across the table to reinforce my change of subject.

'Well, actually, he and you are already acquainted. Remember that night at the dance?'

'The soldier on the gate! Annie, no!'

'Yes! That's him. He came all the way to Imber to find me when we were told to evacuate and arranged for our belongings to be transported to Devizes in a lorry. What a treasure!'

'But . . . is he at war now?' I asked hesitantly.

Annie nodded, looking away and twirling her ring absent-mindedly round her finger. 'He'll be back,' she said eventually. 'And then we'll be married.'

'And do you see the Archams?' I asked. 'Are they keeping well?'

Annie frowned. 'Did you not hear about Mr Archam?'

'No, what happened?'

Annie met my stare over the rim of her cup.

'Why didn't Pete tell me? Surely he knows?'

'Mrs Archam wrote to him to tell him about the pneumonia but he never went to visit, not until after it was too late. She seems fine on the surface, but you know her – the busier she makes herself, the more troubled she'll be inside. You can see it in her eyes. Nobody knows what to do. It's not as if we all live together any more. And the people in Devizes don't give two hoots about Imber. Most of them haven't even heard of the place.'

'Do you think they'll let us go home?' I said, watching her loop her finger daintily into the handle of her cup and lift it to her lips like a lady. 'If we go home, it might give Mrs Archam some comfort.'

'Oh, I don't know, Vi. What does it matter? We've all got new lives now.'

I went quiet, not quite believing that she could let go of the place so easily. 'You have David, I suppose,' I murmured.

She looked up from her cup, puzzled. 'And you have Pete.'

I held up my left hand and waved it at her, bare and ringless. 'Really?' I smiled.

She broke into a grin. 'Just you wait, Vi. He'll be down on one knee before you can say boo to a goose.'

'There's no second-guessing him.' I sighed, placing my empty cup back on its saucer with a clink. 'He'll do as he pleases.'

By the time I saw Annie again, May was nearly over and summer was almost upon us. The sun muscled into the mornings and lingered later into the evenings; the days opened and closed their lids in time with ours. The longer days meant that I could make the trip to Devizes on my day off and catch up with Annie every couple of weeks. It was easy to forget the war when we were together. The air seemed designed for holidaying and harvesting, not fighting. It was harder, somehow, to keep in mind what we were sending the troops to do.

My mother was asleep in bed one evening when I heard the letterbox lift. It was far too late for the postman to be doing his rounds. Still, I ran to the door and found an envelope on the mat. There were footsteps on the street so I hurried outside and saw Sam walking away from the house back down Russell Street towards the Pembroke Inn. The evening was so balmy that he had not brought his jacket. He seemed in no rush.

'Wait!' I called, my voice halting him in his tracks.

He turned and, with a glance over his shoulder in the direction of the inn, he retraced his steps towards me. 'Violet,' he began, in a mumbling tone that I had never heard him use before, 'would you be so kind as to pass my letter on to your mom? I won't be bothering you again.'

I nodded. And he flinched, as if in a quandary about whether to stay or go. Then, making a decision, he turned and resumed his walk without a goodbye. I said nothing more, only dropping my eyes from the silhouette of his back once he had rounded the corner of the road.

Inside the cottage, I examined the letter as thoroughly as I could without opening it, unsure whether my mother would let me read it with her as Sam had implied. I held it up to the light in the kitchen but could only make out the word 'away' and my mother's name at the top of the page. His handwriting was as bold and uncontrolled as his gestures. From what I could see, there was only a single sheet of paper inside the envelope. And there was no address, only 'Martha' written on the front. I ran upstairs and woke my mother, passing her the letter as she rubbed her eyes.

'This came for you. Sam brought it.'

My mother took it from me with a frown. 'At this hour?' she murmured, her voice still cracked with sleep.

'Go on, open it.'

She pushed her thumb underneath the back of the envelope and slid it along the seal. It always frustrated me how she insisted on opening letters so neatly; it wasn't as if she could reuse the envelopes. Once the single sheet had been extracted, she held it close to her chest and ran her eyes across each short sentence.

'Mama, do please let me read it too.'

'Patience, Violet,' she hissed, her eyes not leaving the page. When she had finished, her arms dropped onto the bed, one hand still holding the letter. I sat down on the mattress and looked at her. A sense of reprieve flooded her face. 'He's leaving . . . for good, it seems.' She lowered her head onto my shoulder, all the muscles in her neck unknotting at once. I took the letter from her limp fingers.

You will be relieved, and perhaps a little saddened, to hear that
my infantry will be on the move in a matter of days. I can't say

what for or where to. But it is unlikely that we will ever cross paths again. I cared for you a great deal, Martha, and for Violet. I will miss you both – more, I think, than you will miss me. Rest assured that I will carry your friendship with me until my end – whether it is brought on by the war or by the years that I hope will succeed it.

Take care and may God bless you both,
Samson

He left no address by which to contact him. I was glad of that. I sensed the word 'friendship' had been chosen with care – however tattered its definition had become. Had he been certain that Mama would keep the letter to herself, he might have been freer with his words – if, indeed, something freer had ever existed between them; I was not brave enough to know for sure.

I walked up to Fugglestone the following morning to find the American barracks almost empty. The cook informed me that they had left on a designated military train in the early hours, bound for London. It was not until a week later that we knew the reason for their departure: the Allies had launched an assault – our biggest yet – on the Normandy beaches.

'Do you think he's involved in the attacks?' she asked me, as soon as we heard, her complexion blank as flour.

'He'll pull through, Mama, I'm sure of it,' I replied. I wasn't sure. Not at all. But we were beyond wanting to find out.

Chapter 22

I picked up Mum's parcel from the post office in Delhi on the same morning that I told James about Marc. The events merged like two converging roads, equally potholed and perilous. I could have kept the kiss to myself; the parcel could have been left, unopened, in Delhi.

His anger was deeper than I had predicted. And the heat – the closeness of it – seemed to make everything worse. I had not been able to eat for three days. James said it was dysentery – the fact that I couldn't keep anything down. But the address I had written in Marc's notebook, and the seconds that had followed it, left a stain in my stomach, perfidious, irrevocable, forcing everything else out.

James asked me to draw one last picture of the city before we began the journey home. He only suggested it to take my mind off the sickness but I became obsessed with the detail: every stone and brick had to be right. At dawn, we made our way to the Sheesh Gumbad. The rest of the park was empty. I put pencil to paper but, instead of drawing, thought of lips meeting, of how astonishingly reckless I had been. The shapes that emerged were not my usual solid forms; they did not describe the dome in front of me. Instead I drew bewildered circles: closed, coded, from which there was no way out.

'It might be safer if you saw a doctor,' said James, picking up the drawing and reading it like a diagnosis.

'I'm all right,' I said quietly. The grass in the Lodi Gardens was still cool from the dew – there was dampness beneath my thighs and heat above. He put an arm around me and pulled me in close. 'I'm worried about you.'

I stiffened, wanting to relent but instead withdrawing.

'What's wrong?' he asked gently.

'Nothing.'

'If something's bothering you, you can tell me. You know that?'

I frowned and drew my knees up to my chest.

'Alice . . .'

Nausea swelled inside me, drawing a haze across everything – all the sections of our journey fizzed suddenly into a surge of regret. 'It's Marc.'

James frowned. I dropped my stare to my knees. 'James, I'm so sorry.' The tears, hotter than the air, burnt my cheeks. 'He kissed me . . . we kissed. I stopped it. But not as quickly as I should have . . . I'm so sorry.'

He got up and walked some distance away. The horror of what I had done – the knowledge of what I might lose – invaded the pit of my stomach. I followed him quickly along the path but he seemed to sense my steps behind him. He picked up his pace without turning to look at me. I trailed off, unsure for the first time of where I should go.

I no longer had a route to follow. There was no plan. Just a city, sprawling in every direction. I took myself to the post office to see if Mum had written again. With James gone, I found myself craving her certainty, the relentlessness with which she refused to let me go. When I saw that she had sent me a parcel, I carried it back with me to the hotel grounds. James's things were still in his tent: his shirts, his bundle of postcards, his ruck-sack – nothing had been moved. If I waited here for long enough, perhaps he would come back.

Inside the parcel was an old Church's shoebox. I had seen it once before – at the back of Mum's wardrobe when I was fishing around for a pair of sandals to borrow. Seeing there were no shoes inside, I had shut it and thought no more of it. Opening it again in the tent, I found letters – twenty or thirty of them – sent from my dad to my mum. Most of them had been written when they were children. Silly, meandering things that you'd find in a storybook, with poetry copied out and endless anecdotes about the harvests in Imber. But there was one letter set apart from the rest, in a newer envelope with a neater hand. Mum had laid this one on top of the others. I was about to open it when the tent flap was pulled back and James stepped inside.

He glanced down at the box of letters and saw the envelope in my hand.

'It's from my mum . . . letters between her and my father. I haven't read this one.' I tried to stay composed, lifting the envelope vaguely.

He didn't say anything.

'James –'

'I'm only here to collect my things.' He handed me a booklet. 'And to give you this.' I put down the letter and took it from him. It was a ticket for a flight. Delhi to London.

'You're not coming?'

'I can't, Alice, not after – I'm going down south. To clear my head.'

'But where?'

'I don't know. Kovalam, maybe . . .'

'James, I know I – It's impossible to take back what I did.' He turned as I spoke and began to fill his holdall and rucksack. 'But if you can bring yourself – I don't deserve it – but if you ever feel able to forgive me . . .' I trailed off.

'How could you have let it happen?' he asked. The question hung, stagnant in the tent. It was me now, not Mum, who couldn't give an answer.

'It was stupid . . . a moment of complete stupidity . . .' I sounded pathetic.

'There must have been a reason.'

'I don't know. I was being petulant. It was frightening . . . the idea that you might love me. The thought that one day you might not.'

'It's ridiculous even to say it.' He sighed through gritted teeth. 'After everything. But it hurts like hell what you've done.' He pressed his hands down into the holdall as if to suffocate the clothes inside. 'And the worst part is that I can't stop . . . If only it were that easy.'

I picked out the absent words from his stutter and held onto them as tightly as I could.

'There's a sleeper train heading south. I have a ticket and it's leaving in four hours,' he began. 'I'm getting on it but I need some time to think. Meet me at the station. Either I go or . . . I'd like at least to say goodbye. Just meet me there.'

He gathered up his things, pulled the zip on his bag and left.

I didn't read the letter from the shoebox until I arrived at Delhi railway station. I was alone on the platform, waiting for James. I couldn't think about what would happen if he decided to leave me so I took the letter from my pocket and removed it from the envelope as a way of keeping myself occupied. For the briefest of moments, there were no crowds, no trains. The emptiness felt eerie and scripted, intended for the opening of a letter like mine. The paper was tinted with the faintest of yellows, like a waning summer. I read it once. And read it again. A train came. And still I could not tear my eyes from the letter. The platform filled with bags and families and men with huge urns of steaming tea.

'Alice!' I couldn't trace his voice on the teeming platform 'Alice!'

Finally I saw him, weaving through passengers and luggage. He stopped hesitantly in front of me but I clutched his shirt and brought my forehead to rest on his chest. He took the letter from my shaking fingers.

'Is this true?' he breathed, as he finished reading the page. He didn't need a reply. Instead, he gathered me up and held me still until the platform was empty again.

Chapter 23

'Not far to go, Vi,' Pete called back to me. I followed him through a thin copse up to a stile, which he crossed in three swift movements.

'Tell me where you're taking me.' I swung my right foot clumsily over the fence to join the left and thudded off the plank to meet him in the field.

'It's a surprise.' He grinned, reaching for my hand. He had grown older-looking of late. His chin had gained rough stubble and the hair on his arms had thickened into wire. His voice had deepened as well, imbuing everything he said with a new air of purposefulness. I liked it. The lower voice and the textured face made me feel as if he were moving towards something. Yet I was also fearful – afraid he might leave me behind, trapped in my girlhood. Ever since moving to Wilton, I had stuck stubbornly to my factory uniform, even donning it on days off to avoid the skirts and stockings that I saw Mama slipping into.

Without Freda leading the way, I did not know how to wear the months I had gained since Imber. The petticoats, and the curlers on my mother's dressing-table, had symbolized nothing to me but another outing with Sam.

Yet since Sam's departure, I had examined my appearance with fresh interest; like a stork pecking at its reflection in a pond, I perceived my own gawkiness and was frightened into flight. I was a woman now: with legs and hips to match my breasts. I wondered what Pete saw when he looked at me and, out of curiosity, decided to give him something to dwell on. I picked up an old pair of high-heeled shoes in a second-hand shop a day before we were due to meet and slipped them on in the factory locker room.

'You can't walk back to the farm in those!' He laughed, looking down at my feet at the factory gate with his thumbs tucked into his belt loops. I liked the feel of his eyes on my legs, though; he let his gaze linger longer than usual. Annie sent some of her old makeup to me in the post; a half-empty pot of powder, which was a few shades too light, and a lipstick. I loved watching how the red paste puffed up my mouth into an exotic berry that bounced off the colour of my coat, dress or cardigan. It was like glue for Pete: he barely looked me in the eye any more. Instead, he talked to my lips, listened to them, his expression constantly locked on them as if they were about to cough up treasure. Things between us were much improved since Sam's departure; he seemed pleased that my time was entirely his again. It had never occurred to me that he might have been envious of the evenings I had spent with Mama and Sam. I thought he had better things to do – prettier girls to be going about with.

I tried to ignore all Annie's talk of engagements: it seemed there wasn't a girl in Devizes who hadn't become attached to somebody or other. That the same trend was occurring in Wilton had completely escaped me. Soon enough, I was searching the fingers of the factory girls and starting to feel left out. It seemed the war had made everybody panic.

When Pete mentioned that he had a surprise for me and asked if I could keep Saturday afternoon free, I became nervous. Annie said she was sure that this was it; it was the lipstick that had done it and I had her to thank. She lent me her best day dress and I invested in my second-hand shoes.

'He's probably going to take you to that spot, you know, the one you always go to. On the Downs by Coombe. Oh, it's perfect, Vi! I knew he'd come round – didn't I tell you?'

'If he makes me sit on a bomb again, I'll refuse him.' I laughed.

Annie beamed warmly at me across the table, as if to congratulate me on becoming part of the club. 'And how wonderful that you're in love,' she exclaimed. 'It will make the engagement so much more enjoyable.'

When Pete had set off on a different route from the one Annie had predicted, I was thrown. He wouldn't answer my questions about where we were going. After crossing two sets of fields, I followed him into a wood that carried a dense smell of resin slipping through the veins of trees. The light here fell in isolated pools, crisping patches of leaves while others disintegrated in the damp. A feast of bluebells had been and gone, leaving their yellowed remains to droop and sink into an unkempt carpet underfoot. I scoured the wood floor for a late-coming flower but there were none to be seen. So immersed was I in the town that their bloom had passed without me knowing. In Imber, I awaited the bluebell season eagerly and, come May, I went and lay among them with Freda, leaving two sister-shaped imprints in the middle of the purple sea. I gathered hordes of them in bunches to take back to Mama. Freda said they would never survive outside the cool of the wood; I was determined to prove her wrong. How could something so perfectly formed live only for a day? When, eventually, their bruised heads bowed into a kiss with the side of the vase, I would scurry, undeterred, back to the woods for a fresh bunch. I used to think that, if I could die anywhere, it would be there amid the bluebells, like Ophelia floating in her river. I would lie on my back, stare at the canopy above and picture the sky descending until I dissolved into its hue. Sometimes I imagined the scent becoming so heavy that it sent me into a thick sleep. It took a war to teach me that death was more than a scented evaporation: it arrived with a jolt – a clenched fist that could never again be opened. It was to be feared, not revered or craved or girlishly re-imagined in the depths of a wood.

The trees became taller and thicker in the centre of the wood. Their trunks towered on past us without a thought for who we were or the war we were in; they were all-knowing, oblivious. Perhaps, from up there, they could see an end coming – the end we were all wishing for. In the middle of the wood there was a large crater where a bomb must have landed. There were no trees within twenty yards of the hole, only charred stumps and ash. The pit itself was filled with a cacophony of objects – broken chairs, old car parts and farm equipment.

'Follow me.' He beckoned, stepping onto the pile and picking his way into the centre. He crossed a wooden door with a number three on it and took hold of a rusted metal plough in front of him.

'Wait!' I called, teetering on the edge of the pit.

'Hurry up, then!'

'I'm afraid I might tear the dress.' With a blush, I smoothed down Annie's turquoise pleats with my hands as if to prove how delicate it was.

'What are you dressed up all fancy for anyway? I told you we'd be walking!'

'I'm just tired of my uniform,' I lied. 'I thought I'd start to make an effort after work.'

'Don't tell me that you're going to spoil our fun because of some dress. You'll jolly well start climbing. Come on.'

Reluctantly, I tried to follow the path he had taken. Pete took hold of my hand once I had reached him and went on, stopping finally at a lump of metal that rested on its side as if it were sleeping.

'There!' He brought his hands down to rest on the bronze. Its colours stood out from the rust in the rest of the pit – blue and green patches mingling like oceans and continents on a globe. I frowned.

'Don't you recognize it?' Pete asked.

I studied it again – this time the shape striking me as more familiar. 'How do you know?' I murmured, drawing nearer. 'How do you know it's from . . .'

'The crack – look – it's in exactly the same place as the bell in the church tower. The one with the lowest tone. We used to ring it on its own when there was a death.'

Imber's bell – if, indeed, that was what it was – sat redundant on the heap. It had neither the air nor the space to let out its toll. And what good would it have been anyway when it was not a single man but a whole village that had died?

'It's not the same bell.'

'Well, yes, perhaps the crack is a bit bigger but, then again, maybe it fell.'

'It's not the same one,' I repeated.

'It is, Vi, I know it is! Jim from the farm is going to bring a cart round so we can take it to Wilton. You can have it in your garden. A little piece of home!'

I thought of Imber's fractured cottages and of rifle fire making inroads into the parsonage roof. He meant well. I knew he meant well.

'Go on, touch it,' he said. But I did not need to reach out a hand to feel its coldness. I stood back, not wanting to disturb its rest.

It took an entire hour to hoist the bell out of the crater and onto the back of Jim's cart. I couldn't bear the sight of it sealed tight against the wooden boards. It wasn't supposed to be kept like that – I wanted to suspend it in the tower again so that we could stare up into its hollow and watch it rock.

I was relieved, though, that Pete had brought me here to retrieve it rather than placing it as a surprise in the garden. I could not imagine anything worse than waking up to it unawares, and finding it, inert as a corpse, on the lawn. Every time I washed the inside of a cup in the sink, I would be reminded of its interior – its overturned U a mirror of our valley harbouring nothing but stale air and starved grass.

As we carted the bell home, I shut my eyes and tried to picture it as he saw it. To him it was a project – a way of buying us days in the garden together, repairing it, polishing it, filling in the crack. It was his way of retrieving time – Imber's time – and giving us a reason to spend a piece of it together.

My mother did not speak when we brought the bell through the back gate. She did not even enquire about where we had found it. She accepted its presence as one accepts an unwanted heirloom, issuing instructions about where exactly we should place it as if she had always known that it would one day arrive at her door.

'Don't tip it over just yet,' I told Pete, as he prepared to clamp it into place on the lawn below the apple tree. I crouched and sat in its hollow, staring back at the house. Pete knelt on the grass opposite me.

'Remember Mrs Bexham who used to teach us bell-ringing?' he said. 'What happened to her?'

'I heard she was housed in Lavington, with the Archams.'

Pete stared into the space between his knees at my mention of the Archams and picked at the lip of the bell under my feet with his finger. 'You broke the stay once, remember? And she had to grab your feet to stop you flying off up into the tower.'

'I was always so terrible at it.' I blushed. 'Too enthusiastic, that was my problem.' I pulled my dress over my knees and brought my chin to rest on them.

'That dress suits you more than Annie,' remarked Pete.

My heart knocked around my chest, like a trapped fly. 'How do you know it's Annie's?' I asked, ignoring his other concession.

'She told me,' he said, brushing away my curiosity with his hand. I wondered what else she had told him but did not have to wait long to find out. He stood up so that his face was obscured from me by the upper lip of the bell. 'I wanted to do something to show you I care for you, Violet . . .' he paused, unsure how or whether to continue '. . . because, well, the truth is . . . I can't marry you.'

I fell still.

'Not yet . . . at least.'

'What makes you think –'

He raised a hand. 'I know what you were expecting. Annie let it slip, by accident.' He crouched down to my level and I turned my head to face the inside of the bell. The thought of him and Annie colluding like that, laughing at me, even, made me want to pull at the rim and seal myself inside it for ever. *Not yet*. I tried to stop myself snatching at the only slice of hope he had given me.

'How can you really care for me if you don't want to marry me?' It sounded too simple to be a proper quandary.

'We're still young, Vi, and there's a war on. I don't know where I'll be in a year. I'm eighteen. If things stay the way they are, I'll have to enlist.'

'Well, bully for you,' I quipped. He had been itching to go to war ever since it first broke out – anything to escape to somewhere new.

'Don't look at me like that. I don't want to go. Not even the toughest of men looks forward to war.'

'You wouldn't survive without it, Pete,' I cried. 'What would you do? Stay here with me? Make a home, have a family? Return to Imber, even?'

I watched his face tighten.

'The war suits you and you'll be nothing but glad when it comes your way.'

'Violet –'

'Would it have been different,' I interrupted, 'if we had stayed?'

Pete kept quiet. I listened to the creak of the tree, aching with its burden of apples above us.

'Thought not,' I whispered. Then I stood up from the bell and pulled at its crown so that it clamped down onto the grass with a single, echoless knock.

Chapter 24

I deserved to be left on the platform at Delhi, to lose him for ever. But my mother's letter – while destroying so much – fused us together inexorably. He took me onto the train with him because I was too distraught to be left behind. And we began the journey that he had intended to make alone. I did not ask again for his forgiveness but, as Delhi faded and the stations flashed by, he gradually surrendered it. It took time: fists of words and glass-sharp silences; hours and hours alone together in the carriage. Not the easy bud of a flower. But the pearl-hard grind of something costly.

Mum would say that we were mad to swing so quickly from these fractures into marriage. But it was all or nothing – I had to find a way of showing him I would never be so foolish again.

With his discarded rucksack on my back, I walk from the marketplace to our ruined guesthouse – the only other place that I can think of to look. The bottom half of the building has been stripped completely of glass and doors. Cracks forge valleys down the walls. It seems on the verge of collapse. Rescue workers have left a ladder leaning on the back of the building; they must have used it to reach the guests on the roof.

The door to our room on the first floor is jammed shut – warped against its frame by the water. I shoulder into it until it springs open. A groan heaves from deep within the fabric of the house. I freeze, but it falls silent. Every piece of furniture inside the room – from the bed to the chairs to the wardrobe – has amassed against the right-hand wall. It is as if someone entered in a rage and, with a single movement, swept it across the floor.

The french windows have disappeared completely, leaving nothing but air between me and the bare sea. We paid a few extra rupees for a sea view; now I would do anything to shut it out.

Two of James's shirts and one of my kaftans are draped over the blades of the ceiling fan. Their colours are barely discernible under the silt. I find another shirt and a wave-beaten copy of *Moby-Dick* under the upturned bed. James confessed to me once that he had been trying to finish it for years. Every time he made an indent in its spine, he'd put it down for a month and forget his place. I'm surprised the wave hasn't washed its pages clean of words. Instead the sentences have thickened and mingled into a deep bruise of ink. Half his bags were taken up with cigarettes and books; he left little room for clothes. Unlike his No. 6s, whose fumes he inhaled religiously, he could never settle on a single book but dipped in and out of several, depending on the time of day. I was not much help. Whenever he started reading at a border or in the van, I'd find a reason to wrestle his attention away from the page. We could share the world outside the window but the one in the book was his and his alone. I didn't like it. I wanted his eyes, his thoughts, his words. Even if I didn't give him mine.

I bend down to the wardrobe and place my hands on its side. It is difficult to lift but eventually I manage to roll it over so that I can flip the doors open. The sari I'd bought for our wedding fills the inner space, looped over the rail and threaded through the clothes hangers. Silt has greyed the silk and the gold borders are inlaid with mud, like the crest on James's passport.

'White is for funerals,' the tailor in the shop had told me. 'It is inauspicious, sister, to wear this on your wedding day.'

'I don't mind. White is what I would wear at home.'

He shook his head at me as he handed me the bag across the counter. The next day, he sent Mala, his daughter, across to the hotel to dress me for the ceremony. I did not know how to put on a sari myself. Before she began, she handed me a pile of pleated red material.

'A wedding sari, sister. Gift from my father.'

I take the silted, unworn sari from the wardrobe now and lift the silk to my face. The red one is nowhere to be seen. I imagine it being drawn out to sea, like I was, weaving its way through the waters like a new breed of python. Perhaps somebody is bending over it on the beach, wondering where the bride has gone.

On the morning of our wedding, the scarlet sari looked so rich in Mala's hands. I forgot about home, about the white I had always had in my head when I thought of marriage. And I wore red – fire red. James grinned when I met him at the beach. He should have known that I would do something different. But for every mould you break, you are filling one elsewhere. As Mala and her father stood watching, I could see in their faces the pleasure at having guided me into a custom – not my own, but a tradition nonetheless.

I unravel the sari from the rail. Taking his rucksack from my back, I put it inside. This and the ring are the only proof that we were ever married.

There are more clothes under the bed – a Genesis T-shirt, which he is too old to wear, and a pair of brown shorts. Inside the pocket, there's a piece of card. A photo – wave-beaten and faded. It's of us at the bottom of his parents' garden in Kew. It was one of those evenings that takes you by surprise in England, making all the muscles in your body relax with its warmth. James's mother was putting on an open-air concert. She always wears the most beautiful clothes – fresh off the peg from Liberty. She hosts high tea for a hundred as if it were as simple as combing out her elbow-length hair. James gets his poise from her; he can befriend anyone.

It seems ridiculous now, the idea of sipping wine next to a clematis-clad summer-house, wishing I could exchange my family for his. If I were to whisper to the girl in the photograph exactly what she would come to feel – the ache of home, the need to bind herself fast to something – she would only laugh and take another sip.

I feel it before I hear it: a slow crack spreading its capillaries through the core of the building. I run to the landing to see the stairs give way, falling with the wall into the lobby. There's no way down. I bundle our things into James's holdall and make for a window.

'Get out!' shouts a passer-by from below. 'The whole place is about to go!' I throw the bag down to him. It's the American whose room was on the same floor as ours. He grabs the ladder from the other side of the building and props it up against my window. I clamber down, hands slipping on the bamboo.

'What the hell were you doing up there?' he yells, taking my arm and pulling me away from the building. 'You'll get yourself killed.'

'Wait! The bag!' I break free of his grip and run back to grab it. The house quietens. There are no more groans, only widened cracks.

'What's in there anyway?' He points at the holdall. I frown and pull it close to my chest. 'Your husband . . . I'm sorry, I don't know his name. Have you found him?'

I tell him no.

'Have you tried the hospital?'

The hospital seems so obvious. Why did I not think of it?

'It's on the far west side of the town. They're taking everyone there who they find alive.'

'Thank you,' I murmur. I turn to go and then pause, remembering that he wasn't travelling alone. 'What happened to your . . . ?'

'She's in the hills. Safe. Thank God. I came back down to see if I could help with the rescue operation.'

I look at him, incredulous. If I found James alive and in one piece, I wouldn't leave his side again.

I leave the American by the guesthouse and follow the stretchers being carried out of the town. After a mile or so, the hospital – a concrete oblong with impossibly high windows – becomes visible at the end of the road. Inside, the central corridor is clogged with victims on trolleys. I check every one for James. Then I push my way through the crowd into the ward. Sunlight falls in shafts through the glass, spotlighting particular mattresses. The rest of the room sits in clammy darkness. Beds are separated into sections by threadbare curtains, which have been hauled back and pinned to the wall to make room for more patients. The nurses have given up trying to keep the aisles clear, instead filling the room with as many mattresses as possible. I pick my way through the maze of furniture, scouring the beds for a sign of him. Nurses weave through the hall and stop indiscriminately to wrap steam-white bandages over darkening wounds.

I ask a nurse carrying a clipboard if she has a list of patients. 'His name is James. James Peak.'

She flicks through her papers and runs down the length of the margin with the lid of her pen but I'm told there is no record of him. A fly dizzies itself on the ceiling above me. I want to sit down but there is no room. I have noticed that the doctors stay out of sight.

A woman with a thick Tamil accent, sitting on a nearby bed, starts telling me of a snake, ten feet long, which pulled her through the water with her children. It took them to the edge of the wave and deposited them in the shallows where they could scramble, bedraggled, onto higher ground; her daughter could not have swum without it, her leg ensnared as it was in a ball of barbed wire. I ask her if maybe it was a rope they held and she laughs and says, no, it was not a rope, it was a snake, and why would I not believe her? Just days ago, nobody believed in waves the size of houses. Today anything goes. It was a snake, she repeats; she has never been more sure. I ask where her children are and she points to the next bed. Two sisters lie head to toe, eyes wide open, incapable of sleep. The second girl tries not to look down at her leg, which has yet to be freed from the wire.

It is the dead, not the living, who garner the most attention from the staff. As soon as the life leaves a person, the nurses pounce, carrying them off to the courtyard at the back of the hospital where the body joins a line and, if fortunate, is covered. I check the corpses outside but he's not among them.

A man comes into the courtyard to speak with a nearby nurse.

'Ravindra?'

He's so desperate to speak to the nurse that he barely notices me at first. He clasps her uniform and pleads with her.

'Ravindra! It's me, Alice.'

The nurse moves on. He starts towards me, taking me by the arm and pulling me back inside the ward. I can't understand what he's saying. The woman who told me of the python frowns and gets up from her bed. I beckon her over and ask her what he means.

'His wife. She is not well.'

'She's alive?' I ask, following him to a bed by the wall. The colour has drained from her face and her pupils are unfocused, void of movement. Her lips have morphed from brown to blue. I can feel her coldness without even laying a hand on her. A nurse shouts something across the ward and Ravindra looks up, panicked. Two more nurses approach us and delve under the mattress on the bed. They lift his wife and carry her towards the double doors that lead into the courtyard. He clings weakly to the mattress.

'But he doesn't even realize,' I murmur.

'He knows,' says the woman saved by the python. 'He knows.'

Chapter 25

Freda sent word that she had been granted leave and was to come home for two weeks. My mother fussed terribly about the house, sweeping and dusting for days before my sister's train was due to arrive. She kept pulling me over to fret about holes or patches of damp, which I knew had always been there but to her seemed new. No amount of scrubbing or shifting of furniture would hide them.

On the afternoon of her arrival, Mama buttoned herself into her best dress. She painted her face and saw to her nails. But the more immaculate she made herself, the more it seemed as if we had something to hide. The dress I had borrowed from Annie for my trip to the tip with Pete was still hanging in the wardrobe. I decided Mama would look even more out of place if I did not put it on.

We arrived at the station almost an hour before my sister's train was due, just in case she came early. At twenty-nine minutes past five, a flurry of air pushed itself along the tracks. We took each other's hands and Mama held her breath. I wanted to tell her that she did not need to worry that I would talk to Freda about Sam. Yet I was not entirely sure of what it was that I was vowing, however silently, to keep secret.

Mama, I knew, would change the subject instantly if I reassured her about it directly; she would simply have denied that we had anything to hide. So I stayed silent, hoping that she would deduce where my loyalties lay from the affection that I had stowed in a fresh batch of tea, chopped firewood and a swept hearth. And it was just a visit – Freda had made that clear in her letter. How hard could it be to keep a secret for two weeks? She had no intention of returning to us for good and, besides, there was no home to return to.

Father's death had sent my sister off kilter in a way nobody could have imagined. I tried to reassure myself that, had she stayed, she too would have taken to Sam; she would have acted exactly as I had done. I kept scanning the house for any remnant of his presence; my mother, I discovered, had already seen to his note, hiding it under the lining of her chest of drawers. She could have found a better place for it or even taken a match to it; a simple search of the house had yielded it easily into my hands and I was worried that, should her suspicions be aroused, Freda might be rewarded equally readily. I took it from the drawer and hid it under the mattress.

I checked myself. She had no reason to suspect that anything was amiss. She was too wrapped up in London, I surmised, to spare a thought for the changes that might have occurred in Wilton.

Not a word passed between us as the train approached, only a tightening of the hands.

'I'm so happy she's coming home,' Mama whispered, her voice conveying a different message from her muscles, which flexed and tensed, shifted and stiffened. It took us a while to pick out Freda from the other passengers, the steam and the porters' bronze trolleys.

'Mama! Vi!' We heard a shout from the other end of the platform. There she was, still in her nurse's uniform, walking towards us, bag in hand. She embraced us tightly and planted a kiss on my cheek as if no time had passed at all.

'Oh, I have missed you both!' she cried, taking my mother's arm and handing me her bag when I offered to carry it for her.

'Wait, Freda, we must see to the rest of your luggage.' My mother cast an eye around the platform for a suitcase.

'Don't you worry, Mama. A weekend bag is all I need. I can't stay long, you see. There's so much to tell you about. I hardly know where to start!'

I glanced at Mama, who looked away.

Freda barely stopped to take a breath on the bus from the station. She told us about the dinner dances she had been to and the soldiers that she had treated on the ward – how brave they were, and charming. I thought of the jar of pickled onions she had devoured before leaving. She described the bomb scares and how everyone took shelter together in the Underground and what an atmosphere there was down there. She told us how dear the other nurses in the hospital were to her. She had made the best of friends – so many people to choose from in the city. 'Not like Imber!' I could almost hear her say.

'And how is Wilton?' she asked, after a while, the pace of her chatter slowing for a moment. I waited for my mother to answer but she stayed quiet.

'It's perfectly adequate. We have all that we need here, don't we, Mama?'

We stepped off the bus on North Street and completed the short walk back to the cottage. On the doorstep, Mama fished in her handbag for the front-door key. I watched as Freda glanced to the end of the street where some soldiers were making their way into the Pembroke Inn.

'What are troops doing in Wilton?' She frowned. 'I thought you'd be out of the way here.'

'Wilton House is the army's Southern Command,' explained my mother. 'Although nobody is supposed to know, of course.'

'And we make equipment for the troops in the factory,' I added, 'tarpaulin and camouflage mainly.'

Freda tutted. 'Mama, that kind of work is for labourers' daughters, not for girls like Vi. How could you let her do it? She should have come to London and become a nurse with me.'

'Not all of us have the privilege of waltzing off to the capital at the first sniff of a war,' responded my mother. Freda fell silent.

Having found the key, Mama fumbled with the lock. She frowned at the door as if it were new to her and we were just moving in. Sensing Freda's eyes on her, she could not steady her fingers enough to match the key to the lock. When the door finally swung back to reveal the damp on the walls and the cracks in the ceiling, Freda could only offer a sharp intake of breath. We showed her upstairs and deposited her bag in the one watertight bedroom, where my mother and I usually slept.

'You'll have to share the bed with Violet, I'm afraid. Unless you want to wake up with rain on your face.'

'Or worse.' I laughed. 'There are pigeons in the roof.'

My sister did not look amused. 'But where will you sleep, Mama?' she asked, running a hand over the flaking paint on the doorframe.

'Don't worry about me. I sleep lightly these days as it is. I'll be comfortable enough in the living room.'

Mama made potato floddies for dinner. Freda was full of questions about the evacuation and the factory and, worse, my mother's work at Wilton House. I scraped my fork around my plate to try to cover up our lack of answers. By the time we reached pudding – stewed apple – she had given up.

'Whatever became of that Pete fellow?' she asked, in an attempt to make one of us talk. It was a poor choice of subject. I felt my face whiten.

'He's working on a farm near Coombe,' replied my mother – resolute in volunteering no more information than was required of her.

'Do you see much of him?' Freda directed this question towards Mama but I knew for whom it was meant.

'Violet and he go walking sometimes . . .'

I felt exposed suddenly, and wished Mama had not spoken.

Freda let out a sigh. 'You can do far better than a farm boy, Vi. You're eighteen, you have a good figure. You should be out and about with an officer.'

'I don't –'

'They aren't exactly in short supply here.'

'That's quite enough,' exclaimed my mother. 'Not at the dinner table. Anyone would think you'd left your manners behind in London, Freda.'

'I shan't waste niceties on Violet, Mama. She needs to be told. Otherwise she'll end up old and alone.'

'Better old and alone than a good-for-nothing busybody,' I muttered.

'I'm going to fetch some firewood from the shed,' Mama began, ignoring this last exchange and picking up her empty bowl. 'When you two have grown up enough to join me in the living room, I would welcome the company.' Then she scraped her chair across the tiles, deposited her cutlery in the sink and left the kitchen.

'Don't tell me you *actually* care for him?' Freda leant across the table.

I looked up from my bowl. 'As a matter of fact, I do. I cared for him as far back as that daft dance you made him take you to. And I care for him now. More than ever.'

I watched as Freda's features became unsettled. She rearranged them, seconds later, into a picture of calm.

'You're not still upset about all that, are you? It was years ago, Violet!'

'I didn't say I was upset.'

'Look, Imber was such a small place. I wasn't exactly spoilt for choice back then. London has taught me to be more . . . what's the word? Discerning.'

'Listen to yourself! What would Father think?'

Her gaze flitted away from mine and found it had nowhere to go. Eventually it settled on the kitchen floor. 'He'd warn you not to repeat your sister's mistakes, that's what he'd do,' she said quietly. 'To keep your heart safe for someone worthy of it.'

'He wouldn't mind who I loved, Freda, you know that. As

long as they had a good character. He wouldn't care if they were a Whistler or an Archam, landed or penniless.'

She frowned into her bowl. 'You do know he'll never marry you.'

'You can't be sure of that.'

'He's a drifter,' continued Freda. My hand tensed around the handle of my spoon. 'You knew that from the start. He won't settle, Vi, least of all with you – you belong back in Imber.'

'How do you know? You haven't the foggiest idea what it's been like. You've been away.' I could feel myself reddening and, in spite of my resolve, my eyes filled. She crossed to the other side of the table and slipped her arms around my neck. I tried to push her away but she leant into my ear and made the same ssshing sound she used to make to her dolls when putting them to bed in the parsonage.

'I wish I'd been here,' she mused. 'But I can't very well undo it now, can I?'

Later, in bed, she rolled over and whispered, 'The parsonage, Vi-vi. What's become of it?'

'I don't know,' I muttered, keeping my back to her. 'Don't pretend to care. You didn't even write.'

'That doesn't mean I don't miss it.'

I pulled the eiderdown further over my shoulders.

'I'm sure they'll keep everything in order, Violet. The Major wouldn't let anything happen.'

'The Whistlers left too. Everybody did.'

'But what about Imber Court?'

'They boarded it up.'

Freda's breath became weightier.

'We're not allowed on the Plain any more,' I continued, 'but I went to one of the beaches they've taken in Dorset. You should have seen it. It was all cut up with wire and cartridges and concrete. I hate to think what they've done to the valley.'

'Oh, don't.' She sighed. 'How awful.' I felt myself getting angry at this outburst of concern for a place she had been so ready to discard. 'And to think Father's buried there.' She paused. 'Where are his things, Violet? They weren't downstairs when I looked.'

Throat tightening, I turned away and feigned tiredness.

'They must be somewhere . . .'

'It's late – you're exhausted from your journey.'

'Violet, you didn't leave them behind, did you?'

'No . . . Never.'

'Then where are they?'

'Mama put them in the cellar . . . for safe-keeping.' I gripped the edge of the quilt.

'The cellar?' she exclaimed, sitting bolt upright. 'Haven't you seen the damp?' She clambered out of bed and pulled on a dressing-gown. Taking a candle from the chest of drawers, she swept towards the stairs. I had no choice but to follow.

'How could you let her?' she cried, as she descended the cellar steps and held her light over the boxes of books. Thrusting the flame at me, she bent down and tore open the cardboard, picking up a slim volume of Gerard Manley Hopkins from the top layer. Its blue cover had been defaced by a watermark that ran like a wave from corner to corner and darkened the binding of the spine. The pages inside rippled up from their neighbours instead of lying flat – backbones crooked from the constant cycle of damp and dry air.

I couldn't answer her. Instead I turned and left the cellar for bed. Upon reaching the landing, I felt the inside of me sink down towards the boxes. It was worse than I had feared; the absence of light. In bed, I shut my eyes but did not sleep; I thought only of Mama and Sam, lifting the boxes and carting them down the cellar steps – with me, a shadow, watching in the hallway, unable to say a word.

Freda did not come back to bed that night. I awoke to find her side of the mattress empty. I dressed quickly and went down-stairs to make the tea, hoping that I would find her in the kitchen. As I descended the stairs, my hand came to rest not on the banister but on a book: its cover and spine were splayed like a seesaw across the wooden rail. There were more following it. Downstairs, the window-sills, the crown of the grandfather clock, the sofas and the backs of the chairs were all covered with open books. It felt as if a bomb had been detonated in the cellar, causing the contents of the boxes to sparrow up into the body of the house and come to rest on every spare surface they could find. A fire had been lit, although it was only eight o'clock in the morning, and the books basked in the heat.

I tried to gather them together quickly from their drying places but already I could hear movement above me. Mama's footsteps sounded on the landing.

'Violet?' She put a hand on the banister to steady herself, knocking two books from their perch. 'What in the name of −'

'I'm drying them,' Freda interrupted curtly, from the kitchen doorway. 'You're fortunate. Most of them can be salvaged.'

'Put them away this instant!' shouted Mama. 'Do you hear me?'

'But they're Father's −'

'I said put them away!' she cried, tears journeying down her cheeks.

Freda stooped in practised obedience towards one of the books on the hall floor. Then she paused. 'No.' She retracted her arm. 'They're not going back in the cellar. Not on my watch.' She stood up again, empty-handed, and shot me a glance.

'You insolent girl!' shrieked Mama. I had never seen her in such a state. My mother picked up the book nearest to her − a slim French dictionary that had fallen from the banister onto the stairs − and hurled it towards Freda. She tried to duck but it struck her clean on the temple. She put a hand to her head and stared up at Mama with incredulity. Mama sank onto the step beneath her and let her head drop into her hands. As I hurried to the stairs to comfort her, I heard the front door open and close with the smallest of clicks.

'I'm sorry,' breathed Mama. 'I'm so sorry.'

'Don't worry,' I whispered. 'I'll see to the books.'

I spent the rest of the morning ferrying armfuls of my father's library down to the cellar again, savouring the feel of their fire-warm covers on my fingers. The heat they had gained from the house quickly dissipated in the cool of the cellar and it took several journeys before the final pile of books was laid to rest. I kept back *The Secret Garden*, which Freda had read over and over as a girl. I put it under her pillow, like Mary's key behind its brick.

Later that day, Freda came to meet me at the end of my shift. I emerged from the factory to see her standing next to the gate. Even from a distance, she did not look herself. Her shoulders were hunched and her head drooped. She had always been lanky, but the years had taught her to wear her height well and with grace. Today it seemed that her limbs had grown too cumbersome and heavy for her; she held herself in a way that suggested she wanted, just for an hour, to consume less space.

As I began my approach, I saw Pete rounding the corner of the road outside. I thought about carrying on. Of meeting them there – of suffering his awkwardness and her disdain. And afterwards I thought about what might have happened had I joined them sooner. But, feeling my face burn at the sight of them, I slipped behind a wall and watched him draw near to the gate.

He stopped short of Freda and nodded a stiff greeting. When she looked up, something strange happened. All her fancy ways vanished for a moment and she seemed lost, suddenly, like a child. Pete drew closer. He raised a hand to her temple – the place where the book had struck. I flinched against the wall, heart knocking at my ribs, as if asking to be let out. When I stole another look at the gate, they were talking normally again – an indifferent distance installed once more between them. I wondered for a moment whether I had imagined his touch.

I left the wall and walked towards them. Pete must have felt the silence frost up between Freda and myself because he made his excuses and arranged to call round the following day. Like Pete, I found my eyes jarring on the purple knoll of flesh that had puffed up above Freda's eye. I, too, wanted to reach out and nurse it, cover it, undo it.

'Is Pete living in Wilton?' she asked, watching him make his way down the road.

'Are you all right, Freda?' I reached towards her temple but she raised an arm to stop me.

'I'm catching the early train back to London tomorrow. I shan't bother you and Mama any longer.'

We walked in silence back to the house. As we reached the front door, she turned to me and said, 'Pete comes to see you at the factory quite often, doesn't he?'

I nodded.

'A boy doesn't do a thing like that unless he likes a girl. You should know that.'

She left for London without saying goodbye to Mama. She would not let me accompany her to the station. But when I went to strip the bed and wash the sheets, I found that the book under her pillow had gone, along with the key to the locked cellar. If his books were to be consigned to a slow, damp death, then the least she could do was allow them to rest in peace.

Chapter 26

Terse waves nudge the shore. The sun suspends its bulb at the apex of the sky and lights the sea in a coral blue. If it weren't for the debris, you would be forgiven for thinking that the waves were harmless – a watchful mother singing to sleep the bodies on the shore.

Here, on the beach, I can see the spot where James and I deposited our bags on the sand and sunbathed the day away. Having been boxed together in the train for two days, we stretched out our limbs in the breeze and absorbed the sky. *Getting married in the morning*. Even I was dizzy with the thought of it. He asked whether he should telephone my mum to ask her permission. I ignored the question. But he rolled over on the sand and repeated it.

'It's traditional to ask the father, isn't it?' I sighed.

'I think she would appreciate it.'

'We don't owe it to her, though.' I sat up. 'Not after . . .' The movement covered him in a thin shower of sand.

'She still cares for you.'

'I've told you how paranoid she gets. It's not worth the bother.'

'True. She might panic . . .' He propped himself up on his elbow and dusted the sand from his shirt. 'What about your father? Do you have any way of contacting him?'

'He could be dead for all I know.'

'She must miss him, in spite of everything.'

'Yeah, well. What's done is done.'

'Have you ever thought about looking for him?'

I pulled my legs up to my chest and rested my forehead on my hands, nursing my eyes in the shade of my own limbs.

'You must have thought about it . . .'

'I used to.'

'What's changed?'

'He wouldn't want me to find him.'

'You don't know that.'

'Yes, but . . . I kind of do. Someone once showed me this photograph of him . . .'

'And?'

'I don't know . . . I guess, just seeing him older . . . it made me realize that he'd survived without me all this time. I realized he actually existed. Before that, I could sort of get away with treating him as if he was imaginary, or something.'

'Who showed it to you?'

'I was only twelve. I can't remember,' I lied. I leant back and dug my elbows into the sand. 'It doesn't matter now, does it? Not really.'

'Did your mum see it too?'

'It doesn't matter. I have you now.' I reached for his hand and laid my head on his shoulder.

I thought of James's family, of the bustle around their kitchen table in London, the meals, the holidays and the bare-faced arguments about things as small as who borrowed whose socks. Mum and I must strike him as an offbeat pair – my mother as fixed as a limpet and me as absent as my missing dad. We don't fit together like a family, the pair of us – even with Tim around to masquerade as a father. I couldn't bring myself to tell James that the meagre facts I'd been given about my dad had been frayed by his sister's visit. How, when I was older, I'd dug out the telephone number she had given me when I was twelve and asked everything that I was burning to ask.

I should have told Mum but it would have made her worse. If I gave her another layer, another knot to set about untying . . . she'd crack. And I wouldn't be able to handle it. I didn't understand then that it was she who had the bigger secrets.

At the foot of the beach, the sea heaves itself onto the shore and unloads more water onto the sand. It has been three days since the wave came and still new debris washes up. I do not sit down to watch. I stay on my feet so that, if the water keeps coming, I can turn. And run.

It didn't take much to convince my father's sister to tell me what she knew. I was nineteen when I called her. I had hoped that my curiosity about him would vanish with age. But, like the debris, my questions seemed to keep arriving.

Another wave breaks. It nudges at a girder on the sand. Spills over it. And then retreats.

She had told me that my father was given away when he was born. She'd said it would have been better for 'Peter' if his mother had never tried to contact him again. *Mum was a complicated woman, Alice.* Complex. A complicated character. She kept repeating it down the phone, as if she herself needed reminding.

The sea lets go of its breath for a second time. It sifts through the contents of the beach, drenching my feet and departing again, in seconds.

Even as a boy, Dad had tried to remove himself to places that his mother's letters couldn't reach, marooning himself in Imber in the hope that she might leave him alone. But she kept on burdening him with her regrets, sending him note after note but never once visiting. The child in him couldn't quell the thought that she might one day come to fetch him.

This time, the water brings more debris with it – a net, a wooden beam and a saucepan that it fills and empties, fills and empties.

My father, she told me, left Wiltshire the moment his mother asked to see him in London. He was a grown boy. The war was ending. And she thought he deserved the truth.

Water gathers. And pauses. The sand glistens like a mirror.

Pete traced the address she had given him and found her in a flat near Clissold Park.

The wave breaks. Expires. Shrinks.

Inside his mother's flat, living with her all this time, was a daughter she had kept and loved and reared. And Pete, whom she had left to roam, could not be consoled – least of all by a family he had never known.

The sea leaves. Empty. I have no pity left to give him – this strange, misshapen shadow, who gave me breath and left me, as if I were simply another piece of debris.

I continue down the beach to search for James. If only I could find him we could start something new. Something fresh and simple, with no ties to before. But there's always the sea. Always the wake. With its washing up of things that we can't forget.

'Check the lost-and-found board,' a rescue worker tells me at the neck of the beach. 'They will not have dealt with his body unless it has been named. And if he's alive, it might be listed there.'

The board is already thick with hand-scrawled notes: newspaper, book covers, fragments of posters have all been reclaimed from the debris and written on with whatever pen the rescue workers provide. Each note details people who have been found alive or dead or others who are missing. People are dividing them into two sections: missing and found. The missing board is five or six layers thick with paper. But the found board is all but empty; the lines of bodies in front of the boards need no note.

One of the rescue workers holds back a crowd clamouring to get closer. Arms outstretched, she lets two or three through her grasp at a time. Once at the board, they rifle through the paper, lifting each scrap, like the lid of a box, to peer at the note underneath.

I tear a page from James's *Moby-Dick* paperback and, taking a pen from the woman in front, scrawl down the bare facts – bones without flesh. He has sandy hair, I write. He is British. Tall. Last seen in a blue-and-green-striped shirt. It has become harder and harder to picture him alive and well in front of me so

I resort to listing anonymous colours. I am not the only one. Most of the notes are written in a giddy mesh of Tamil. But there are three I can understand:

Natasha Farrant. Blonde hair, tight short curls, British, 24 years of age. Brown eyes. Has a one-inch scar on her left ankle. If found, please bring to the hospital.

Francois Dupont: Il a les cheveux maron et il portait une chemise verte le matin du vague. Nationalité: français.

And underneath the note in French, I read:

Alice Peak (née Fielding), wife of James Peak, disappeared from the Saravo guesthouse on the morning of the wave. British. Red hair. Pale complexion. Please contact the British Deputy High Commission in Madras if found. Telephone 42192251.

I snatch the paper from the board. Somebody knows I'm here. It's not James's handwriting but they mention him by name. They're calling me his wife. He must have spoken to them. Is he in Madras? I don't even know how to get to Madras from here. *Telephone 42192251.* My heart sinks. All the lines are down: surely they know that? My only hope is the woman at the tea stall. I push through the crowd and make for the hill. I'm not running from the wave this time but towards the thought of him living and breathing in another, untouched, city.

'Please, I'm begging you, you've got to let me use the telephone again,' I plead with the man at the office. His wife isn't with him. He reads the note in my hand, squinting at the telephone number. Then he beckons me inside.

Back in the phone booth, I hold the receiver to my ear and dial the numbers from the note.

'British Deputy High Commission in Madras.'

It is the first composed voice I have heard in days.

'I – Hello, it's – I'm – My name is Alice Peak. I'm calling from Kanyakumari –'

'Mrs Peak. Hold the line, please.'

There's a click. A clouded silence shifts for minutes down the line.

Then a voice cuts in: 'Mrs Peak?'

'Yes?'

'Hello there, my name is Derek Wright. I gather you're in Kanyakumari.'

'Have you heard from my husband? His name's James. James Peak.'

'Let me check for you.' His words are clipped and precise, like the folds of an origami swan. 'One moment.'

There is a pause. I can hear other phones ringing in his office and the swift flick of fingers running through a paper file.

'Mrs Peak?'

'Yes, I'm still here.'

'A rescue worker called on behalf of Mr Peak yesterday from the hospital.'

'He's alive?'

'I'm afraid we have no more information. I'm sorry but I can't be sure.'

'But I checked the hospital and he's not there.'

'As I said, Mrs Peak, our records show that we received a call from the hospital but that is all the information we can give you.'

Stop repeating that name. I'm not used to it and I just think of James. 'Can you send someone to help me find him? Please.' My voice starts to falter.

'We've been in close contact with our rescue team at Kanyakumari, who are doing their best to ascertain the whereabouts of each missing person. I will inform them about your husband. We will make travel arrangements to Madras for every British citizen. You will need to contact us for a passport – I'm assuming that, like others, you lost yours in the tsunami. Are you injured in any way? We've dispatched a medical corps to the marketplace should you need any assistance.'

'Tsunami . . .'

'The wave, Mrs Peak.'

'I've – If the rescue worker or James . . . if they call again, please, I'm begging you, tell them I rang and that I'm searching, and that I'm all right, will you?'

'Of course. I'll make sure I add it to the file. When are you due to fly home?'

'He wasn't in the hospital . . .'

'Mrs Peak, your flight?'

'I – I'm sorry, I don't even know what day is.'

'It's the eighteenth of August . . . 1971.'

'I know the year,' I say abruptly. 'Our flight is on the twenty-third – from Delhi. We moved it. We weren't even going to come down here . . .'

'Then you'll need to get to Madras before then. We will arrange your onward travel to Delhi once an emergency passport has been processed for you.'

'I'm not leaving without James.'

'We will be of assistance where we can, Mrs Peak, and I understand how distressing the last days will have been . . . but I would recommend travelling to Madras at your earliest convenience . . . We will be able to help you with your search at the very least. And with your onward travel.' He pauses. 'Is that all, Mrs Peak?'

I don't reply.

'All right, then. Please call this number again when you reach Madras . . . and we will try to gain some clarity on the whereabouts of your husband before you arrive.'

The line resumes its hum and I lower the receiver.

Chapter 27

We heard about the end of the war in the same way as we heard of its beginning: on the wireless. It should have been momentous – the dancing, the embracing of strangers – but by the time VE Day came, Pete had been missing for two weeks.

Mama rushed into the house to say that someone outside the Pembroke Inn had told her to tune into the news and quick. We sat at the kitchen table, waiting for the old box to settle on the right station, Mama peering into the speakers periodically as if trying to speed it up. We caught the tail end of the announcement – enough to hear what had happened. I expected to feel relief. To think suddenly of going home. But I could only fix my eyes on the empty chairs – the places where Freda and Pete should have been – and remember Father, left behind in Imber. We would be going home to nothing more than vacant rooms.

We tried to telephone Freda from the box at the end of the street, but nobody answered. It had been nearly a year since she had last been with us and I wondered if, even now the war was over, she would ever return to us. After one more failed attempt at the telephone, Mama took me by the hand and tugged me out of the box towards the Pembroke Inn. All along the street, people were coming out of their houses and looking this way and that, as if to taste the air for any sign of change. Inside the inn, the landlady balanced a gramophone on the bar and set a Charleston tune playing. Boys in clean uniforms – yet to be sullied by fighting – knocked together glasses, toasting their luck. And the entire place was filled with bright noise, brighter than I had heard in months.

'Cheer up!' A soldier took a seat on the stool next to mine.

'Haven't you heard the news?' He placed his cap on the oak bar and kept a hand on it out of habit. I wanted to tell him that he could let go now, that there would be no ticking off from the sergeant if he lost or damaged it. But instead I let him hold it: it seemed easier to carry on as we were. He smiled expectantly, waiting for me to answer. I couldn't quite reconcile the youth in his features with the moustache on his upper lip: the two did not fit comfortably together.

'It won't really be over until we're home,' I murmured in reply. It was a foolish thing to say: places can die, just like people. The air can leave them and they grow cold.

'You're not from these parts, then?'

'No, not quite.'

'I know the feeling. My mother and father are in York and my brother is already at war. Wouldn't it be perfect if they were all here with us now?'

I scraped together a weak smile.

'To loved ones,' he said, holding up his glass.

'To loved ones,' I echoed, letting the lip of mine kiss his. A soldier in the far corner dragged an ATS girl into the middle of the room and they began to dance, feet picking out the rhythm of the Charleston. My companion at the bar held out his hand. I glanced towards Mama, who was laughing with Mrs Hunt, the landlady, and before I knew what I was doing, I had placed my hand in the soldier's. It was the end of the war; perhaps if I danced, if I marked it in some way, it might feel more real.

I followed the soldier through the other dancing couples to the centre of the room and thought of Freda practising her steps in the parsonage: she used to put on high-heeled shoes and dance on the parlour floor with the mop. Yet when it came to the dances themselves, she acted as if she couldn't care less. I remembered how, in the hall at Warminster Camp, the steps seemed so natural to her, as effortless as sleeping.

I bobbed along as best I could in the middle of the inn with the soldier. I kept my head bowed over my feet, which Freda had told me was an awful habit. I was supposed to look upwards and into my partner's eyes, but I was too embarrassed to meet his stare and I feared I would lose concentration.

'I'm jolly glad to see that neither of us are dancers!' he called over the music. I blushed and tried harder. How elegant Freda would have looked if she were here. Everyone in the room would have wanted to be her partner. She was probably dancing somewhere in London at this very minute – under Big Ben or along the Mall.

'I hear they're showing a picture in the theatre in Salisbury this evening.' The soldier spoke into my ear, hand still on my waist. 'Would you like to go?'

'I beg your pardon?' I called, over the sound of the gramophone, pretending not to hear.

'I was wondering if you'd like to see a picture with me.'

I tried to smile gratefully. 'I'd love to but . . . there's a boy, you see. And we're –' I didn't know what we were. Or if he would even come home again. He had been gone for a fortnight. In town I'd managed to corner one of the land girls, who'd said he had not been at the farm since a week last Tuesday.

'I see,' said the soldier, rubbing the back of his head awkwardly. 'Well, he's the lucky one.'

'I'm sorry,' I replied, stepping away. 'Thank you so much for asking.'

I returned to the bar to find Mama, who had been watching me dance.

'He seemed like a nice boy, Violet,' she began.

'Can we go and ask after Pete at the farm?'

She sighed and rolled her eyes. 'Violet . . . the war has just ended. What are you doing thinking of Pete? I've no doubt he'll be back before too long. Especially now the fighting is over.'

'But, Mama, it's been two weeks. And he never mentioned going away. What if something's happened?'

'Darling, nothing's happened. He's his own man, that's all. But if it will put your mind at rest, I'll come to the farm. Just as long as you promise to forget about it after that.'

'I can't promise. You know I can't.'

She held my gaze for a moment, then looked with dismay at the soldier I had been dancing with, who had found another partner on the other side of the room.

In order to reach Pete's farm, Mama and I passed through Fugglestone where Sam and his American troops had been billeted in the run-up to the Normandy attacks. The barracks, once temporary, had not been removed since the departure of the Americans but fortified with bricks and tiles. It seemed that the military were planning on moving in for good, despite the war being over. It made me fear for Imber and I wanted to tell my mother as much. But she remained taciturn, marching as quickly as she could past the entrance without turning to look inside.

We followed the river and passed under the railway line, which shuddered with the weight of an approaching train.

'You shouldn't worry for him, Violet. He'll turn up. He's a grown man.' She put out an arm to still me and we waited for the train to arrive.

'I know. But I appreciate you coming with me.'

The carriages rattled over the bridge and steam poured down towards us in voluptuous plumes before rising up again towards the churning breath of the engine. For a moment, we were enveloped completely in its cloud – just Mama and I and whiteness. I inhaled its metallic perfume. It was the only scent I had taken to heart here in the town. All the others – petrol, wet cobbles, chimney smoke – were pollutants to the hay and wool and yarrow that I remembered from home.

Upon arriving at the main farmyard, we were met sternly by the farmer's wife who, at the first mention of Pete, promptly enquired after his whereabouts. 'The boy knows he can't leave without serving his notice,' she barked.

'I'm afraid we don't know where he is either. We assumed you might be able to help,' I ventured.

'Well, I wouldn't be asking you if I knew where he was, would I?'

'We're sorry to have bothered you,' Mama apologized. 'Violet was only concerned for his well-being. That was all.'

'Listen here. If he dares show his face in Wilton again, you tell him that he's to look for employment elsewhere. I've plenty o' lads who'll take on his chores – lads who are reliable and don't take off at half a second's notice.'

'Has he done it before, then, Mrs Hooper?' I asked. Mama squeezed my arm, afraid I might aggravate her further.

'You bet he has. And his favour's worn too thin this time.'

'Thank you. We'll be on our way –' began my mother.

'You might as well take his things,' she interrupted, as we turned to leave the yard. 'I shan't be wanting him back.'

My mother and I exchanged a glance. 'If you would be so kind as to show us . . .'

'He's pushed his luck too far this time,' she muttered, bristling past us and waddling with force across the yard. I assumed she wanted us to follow her so we set out after her. She stopped at a stable block with a ladder leading up to the top floor.

'Up there.' She pointed. 'I'll be leaving you to it, then.'

I was not familiar with his accommodation at this farm. He had kept quiet on the subject, saying only that he did not plan to stay for long. As we pushed back the door at the top of the ladder, I was appalled to find there was no fire or heating or any bed to sleep on – only a single, straw-filled mattress resting on cold, bare boards.

'Imagine doing a hard day's work in the weather we've had, then coming back and sleeping in here,' said Mama. 'It's a wonder he's still walking.'

'Where are his clothes?' I asked, scanning the room foolishly for a cupboard.

'There's a box over there.' My mother pointed towards a trunk in the far corner. I walked across the room and pushed back the lid. Inside were all his belongings – three shirts, two pairs of cords and an officer's coat he had picked up from Wilton House after the Americans had left. I was familiar with the cut and weave of each item. And yet I had never considered how small the sum of his possessions would be once they were assembled – how they barely filled even half of a single trunk.

I delved further inside. My fingers stumbled on what felt like a stack of papers beneath a layer of clothes. Freeing them from a tangle of shirts, I tried not to attract Mama's attention. They were letters: my letters, from Imber.

'That can't be all of it!' my mother exclaimed, coming over to my side of the room and bending to inspect the contents of the trunk.

'What do you mean?' I asked, pulling a shirt over the letters to hide them.

'Nothing . . . no, of course.' She collected herself. 'I shouldn't have been so surprised. For all we know, he could be an orphan, God bless him.'

She paused, pressing her lips together as if deciding whether to go on. 'You're not still thinking of . . . marriage, are you, Violet?'

'If he'll have me,' I whispered. 'I'd be miserable without him.'

'You'll be miserable *with* him, my darling. Just look.'

She gestured towards the trunk but all I could see were my letters, grouped carefully in chronological order, each one filed in its correct envelope.

As his trunk was too heavy to carry, we took his belongings in sacks back to the house. I made neat piles of his things and stored them under our bed. Remembering Sam's note, I removed it from under the mattress, where it had torn slightly, and kept it with Pete's letter in my drawer.

Another week passed and I was still hopeful of Pete's return. He had probably gone to scout out work at a nearby farm: it was not difficult to imagine him tiring of Mrs Hooper's briskness in Coombe. Two more weeks went by and I started to worry. I feared that he had left for good and wondered what I had done to deter him from calling to say goodbye. I took to sitting by the bell, running my hand through the thin skin of dew that was deposited on it each morning. It had become so embedded in the surroundings of the garden that it now stirred in me only the faintest memories of Imber. Moss had begun to attach itself to the rim and spread across the surface like a knitted garment. At first I had scraped it off dutifully every couple of weeks, washing the bronze with a sponge until I could see its green and umber markings once more. But I had given up of late, letting Nature have its way. As the moss thickened, so the separation grew between the mute bell in the garden and the ones in my memory – strung up high and full of song.

One night in June, when Pete had been gone six weeks, there was a knock on the door. Mama did not rouse so I crept down on my own in the hope that it might be Pete.

At the door, I could just make out a nurse's cape through the flap of the letterbox.

'Hello?'

'Hurry up and open the door!' Freda hissed at me. 'I've been out here for ages.'

I lifted the latch and she pushed past me, depositing her suitcase on the hallway floor.

'Freda, what are you doing here? Are you home for good –'

'Where's Mama?' she interrupted coolly.

'It's past midnight. She's asleep upstairs.'

My sister let out a frustrated sigh and paced the hallway. Then she turned towards me and grasped my arm, her hand cold from the night air outside. 'Violet, please tell me you didn't know.'

'I don't underst–'

'You know perfectly well what I'm talking about.'

'I –'

'I've heard talk, Violet, in town, about an American officer.'

My ribs tensed.

'An American officer with whom Mama . . . became acquainted.'

'I never heard . . .'

'Will you swear to me that you don't know anything about it?'

'It's just aimless chatter, Freda. You know what people in Wilton are like. Everything has to be taken with a pinch of salt around here.'

'Except I didn't hear it from anyone in Wilton.'

'Then where?'

'Never you mind.'

She did not drop her eyes from my face, not even when I looked into the living room towards the hearth, which was in need of sweeping.

'There's nowhere for you to sleep,' I mumbled weakly.

'I'll make do with Father's chesterfield.'

Her words made me colour. I walked up the hall under the pretence of fetching a blanket and pillow. Then I climbed the stairs with dread in my stomach that I felt certain would only be compounded in the morning.

Freda could stay for two whole days. After relating the severity of her family's situation to her matron, she had been granted emergency leave for the weekend. For the entirety of Saturday and Sunday, my mother and sister became like figures in a weather house – Mama appearing only when she was sure that Freda was out of sight. She seemed to sense instinctively that Freda had heard something.

I expected her to intervene and pre-empt a confrontation but instead she hid herself away guiltily. She kept disappearing to run errands around the town, anything that kept her away from the house. For her part, Freda became increasingly frosty towards me. Now that the war was over, my shift at the factory had ended, and I could hardly avoid her in the way that Mama did: it would only make us seem more culpable. Mealtimes were the worst – a million and one silences passing across the table as one of us conveyed the salt to another, poured water or enquired hesitantly after a second helping.

Our stalemate finally fell apart on Sunday. I had stayed on to attend to the flowers at church and, through an unlucky lapse on the part of my mother, she and Freda had been present in the house without me for over an hour. If either of them was hoping that my return would relieve the tension between them, I was to be a disappointment. We sat down to eat in silence, the pressure rising like the damp on the walls with every conversation that refused to start. It was left to me to break the silence.

'How wonderful that the war is over, Freda, and that you can be with us for Sunday lunch,' I said. Mama looked up and smiled tensely at me. My sister said nothing. 'I imagine London was quite the place to be. Was there much celebrating?'

Instead of launching into the merits of London, I was surprised to see my sister whitening and staring down at her plate. 'I suppose so . . . I wouldn't really know. I was on a shift . . . I had work to do.' I sensed I had upset her but couldn't, at the time, work out why.

'But there must have been some celebrations on the ward. With the other nurses?'

Freda shook her head. 'The sick still need tending, regardless of whether there's a war on or not. There's always work to do.'

'Oh, but I was reading in the newspaper that everybody went out on the streets. I saw a picture of a nurse in her cap dancing with a soldier on the Mall. It made me think of you,' I pressed.

'I was certain you'd be joining in with all the dancing. You love to dance.'

Freda set down her cutlery a little too vehemently. 'I told you I was working . . . I don't have the time to swan off and go dancing in the street.'

'Nonsense, Freda! Since when have you been such a prude?'

'I'll tell you since when. Since I discovered that, while the rest of us were doing our best for the war effort, my mother had taken up with a Yank.'

I didn't know what I had been expecting, but it wasn't that harsh assertion of the facts. They seemed all the more horrible, the way she had set them before us. And yet she hadn't been here. She hadn't been here to stop it. Mama stared at her plate intently, refusing to look at Freda. I tried to think of a change of subject for her sake but there seemed nowhere to go. I waited for my sister to speak again.

'I was in town yesterday, Mama, and I came across a Mrs Grey. Do you know of her? I'm sure you do. She worked at Wilton House with you – as a cook.' She clipped the consonants in the word as if it bore a world of significance and leant back in her chair, waiting for my mother's response.

'Yes, I do. A very generous woman, always passing on spare carrots and potatoes from the garden at the house.' She held onto her composure so well that I started to doubt whether she had anticipated the direction in which Freda intended to take the conversation. Then she shot me a frightened look from across the table, which quashed the doubt.

'It's just hearsay,' blurted Mama, before settling herself as much as she could. 'Whatever you've heard, it's just talk.'

'What is hearsay?' Freda looked at our mother, her eyes wide with contrived innocence.

My mother tightened her grip on her knife and fork. 'I don't think you can be in any doubt as to what I'm referring.' She put down her cutlery as she spoke, pushed her plate to one side and leant into the space across the table. 'Whatever they have said at the house, it is not what it seems. Violet will tell you.'

I stiffened, glancing at Mama, who avoided my eyes, abashed at having to bring me into the debate.

'Oh, yes! Of course.' Freda turned in her chair towards me so there was no escaping her glare. 'There you were, Violet, looking *genially* on as Father was betrayed in broad daylight and Mama made herself the talk of the town.' Her eyes bored into me until they had extracted a deep blush from my cheeks. I wanted to hide my face from her, run upstairs and bury it in a pillow. But I knew what it would mean for Mama if I looked away. Freda had only heard gossip: she had no proof and nor would she find any.

'It isn't just gossip,' she continued, her voice becoming angular. 'Everybody here *knows*. I have it from a reliable source.'

Mama turned rigid.

'Why do you care, Freda? You left us!' I cried, standing up and moving round to our mother's side of the table.

'Oh, that's just perfect, isn't it?' she snapped, jabbing a finger in my direction. 'How can I be responsible for an affair that happened entirely in my absence?'

'Don't use that word,' my mother retorted. 'There was no such thing.'

'That is not what the town is saying, Mama!' my sister exclaimed.

'The town?' Mama repeated with alarm. 'We're decent people, Freda. Nothing untoward happened.'

'Would you have any old Tom, Dick or Harry read this, then?' She pulled a piece of paper out of her pocket and cast it onto the table. It came to rest by my mother's plate. I looked down at Sam's note and knew the game was up.

Mama picked it up. 'Where did you find this? You had no right to rummage through my belongings.'

'Ask Violet. It was in her drawer.'

Mama stared at me, forlorn. She took a breath. 'Freda, you

must realize . . . how hard it was for Violet and me after the evacuation, without your father . . .'

Freda's eyes narrowed. 'Forgive me, Mother, but I don't see the other widows pouring out their grief to any willing soldier who might happen to drop by.'

'How can you be so unfeeling? He was a friend! He was a good friend to both of us.'

'Oh, please!'

Mama's voice was wavering now, her eyes rabbit-wide. 'There might have been more to it had it been allowed to grow . . . But I dealt with the matter swiftly as soon as I realized the extent of my feelings.' She nodded in my direction, as if remembering my words to her in the kitchen on the day she had brought it to an end.

'So you did love him.'

'That is not what I –'

'But he said in the note that he cared for you.'

'Did he not also say that he cared for Violet?'

'That is not –'

'And do you not care for me as a daughter? It's the same, is it not?'

'But he's a man, Mama, and you're a woman!'

'I know I've been blind to how others might have interpreted the situation. But for your part, Freda, will you not see that I meant no harm by it and I put an end to it as soon as I grasped what it might become?' Mama extended a hand towards her.

Freda wavered. A few seconds later, she was on her feet and moving towards the door. 'How are we to go on after this?' she asked. 'What would he think?'

Then I let slip what my sister had been baiting us to admit: 'Father's dead, Freda. It wasn't . . . it wasn't wrong . . . because Father is dead.' I was crying. 'Soon we'll go back to Imber. That way, we'll be near him.'

Freda dropped her voice to a murmur, her eyes stone cold.

'Do you honestly think that all this can be magicked away just by going home? Nothing will ever be the same again.' Then she left the room, taking Sam's note with her. We listened to her steps, bullet-like, on the stairs.

I waited a while in silence with my mother. Then I readied myself to go and fetch her. 'Be kind, Violet,' my mother murmured, as I stood up. 'Be kind to her.'

I crossed the landing to find our bedroom empty. Sam's note had been shredded and discarded in the fireplace. There was no sign of Freda. I should have burnt the note before she had a chance to find it.

I collected up the paper from the grate and put it in my pocket. I would have held a match to it there and then, but the fireplace in our bedroom did not work: the chimney had long since caved in and the chute was full of bird nests. A single glance out of the window told me where Freda had gone. She was sitting with her back against the bell in the garden, knees pressed up against her chest, crying like a little girl. I could hear her sobs from the window. Downstairs, I padded across the lawn past the bomb shelter and over to the apple tree.

'Freda, please come inside,' I said softly.

'It's ruined everything. *Everything*,' she cried. 'We haven't a home, we haven't a father – we haven't even a proper mother any more. And I've . . . It's my –'

I waited. But she didn't finish. I knew what I should do: I should stoop down and touch her, let her know that, for her part, she was forgiven. But I remained standing.

Chapter 28

'It was auspicious, sister. All my family live in the hills. There are no fishermen in my family. Only shopkeeper. None was taken, sister, none. They are all alive,' explains Suganthi, the woman from the hill. 'So I help you. I will help find your husband.'

Her husband had sent for her after I had telephoned the deputy high commission from his booth. I was inconsolable, and I could tell he didn't know what else to do. I'm grateful she's with me. She speaks Tamil, for one thing, and can ask the nurses at the hospital about James. Yet I can't understand how she can muster up such kindness towards a stranger when her town – the place she has lived all her married life – has been swallowed whole by the sea. I think of the letter Mum sent me. *Such selflessness would have left me aghast.*

'My mother lost her home once,' I say, as we cut a path towards the hospital.

'How, sister, in a fire?'

'No, it was taken from her by the army. But she only had to move to the next town.'

'A home is a home, sister. When I left my family to live with my husband, I cried for days in secret. And they live only one mile! But my daughter goes to live in London. So far away. I visited two years. My first visit. She didn't say it on the telephone, sister, but in London, every day is monsoon day. Rain, rain, rain. They live in a small, small house, with fifteen family. There is no space for her children. Where will she put them? In the cupboards? She wanted to find us work there. But I tell her, no. It is a bad plan. I see life is good for me here – auspicious, sister.' She clasps her hands together as if to thank God. 'Your mother, did she ever go back to her home?'

'No, never.'

Suganthi frowns at me.

'She can't settle in her new home. She thinks her old home would have been better.'

'Ah, but if she stay in her old home, she could not have such a beautiful daughter.' She stops me in my tracks and cups a hand around my cheek with a wide smile.

She is what I would have given you, had I been a better man. I keep quiet, thinking only of the letter.

Suganthi turns to face down the hill, breathless from our walk. 'Alice, the wave brings bad things,' she spreads a hand across the view of the debris sprawled beneath us, 'but your Amma, she cares for you. You go home and see. The water, it comes and goes and everything changes.'

If I am to stand any chance of reaching the deputy high commission before my flight, I must leave Kanyakumari today, travelling first to Madras and then to Delhi. There was still no sign of James in the hospital. I telephone the deputy high commission again to see if they have received any further news. But the call yields nothing, only a repeat of the information I heard yesterday.

'I did take the liberty of calling the airport to confirm your flight,' says the man at the end of the line. 'If you do intend to travel home, we can make arrangements for your journey from Madras to Delhi airport. You can telephone your family once you arrive here to let them know your plans.'

I avoid an affirmative answer and hang up. There are very few buses travelling between here and Trivandrum. They are still clearing the roads. I don't even know if the trains are running.

Suganthi arranges for a driver to take me to the station in

exchange for a handful of rupees – worthless since the wave – and a packet of Ceylon tea from her kitchen. I don't even know if I'm set on going yet but I climb into the car with the holdall full of James's things and head for the station all the same. Tree after tree has been felled and laid to rest along the road. We frequently have to turn off the tarmac and drive through the dirt to avoid them. This place used to be so green, as if it did nothing but rain. But any foliage that has survived has lost its colour to the mud and silt and travelling sand. The entire landscape looks sick – like something that should have long since been buried.

The station is packed with people trying to get away. There are guards blocking the entrance to each platform. Whole families sit perched on the contents of their houses. People have loaded their remaining belongings into vegetable crates and flour sacks – any container they can lay their hands on. The luggage has a watery look – suitcases misshapen by the sea, then cemented in the sun; salvaged papers and photographs, all carrying the trace of the wave in the ripple of their skin. A couple of people stand with nothing but the clothes on their back in the ticket queue, casting an eye at the belongings other people have brought and realizing they have nothing to barter with. One man offers his watch, miraculously still ticking on his wrist, and is given a ticket. A murmur jostles through the queue and people root around for similar objects. The next woman can hand over only a twenty-rupee note, its ink half erased. She is turned away. A husband approaches the window offering the gold from his wife's ears. James said an Indian wife carries her gold everywhere except to her grave, her family's inheritance judged safest when fashioned into jewellery and pressed against the warmth of her skin. The man behind the desk nods and holds out his palm. The wife nurses each of her earrings from her lobes and drops them, with hesitation, into the outstretched hand. In exchange, they are given two paper tickets.

I wait my turn in the queue and pull out my ticket to Madras from my pocket once I am beckoned forward to the window. I have been told it requires a stamp from the ticket office before I can board the train. The sight of the ticket elicits a muttering from the crowd. But the man behind the counter remains stern.

'No gift, no stamp,' he tells me.

'You've got to be joking!' I cry. 'I already have my ticket.'

'Okay, okay, madam, that is fine, you will not be travelling. Move aside, please.'

'No. Wait.' I unzip the suitcase and fumble around inside for something to give him. My fingers pause over the cover of James's passport, feeling its permanence.

'Madam, if you please, there is long queue here.' He is pointing not at the passport but at my wedding ring and motioning for me to hand it over to him. James bought it just before the ceremony from a man whose shop sign claimed with much bombast that he was the best goldsmith in Tamil Nadu. Every surface in his beachside cabin was drenched with jewellery. The walls shimmered so vehemently that they looked wet. The shopkeeper had strung up a strip light along the length of the ceiling and the brightness of the gold inside had made our eyes ache with delight. This was what it had felt like, marrying James: the smallest of acts stuffed full of the shiniest treasures.

'I can't. My husband gave me this,' I tell the ticket officer.

'Then move aside, please . . . Madam?'

I slip it off my finger, dropping it onto the map of my open palm. It is only four days old. You can't form an attachment to something in four days. It's just a cheap piece of metal. I hold it out towards the counter. I try to let go. The clock in the station stutters into its fifth hour. The queue throbs behind me. It is only a matter of unclenching my fist.

Chapter 29

Imber's parsonage, which used to house our every hour, now gives birth to egg-yolk yellows, ether blues and bulging greens: a greenhouse that breeds verdant rooms – great webs of ivy that string themselves up over the ghosts of old walls to form inner chambers of their own. I touch the remains of the doorframe. The brickwork on either side of it has buckled and crumbled to reveal haggard cracks out of which nobody looks and into which nobody stares. I shouldn't be here. Somebody should have stopped me entering. Had I known how easy it would be to reach this place, how little effort I would need to exert, would I have come back sooner?

Inside the house, the bottom half of the staircase is missing, leaving steps that lead up to the sky. I cannot reach my bedroom, in ruins, upstairs. The glass that remains in the windows downstairs has splintered into muddied blades, and ivy twists across their vistas. A knit of goose grass has prised its way through the fireplace in the drawing room and milkwort cleaves to the cracks in the hearth. Everything conspires to pull the house down into the earth for burial. After all my fears of shells and bullets, it is Nature, not war, who has had her way. And I find that I am pleased for her.

In the centre of the drawing room, gangling stalks of hoary plantain tower up towards the ceiling. Their lamps of eerie violet bend whenever there is a gust of wind, surrendering their wisped petals, like strands of ageing hair. The entire house reminds me of an old face whose skin, no matter how thin, will not surrender its secrets – will not give a name to the little tremors that carved each wrinkle and deepened each crack.

The flowers cluster into a space no bigger than an armchair in the far corner of the room. They are fed by a pure bath of sunlight. If I stand among them, I can see right up through the first floor above and the roof: an ellipse of sky has emerged eye-like among the rafters, light flooding through the gap onto my upturned face. The rest of the room sits in darkness.

In the kitchen I find a rusted can of pears, teeming with ants searching for an opening. I remember my mother leaving a host of food in the larder – a seal of her ownership, perhaps, or of her will to return.

With difficulty, I cross the field opposite the parsonage, stamping down great swathes of grass to forge a path back to the car. To my right is the empty casket of the church – as weathered by the passing years as my own body. Despite everything I witnessed there, it is the only building in Imber to harbour a soul in its ruined frame. It still quietens me when I pass. The bells in the tower are long gone – looted, melted down and sold, maybe. Or rusting in my mother's old garden.

I didn't take the bell when I moved out of my mother's house. Once all hope of going home had been extinguished, she grew quite attached to it. I could not ask her to give it up. And Tim would not have understood. He knew about Imber. But he did not ask questions. He was not the kind to pry: he had a past of his own – women I did not care to know about – that he preferred to keep to himself. It felt strange, at first, to share a life with someone whose ways were so different from my own. I had not witnessed his ageing; his face was creased with unfamiliar folds – singular experiences had ploughed each line. I knew when I married him that a part of us would always remain a stranger – sharing houses and beds and weekends but remaining mute about the past. It was what we both wanted. The unknown part of him reminded me of something I had known before: I liked how he kept things back, how we agreed, silently, to keep secrets. We married a year after meeting, in 1965. He loved Alice as his own and that, for me, was enough. Now I only envy him the way she warms to him, tells him the things that I wish she would tell me. It seemed so effortless: she took to him so quickly. It made me wonder how, after so many years of trying, I could have failed to win her over.

I am on my way out of the village now, retracing my steps past Seagram's Farm and finding my way back to the car. He will be expecting me.

The door is opened; I climb inside, steadying myself on the steering-wheel and not looking back. My hands are ageing by the day, the skin on the backs coming away loosely from the bone, veins mapping an ever-starker path to my wrist. I'm still wearing Freda's band. Then there's my wedding band and my engagement ring and my mother's wedding ring, which I wear on my other hand.

'You've got no hope of floating with that lot on!' Tim cried, when we went swimming in Bournemouth with Alice one summer and I refused to take them off. He's right: it can't be good for you, carrying a whole life, unlived, in circles around your fingers.

I start the ignition and pull away. The road lifts me up to the lip of the valley and over the top of West Lavington Down. I pass the military booth that seals their land like a letter. It is still empty.

As soon as I have passed it I want to turn back and open the place up again, leaf through its pages and linger indefinitely on its last word. The car has carried me away with such fluidity that my coming and going seems as easy as sleep. Last time I came back, there was no car to hush me down the road or cover over the fissures in my nerves. Instead, we had had to walk across the Downs behind Bratton before dawn and come in from the north. The only way to reach the village undetected during the war was by foot; and that was not permitted. A week before he disappeared, Pete and I set off for the Plain in the early hours. Had

I known where he was taking me, I would not have agreed to go. It was only once we passed the well near Wadman's Coppice that I realized we were on military territory – that he was trying to take me home.

'Let's go back, please,' I begged.

'Come on, you'll enjoy it.'

'*Enjoy* it? Do you have any idea what they'll have done to the place?'

'Nothing much will have changed, Vi, don't you worry.' He pressed on ahead of me towards the base of the valley.

'What if there are soldiers around?' I asked, as he joined the chalk track that led into the village.

'There won't be,' he replied. 'It's not even dawn yet.'

A dense mist had descended, shrouding the Downs and the tracks so that I couldn't see Pete if he wandered more than a few yards ahead of me. The fog ebbed and flowed in front of us like a giant tide and I began to notice the ways in which the army had laid claim to the land. Battered tanks pierced the haze like aged rocks; signs denoting 'unexploded military debris' confronted us suddenly from inside the fog's folds. Pete wavered off the path for a moment to examine an overturned tank, sullen and rusting among the dewed grass. He threw a kick at it and the sound bounced from Down to Down. If it wasn't for the echo, I wouldn't have known that the hills were there.

As we joined the neck of the valley, a new body of fog enveloped us. Murmurs of light had entered the sky by now, purifying the mist into a receding veil of white.

The first building that we came to was the Bell Inn, its faded sign fanning the mist on its hinges. The inside was little more than a carcass – a series of hollow caverns stripped bare of their bottles and glasses, tables and chairs, harbouring instead darkened air and gun cartridges. Holes blossomed like moles in the brickwork, letting in the moonlight in pencil-straight shafts. Pete bent down and picked up a cartridge from where the bar would have been; it lay as rigid as a dead finger in his open palm.

'Would you look at that, Vi! It's the cartridges they use in their Number Fours!'

He uttered these last words with such vibrancy that I had to turn away. I couldn't fathom how he could stare at the rifled fragments of his old home with the same indifference that he afforded to dead cattle or a storm-ravaged barn.

I followed him onwards into the village. They had built a metal blockade around Imber Court, so tall that we had to clamber onto a stack of barrels to see inside the grounds. I wanted to vomit. The house had been boarded up with copper-green shutters and a matching roof so that it resembled a face whose features had been gouged out and bandaged. The front lawn was now asphyxiated under a thick layer of concrete and a sign had been stitched to the side of the house: *Nothing of value is kept inside this building*. Only remembrances perhaps, and a life still-born. I could think of nothing but our parsonage and the church and how it would be better for a bomb to have fallen on them than for them to suffer the same slow rape as Imber Court.

Pete jumped down from the barrels and broke into a whistle, carrying on past me towards the church. I stayed where I was. The rest of Imber was hidden from my view by the thickened copse flanking the right side of the Court. 'I can't carry on. I'm sorry,' I called across to him, unable to inject enough strength into my voice for him to hear me. 'I'll see you back at Bratton.'

I turned, but was stopped in my tracks by the sound of air being released from a bottle, only louder and more pressured. A red flare inked through the mist's capillaries and spread like blood through the fog. It drifted towards me, dissipating into flesh pink. They were here.

'Pete!' I called, in a thick whisper. 'Pete!'

Swallowing my fear, I ran back to the village, skirting the

edge of the copse in case I needed to hide. I couldn't find him in the fog. Perhaps he hadn't seen the flare. The sun inched further up into the sky and gained strength. The mist thinned. Soon our cover would be gone. I could see the church tower now, the air around it still tinged scarlet from the flare. Then the gunfire started: it barked its way from one side of the valley to the other, producing so many echoes that it was impossible to distinguish the original sounds from their offspring. A sudden flash lit the mist. I heard the shuffle of feet and buried myself in the trees.

There was a break in the firing. A slow droning sound seeped from somewhere beyond the church, like a tractor, only deeper. The growl carved into the silence, stalking the Plain like an injured beast.

'Violet! Psst!'

I slipped from the wood to see Pete scurrying down the track towards me.

'They've got three Shermans and about fifty men – that's just the ones I can see! Come and look!'

'Pete!' I cried. 'Please take me back!'

'But it's too good to miss!'

'Good?' I echoed. 'What do you know about good?'

He took hold of my hand and bolted towards the church. I resisted, but the strength of his grip forced me into following. Pulling me into a bush, he caught his breath and then peered eagerly out at the Plain. The fog began to part. I thought of the rising folds of a theatre curtain – the pattern made by a receding wave.

Then it began. In full. Boots thudded on chalk. Gunfire rebounded between walls. A shell was fired in the direction of the parsonage. Smoke billowed. Soldiers ran. A boy – no older than twenty – snared his leg in wire outside the school. I imagined him bleating, a flailing lamb caught on a fence. There was a smashing sound. I looked up as a soldier put his elbow through the glass of Mrs Mitchell's upstairs window and aimed his gun downwind. I thought of the laundry press – her pride and joy – broken and in pieces on the floor.

Before he'd left, Sam had told me there were ghosts here, hidden in the hearth of every house. He said the Yanks drew lots to decide who would keep guard and sent the others to sleep rough on the Plain, so perturbed were they by the voices they heard in the cottages. He talked of words – chalk-white – that appeared on the ruined walls in the morning, words listing the purpose of each room – 'Pantry', 'Larder', 'Bedroom', 'Hall' – as if staking a claim to them again. He did not know that the ghosts he believed in were of the living, breathing kind.

'I can't watch,' I cried to Pete, leaving him in the bush and stumbling away in the first direction I could think of. I ran as fast as I could to the track that led to Coombe Hill. He didn't come after me. But I could feel his eyes on my back. I didn't know it at the time but things would never be the same between us, just as Imber would never take on the same shape in my mind. Unknown to me, it was the last time I could fool myself into thinking that this place – and that boy – were mine.

Perhaps it would have been different if I had gone there with Mama, or even Freda. Pete was too enamoured of the guns and shells and bullet holes to see what had been taken from us. To him it was just broken stone.

I kept thinking of Father, of how his grave had witnessed these assaults day in day out, how he had watched as stray shells embedded themselves in the thatch and bit through wall after wall. Even if we were allowed to return, there would be nothing left to inhabit. We had lulled ourselves into thinking we could mend things. But it wasn't merely a case of damp and rain, floods and storms. Now there was the damage of an entire army to contend with.

And there were other ruins – gifts of the war – that had different shapes. A daughter, a husband, a marriage, a home: there was nothing the war couldn't invade or appropriate as its own.

The White Horse tattooed into the chalk skin of Westbury Hill met me as I emerged at Bratton. Gunfire continued to stutter across the Downs. I curled up in the nook of the horse's hoof and felt the dawn roll in behind me, sleep arriving just as the sun began to whiten the horse and bleach its mane. The light brought rest and, with it, the thinnest of dreams. The horse gained breath and a kick in its feet and galloped away without me. Its flat shadow skimmed like a travelling cloud across the length of Salisbury Plain. And, with a shake of its mane, it quilted the ruins of Imber in an ashen layer of dust.

Years later, when I took her up the hill to that same horse, she complained about the walk. The view at the top silenced her, as I'd known it would. We sat in its eye and she said she could see all of England. The berries we picked from the bushes on the way up darkened our fingertips; we licked them so that they turned from dusk black to dawn purple. She asked about her father. And for once I managed to meet her eye and tell her what I could. I was happy. I felt brave for having brushed against the truth. There is something about seeing England from a height – years of buying and selling, growing and reaping mapped across the fields – that makes the past easier to understand. I told her I'd loved him and that he'd left of his own accord. There was nothing else I could say. She could not know, at that age, that her mother was as much to blame.

Chapter 30

The village sinks back into the valley. In the rear-view mirror, I can just make out the spire of the church, submerged under the brow of the hills. The Cortina completes the curves and dips of the firing range, passing through the unmanned military barrier as if it were perfectly permissible for me to be there. With Imber behind me, I thread my way back to the suburbs.

Lines of houses with matching doors and windows duplicate themselves along streets named after flowers. Ours has always been difficult to distinguish from the others, even after several years of living there. It is newly built with thin, oblong windows and a garage that juts out at one end. Tim bought it for practical reasons – the space, the neighbourhood, the short commute. Returning to it evokes no sense of homecoming. I used to worry about this inertness until it dissolved into habit and I no longer gave it thought. Alice's room is at the front of the house, although I don't know why I still refer to it as that. All that is left of her is a couple of boxes of records set down next to the player, a few clothes she no longer wears hung in the wardrobe and a bed made up with fresh sheets for when she needs it. On the back of the door is a jaded newspaper cut-out of Joni Mitchell sitting cross-legged with a guitar, which she has forgotten to take down. We moved into the house when she was nineteen and she never properly unpacked. Once, when she was in Salisbury with friends, I discovered a drawing under her bed that she had made. She was always artistic as a child but I thought she had long since given it up. I tacked it to the wall, thinking it would make her feel at home. The drawing was of Westminster Abbey – full of thin, spindly pencil marks: frightening in their precision. As I looked more closely, I saw that the Abbey was ruined: roofless and crumbling with an invasion of creepers scaling the walls. The structure was so convincing, it was as if she had witnessed its destruction. Staring at it on the wall, I felt something inside me unravel uncontrollably: for a moment, it was as if she and I shared the same fears. The pictures were almost spectral – her pencil ghosting the paper with lines that were sometimes barely visible. It frightened me, yet I did not want to tear my eyes away from it.

There was another drawing under the bed that I did not pin to the wall; instead, resisting the urge to screw it up, I folded it into four and placed it back where I had found it. It was of our house, with its insubstantial walls and doors, its modern fittings and close-cut lawn: the windows were glassless and a thickly scrawled darkness reigned in the inner rooms. Here her pencil had pressed hard into the paper. No ivy, no wild flowers bloomed from the foundations. The lawn in front of the house was clipped and in order. The roof in the picture remained in place, as did the bricks, but everything else was vulnerable and hollow. There was no life inside the walls – just a dark absence.

Her drawing of our house coloured my view of it irrevocably – so much so that when I approach the drive now I can no longer discern whether the drawing caused my ill-feeling towards it or simply brought to the surface something that was already there. I reverse the car onto the drive, turn off the engine and breathe out. Tim is coming out of the front door. He's running. He never runs.

'Get out,' he mouths, through the glass, pulling at the locked car door with one hand. He's sweating. 'It's Alice.' He takes my arm as I step out and guides me towards the front door. 'It's Alice. She's in trouble.'

We're inside the house now. I try to ask what he means but the words won't arrange themselves in the right order. 'She's in Kanyakumari, Vi. Tamil Nadu.' He pushes the name out as if I should know it.

'Kanyakumari . . .' I scramble around for a recollection of the word. 'What do you mean?'

'The tidal wave on the news. It hit India,' Tim answers, 'and Alice is there.'

'But . . .' I think of the television report – how we had heard about the vanishing of a whole town, without a thought for our daughter.

'She telephoned just before you got here. Thank God she's okay but we need to get her out. She's refusing to leave until she's found James.'

'James?'

'James, her boyfriend. You met him, remember?' He points to the home-sweet-home heart that hangs above the sink.

'Of – of course.' I frown. 'Her boyfriend.'

'What do we do?'

I want him to be quiet with his questions. She's halfway across the world and she hasn't spoken to me in more than six months. I can't even think of where to begin.

'But we've no way of contacting her. No number, no nothing.' It is as if he's objecting to a suggestion I have made. I keep silent.

'There must be a flight we can book for her . . .'

I tell him that she won't get on a flight if James is still missing, that we need to go and fetch her.

He mutters under his breath. *She could be anywhere.*

'You stay. I'll go,' I say.

'Are you sure that's wise given – Maybe we should go together, darling.'

'One of us has to stay. In case she tries to get in touch again.' I'm insistent now, my voice stiffening.

'Yes, but –'

'I can do it, Tim. I have to. I'll be okay, I promise.'

He says he'll call to see when the next flight is and tells me to start packing. We clasp each other tautly for a moment, but there isn't enough time. He doesn't even know where I've been today. But I can hardly explain now. He reaches for the phone and dials Directory Enquiries. I leave the kitchen and climb the stairs two at a time, fumbling under the bed for a suitcase and filling it with whatever comes to mind. In all my life, I've gone no further than London. The only time that I have packed a full suitcase is to move a few miles away – from Imber to Wilton, then out of my mother's house and into Tim's. And now, instead of unstitching myself slowly from this place, I am leaving with one swift rip. Tim must think I'm mad; he's stayed tethered to me all this time, travelling the country with his job, making sure everybody can still turn their lights on. And I, all the while, have folded myself away into my own peculiar shade of darkness.

How do I even begin to fill a suitcase? And what will she need? Not me; she doesn't need me.

Inside her bedroom, the walls are bare. The drawing of Westminster Abbey is long gone: when she came back to find the picture on the wall, she was furious with me. She kept her drawings hidden after that; I never saw them again. The room became gradually sparser – as if, out of spite, she were removing herself a fragment at a time.

There is a box of records by her bed, some in their sleeves, others propped up, scratched and naked, next to the player. Inside the wardrobe, I push past a sun-bleached gypsy skirt and retrieve a few T-shirts and a pair of bell bottoms; the sensible trousers that I insisted on buying her are nowhere to be seen. In spite of the tidal wave, I'll probably have picked the wrong things. I can picture us now, in the wake of the wave, arguing about the outfit I have packed. When she was born, I couldn't help myself, she was the most delicate thing I had ever held. But as she grew, she became more and more like her father, flitting from place to place, person to person, never quite able to settle. She told me I spoilt everything, pulled her back, tied her down; if her father was around, she said, he wouldn't put up with it; he wouldn't put up with me. She was all I had left of him. It was no wonder I held on too tightly.

A few weeks ago, in a moment of rashness, I had bundled his letters into a parcel and posted them to her in Delhi. It left me swollen – letting go of secrets that I had stored still-born inside me all these years. And yet I had acted out of cowardice. I did not have the courage to tell her to her face.

His last letter – which I had placed at the top of the box – contained everything she needed to know. Rereading it for the first time in years, I had felt its bite as if it were written yesterday. I wonder, now, whether she has felt it too – whether she has understood why I acted in the manner that I did. To her, he's just a ghost. And it took everything in me to give flesh and bones to what he had done. I don't know if she has received any of my letters along the way – the ones I sent to Istanbul, Tehran and Lahore; she could have passed through Delhi oblivious to it all. She and James were due home soon and I had wondered for a while if they had received my parcel. It was always my fear that in sharing this clot, this marker, of things I couldn't undo, I would lose her for ever:

Dear Violet,

I learnt of Freda's death yesterday. Mrs Archam sent word. There is nothing I can say to comfort you. To tell you I'm grieving would only break your heart and to say that I am sorry for your loss falls short of what you must feel.

Mrs Archam has told me of all you intend to do. Had I never known you, such selflessness would have left me aghast. But I have come to expect nothing less.

I will not waste ink over an apology that I know you will rebuff as untruthful. I can't recover what I ruined any more than you can rebuild Imber. But you must know that I did care for you. I ask you to raise her as your own. She is what I would have given you, had I been a better man.

Your Pete

He had penned the letter himself   I was familiar with the handwriting. Yet the unfamiliar script on the front of the envelope and the turn of phrase in his sentences had made me suspect that he had written it under duress; that somebody else had posted it on his behalf. No doubt his major – or some other discerning officer to whom he had confessed his past – had insisted upon him writing to me directly.

I received it a week after my sister's funeral. Mama was not there when I opened it but Alice was. She was bawling and bawling because, unlike Freda's, my chest was milkless and we had only condensed milk with which to feed her. When the post arrived, I put her in her cot and opened the letter in the hall. I hadn't recognized the hand on the envelope so Pete's words came as a shock. I had to steady myself on the banister and sit for a moment on the bottom stair. We had long since given up hope of hearing from him and this was hardly the letter we would have wished for. We would have welcomed any pledge of support, however small and detached: anything to make us believe that he intended to do his duty. He had a military salary now and, although humble, it was more than Mama and I could ever muster. But to Pete – the boy so keen to shed Imber – we were still the family of a parson; he was under no obligation to provide for those whose status and standing he perceived to be above his own.

But you must know that I did care for you. She cried in her cot while I sat blankly on the stair; her tears were not enough for the two of us.

Mama came home to find me still perched there. She took the letter from me and, after reading it once, put it away in a drawer. Unlike me, she thought better of returning to it.

By the time Alice was older, Mama and I had boxed up all of our wounds, thinking it better not to burden each other with the scars that we believed we should have long since overcome. A war never leaves you, my mother would say; only I knew it was not the war that she was talking about. And even if we had wanted to talk, it was not as if Alice would have been the one to listen. She cared nothing for the past, only the day that lay before her. Mama understood her better than I did: 'Give her a little air,' she warned, 'a fraction more air.'

I wasn't going to let her go to India. But I knew it was what my mother would have wanted. So I sat Alice down and gave her my permission, pretending I had a say in the matter. I know now that she would have left no matter what authority I claimed to have.

'Don't take it to heart,' was Tim's advice when she told him – not me – that if she needed anything she would get in touch. She made her own way to the station. The house moved invisibly from one kind of hollowness to another. It was all right for Tim: he wasn't her father. He could treat her with the nonchalance she required. It was no surprise that she liked him more than she did me.

I take a few more of her clothes down from their hangers. Suitcase zipped, I carry it downstairs to where Tim is waiting at the front door.

'She asked for you, you know, when she rang . . . You ought to know that,' he says, taking my bag.

I follow him to the car. If I had stayed at home, I would not have missed her call. 'Where did you say I was?'

'I didn't. I just said you weren't in.'

There's a pause. I know what he will ask next.

'Where were you, exactly?'

'It doesn't matter . . . Let's just get to the airport,' I murmur, eyes fixed on the road.

Chapter 31

I've got to push through seventeen hours of flying, landing and refuelling before I can search for her. On the aeroplane, I keep my fingers sealed around my passport, shielding the virginity of its blank pages. The engine heaves us into the sky above London and I watch, wide-eyed, as the streets and towers and parks shrink into map-like patterns below. Every building and tree seems suddenly intended; everything appears in its place. I'm gripping the side of my seat, aware of nothing but a growing volume of air beneath us.

The passengers in my row seem used to the sensation. They don't start, as I do, when the plane sinks inexplicably, before rising again.

'Is it your first time flying?' asks my neighbour. He has a burnished face whose tan matches the battered satchel under his feet. Even his hands look travelled, worn-in.

'Yes. I apologize, I'm a little on edge.'

'Well, you're throwing yourself in at the deep end with Delhi, that's for sure. What takes you to India?' He runs his palms down the pressed lines of his linen trousers.

The tannoy cuts in to give us an estimated time of arrival. But he looks at me expectantly, after the pilot has finished speaking.

'So, Delhi.' He raises his eyebrows.

'My daughter . . . is in India.'

'Jolly good. She isn't with the Foreign Office by any chance?'

'No.'

He pauses, waiting for more. When I don't speak, he shuffles through the newspaper on his lap. 'Awful, isn't it? About the tidal wave.' He gestures to a picture on the second page.

I nod, trying not to look.

'It's going to take years to sort out that mess.' He points to a monochrome picture of the wreckage.

Raising his eyes from the paper, he frowns at the sight of me. 'Are you all right?'

'Yes, I'm fine, thank you. If you don't mind, I might fetch a glass of water.'

'Just press the button,' he says, reaching up and pushing it before I have a chance to object. 'The air hostess will come and you can ask her to bring some.'

I sit forward, unable to escape as I had planned. Outside the window, beneath us, is sea – the troughs and peaks of which could be mistaken at this height for valleys and mountains. The man flicks his wrists and the newspaper obeys his command with a ripple. I turn to find him still reading the same page. My eyes snag for a moment on a name, halfway down the first column. *James Peak.*

James Peak, a British national, has spoken of the devastation in Kanyakumari where he was seriously injured before being hauled from the water by a fisherman. 'Nobody knew what was happening. The tide came in faster than anything and just kept on coming.' Peak is currently undergoing medical treatment in Trivandrum but, like many others in the hospital, will return to the wreckage as soon as he has recovered in order to search for loved ones.

I'm being looked at. I have intruded into his space without realizing it, bending over the article and moving unsociably close.

'Is everything all right?'

'That's – I think it's someone I know.' I place an index finger on James's name.

The man squints at the paragraph. 'He did well to survive, poor chap. Do you know him well?'

'He's my daughter's . . . I can't be sure it's him.'

He frowns. 'She's not there too, is she?'

I don't answer. Instead I scour the article desperately for a clue as to where she might be.

'Look, if there's anything I can do . . .'

I return my eyes to the window and try to work out how I can get to the hospital in Trivandrum. He's alive, thank God. And he'll know where to look for Alice.

I have never met anyone travelling to India simply for the sake of it, as he and Alice did. They didn't need to go and yet I let them. And for what? For the sake of seeing something new. But she was always like that, eager to explore, preferring to ask questions with her hands and feet rather than her mouth.

At the school gate, the other children were always pestering their mothers with unanswerable questions. Why is the sky blue? Why don't birds lie down to sleep? Could I survive a whole day without my hands? But Alice never asked anything as a child. She was always so assured: nothing caused her to worry or wonder why. She seemed to accept the facts of life with tranquil measure – or, at least, she did not need to learn about them from me. After a while, it began to concern me – the placid silence she cast over every new experience. But then I realized her questions were of a different kind: I saw the way she walked in pace with a river, eyes fixed on a particular body of water moving downstream; the way she pressed her hand to the trunk of a tree until the bark left a mark there. As soon as she could hold a pencil she would draw all these things – small, delicate drawings that barely took up a few centimetres on the page. It was as if she didn't want anybody to see her explorations, least of all give them words. They were hers and hers alone.

When she did ask questions as a child, it was always about her father. What animals did he keep on the farm? What did he smell like? Was he good at sums or spelling at school? These were the things that she was unable to discover for herself. She never asked why he had left, or where he was now – questions I knew she wanted to ask, but to which I did not have the answers.

Chapter 32

The plane hits the concrete with a thump and a bounce, giving its speed to the wind and docking, finally, in a space near the terminal. Passport still in hand, I'm hit suddenly by the heat. It presses into my cheeks, my neck – any part of me on which it can fix its grasp. By the time I reach the terminal, I have broken out in a sweat. Fans ladle the heat around the building, failing in every way to make it cooler. Airport staff produce a *déjà vu* of black bags and leather holdalls, all weathered with the marks of successive journeys. The bags are piled high on the floor and an official presents one bag at a time to the crowd of passengers, asking each owner to step forward. I spot my suitcase near the top of the heap; its unscuffed corners and glistening zip make it stand out from the rest. I wait for it to be handed over, then scour the concourse for the exit.

Outside the airport, the bustle begins. There are taxis crowding the road – huge, bulky yellow-roofed things – and men with steaming trays of fried snacks weaving between the cars. I try to ask a taxi driver for a lift to the railway station and he sways his head nonchalantly, as if he may or may not know where it is.

'Fifty rupees, ma'am,' demands another.

'I only have pounds.' I take out a five-pound note and show it to him. He beckons to another driver and they talk for a moment, thrusting hands out for the note and holding it up to the sun. My pulse quickens at the realization that I am penniless in a country I don't know, with no way of reaching the south. We did not have time to think about rupees before I left home.

'Okay, okay, ma'am.' He opens the door to the taxi and ushers me in with my suitcase. It is so hot that my skirt sticks to the leather seat. The car gives a guttural shudder and we hurtle into the city. The place is heady with noise – horns and engines and drum beats. Roads splinter and join illogically, then disappear into rust-coloured dust. Men in pressed shirts draw trails in the dirt with their bicycles. One carries a caged, squawking chicken; another a stack of newspapers; and another still a garland of jasmine laced over his handlebars.

If I were asked to retrace our route to the airport, I would not be able to: Delhi is a labyrinth. And if the rest of India follows suit, I do not know how I will find Alice. Or James, for that matter.

Before she even brought him home, I had determined not to like him. I had seen him once before – during that nightmarish weekend when Alice took herself off to the Isle of Wight. He dropped her off on the Sunday night. I was so relieved to see her that I didn't glimpse him in the car; he didn't come into the house. Perhaps she had warned him about me. If I had known they were an item, I would have paid more attention. When she finally did bring him home to meet us, he told us that he was a photographer.

'Oh, wonderful,' Tim remarked out of politeness. 'Weddings and christenings, that sort of thing?'

'No . . . more art, actually. I focus on travel, culture – the journeys people take.'

It was hard to make head or tail of him. He wore his hair long – but not so long as to cause concern. I wondered if Alice had asked him to cut it before coming to see us. It was a miracle, really, that she had brought him at all – although I did not see it in that way at the time. Even then, I could tell he adored her. As footloose as he might have been with his travels, he had the look of someone who was beyond the point of going back. I had learnt over the years the hallmarks of the ones who loved, and the ones who left.

Chapter 33

The train inches down the spine of India and pulls into the station at Trivandrum. A tussle ensues among the passengers outside for drivers and taxis. For some reason, they do not seem to be accepting rupees. Pressed at the back of the crowd with a wodge of notes I retrieved from a bank next to the station, I have nothing but money to bargain with. I spot a man on a motorbike at the end of the rank who, perhaps, I can persuade to give me a ride. I lumber towards him with my suitcase, asking for the hospital and showing him the rupees. Just then, a woman in turquoise with a baby on her hip brushes past me and climbs onto the back of the bike – his wife or sister or whoever he was waiting for. He starts up the engine as if to leave. Then he reaches over and, instead of the notes, takes hold of the water-flask protruding from my rucksack, motioning for me to climb onto the bike behind his wife and child. Four on a motorbike, with my suitcase, and no secure way of holding on? 'Thank you! Thank you so much!' I say, perching on what little space is left at the back of the bike and floundering around for something solid to clasp. The woman in front carries my suitcase and gestures for me to put my hand on her shoulder. She murmurs something, which I can only assume means hold on tight for, before I know where I am, we are swerving around a wandering cow and skidding off along the dust-coated road.

Despite my attempts to explain, the motorbike deposits me in the middle of town rather than at the hospital, and it takes me a full hour in the heat to find the right street. I know now why the driver on the bike took the water instead of the rupees – already my throat feels parched.

The man at the hospital desk asks me for James's full name and frowns at his list of admissions.

'Do you have any water?' I ask vaguely.

'There is no clean water in the town, madam. The pipes are broken from the wave. We have boiled water for the patients . . . Your brother's nationality, please.'

'He's not my –' I stop myself. 'He's British. He's around twenty-six years of age and he came from Kanyakumari.'

'A moment, madam.' He disappears into a back room and I hear him slide open some sort of cabinet. He returns with a file. 'Wave victims are Ward Three.'

I check Ward Three, followed by two others, but he is nowhere to be found. The last ward is at the back of the building. There are so many mattresses in the corridor that it is difficult to reach the far end. The last patient I pass is curled in on themselves, seeking out a foetal privacy in the nook between their arms and knees. It is then that I see him, lying on a bed, in the middle of the last ward. A hollow stare is embedded in his face. One of his eyes is sealed shut with a bruise, and a large dressing, soaked scarlet, rests on his shoulder. Every knot of discomfort I have stored up towards him – the blame I have heaped on him for taking Alice away – starts to loosen. For a brief moment, I see the boy in him, as far away from home as Alice. James has not yet seen me. And I am suddenly fearful of what I should say.

Like most of the patients in the room, he stares inertly at the ceiling. It is a look that distinguishes the victims from those who, like me, simply belong to the aftermath. Some of them lie in the same wave-stricken clothes they were wearing when it came. Even if they have been reclothed and bandaged and washed free of the silt, they still seem marked, set apart somehow.

It is the same look that I saw in my father's friends when they returned from the war. I could pick out the men who had been at the pulse of it without even knowing their name or rank.

Wave or war, it doesn't matter: they both leave a ghost in the eyes. It is hard to imagine Alice wearing the same shapeless expression that I see in James now, even though I know that, somehow, she too will bear it.

Freda was right when she said that the war had altered everything. Pete's homecoming was not what it should have been. Things didn't click back into place; they became more fractured.

He returned to Wilton after two months. When I opened the door to see him standing on the other side of it, I felt nothing but relief. Any desire to ask after his absence vanished with the sight of him. He had come back and sought me out and that was all that mattered.

'I've come to collect my belongings,' he said, fixing his stare to the doorstep. Any greeting that he did offer was empty of warmth. I led him upstairs. His pile of possessions rested now at the foot of the bed that Mama and I shared.

'You kept my letters,' I said, pointing to the shoebox, which I had set apart from the rest. He looked up for the briefest of moments and I saw in his eyes a fissure of sadness, or shock, perhaps, at my candour.

'You had no right to go through my trunk.' His manner was uncertain.

'It was too heavy for Mama and me to carry ... and the farmer's wife insisted we take your belongings. She said you'd lost your job.'

He seemed impatient suddenly, as if deciding that he had already stayed too long. 'Where will you find work?' I asked.

'Violet, please, it's best if you don't – If you could help me carry everything down the stairs, I'll be on my way.'

'But where are you staying? I'll walk there with you. You won't be able to carry it all by yourself.'

He fidgeted reluctantly at my suggestion but then, after a pause, relented. He was staying at the Pembroke Inn. We ferried his belongings down from the bedroom until only the box of letters remained upstairs. I turned to go back for them but he stopped me.

'Keep the rest. I've no need . . .'

I reddened and busied myself with his possessions, loading them into two old sacks which I had retrieved from the larder.

'Pete,' I murmured, once we had set off towards the inn. 'Please tell me – what's the matter?'

'Nothing.'

I stared flatly at him.

'I can't. It isn't up to me.'

'Then who is it up to?'

He let out a frustrated sigh and faced the pavement ahead to avoid my stare.

'I told Freda about the American. It was me, all right?'

'But . . . I don't understand.'

'She can tell you the rest. She's your sister when all's said and done.'

'No,' I intervened. 'I'm sure it wasn't just you . . . Freda said she'd heard rumours.'

He did not reply. I tested every excuse in my mind but was left, only, with the certainty of my sister's accusations.

'You won't gain anything taking my side.'

'Pete, it's all right, I – She had a right to know.'

'What do I have to say to get you to stop?'

'Stop?' I dropped the weight of the sack as I spoke. 'Are you bringing this to an end?'

'Bringing what to an end? There never was anything firm. There was no . . . I never promised anything.'

My breath sparrowed in my throat. I couldn't form my words. So I put down the sack and walked away from him, away from his bags of belongings, back towards his letters, upstairs in the house. I shut myself in the bedroom and sat on the floor with my back against the bed. Mama had filled the tin pail with hot water ready for a wash. I did not have long before I was disturbed. I watched the steam drift blithely up towards the beams, its whiteness dissipating somewhere between the floor and the ceiling.

Alice has grown so like Pete in recent years. I wish he was around to see it. Like him, she keeps her cards close to her chest – on good days, pretending not to care; on bad days, creating the pretence of love before pulling the rug from beneath your feet.

When Tim and I first met, long after Pete had gone, she was a picture of indifference. I would ask what she thought of him and be met with an evasive shrug of the shoulders. 'You do what you like, Mum. It's your life.'

I tried to explain that I wanted her to like him, really like him, that it was important to me. But she pushed air through her lips, flashed the whites of her eyes and, shortly afterwards, asked if she could go to her room.

I found out after his proposal that it was Alice who had suggested going shopping for a ring, Alice who had shown him the White Horse at Westbury, and Alice to whom he broke the news first.

She'll be the same with James, if she sticks with him. She won't ever tell him she loves him but it will escape from her sometimes, when she thinks he's not looking. I often wonder whether he and I see the same things in her. Watching him there in the hospital bed, I want to ask him if she still sleeps with her arms folded and whether she has grown out of the sulks that she used to stage if I kept her indoors for too long. I am not afraid to acknowledge now that he is more familiar with her ways than I am.

'James,' I say, without quite intending to speak. He looks up from his ward bed and frowns, trying to place me for a moment. Then he stiffens with recognition.

'You've come to tell me she's dead, haven't you?' he murmurs tautly, fists pushed into the mattress.

'No, she's alive. At least, we had a telephone call from her.

That was all. She's still in Kanyakumari . . . as far as we know. She won't leave until she's found you.'

'She's . . . My God . . . Is she all right?'

'I don't know. It was such a short call. Tim – my husband – spoke to her.'

'Does she know I'm here?'

'No. I came straight from the airport. I saw your name in the newspaper.'

I move over to the bed now and stand at the foot.

'I should never have gone to get breakfast,' he whispers, looking past me towards the bed opposite. 'I should have stayed. Then we wouldn't have been separated.'

'The most important thing is that you're both alive.'

I sit down on the mattress and, unsure what to do next, I reach over and put a hand on his arm. The contact feels like a breach – for both of us. 'She'll be so relieved when she finds out that you're all right.'

He turns his head. 'You've no idea how quickly it came. Masses and masses of it.' He grips my hand out of instinct. 'Everybody's talking about the wave like there was just one . . . but the water just kept on coming. And it wasn't even water . . . It felt like –' He cuts himself off and pulls away from me. 'I'm pretty sure I was underneath for . . . It seemed like minutes – but it can't have been. I would have drowned.'

'How did you get out?'

'I . . . I don't even know. It took me past a building. Something sharp went into my neck. The water was so black I didn't even realize I was bleeding. There was a man who managed to get me on top of the building somehow . . . If the helicopter hadn't come when it did, I would have bled to death. The doctor told me.' He straightens his back and pauses. 'You must find her, Violet. What if there's another wave?'

I open my mouth to dismiss the idea and then, seeing the earnestness in his uninjured eye and the fear married to it, I keep quiet. If you have been caught by one, it is only reasonable to fear that you may be caught by another.

'Please. You've got to find her.'

He doesn't need to tell me to go. I ask him where I should look and to describe the places where she is likely to search for him.

'They've told me about a lost-and-found board in the market-place,' he explains. 'One of the rescue workers said they'd put up a missing note for me. He said survivors come and check it every day for new notes. She's bound to go there. And try our guesthouse. The Saravo.'

I stand up and turn to leave but he says there is something he must tell me before I go. She may not have had the chance to share the news on the phone but Alice and he are married.

I stare at his hand and imagine a ring on hers – its meaning fixed. A closed circle.

'It happened about a week ago.'

Happened. He is talking about it as if it were a freak accident, like the wave. Married to a man I barely know. *You may do as you wish, but do remember it's for life.* My mother's words to Freda come cantering into my ears. She can be a stubborn, unthinking girl sometimes.

'I sent a parcel . . . to Delhi. Did she –?' I stop in an attempt to compose myself.

'Yes, she did.'

I glance at him only once to say, 'I must find her,' and then I turn and walk out of the ward.

Even if, before the wave, they married on impulse, it will carry more weight now. I think of Pete and the war, Freda and the arrival of the wave. Things that perhaps would have drifted apart or never touched have been thrown inseparably together.

Chapter 34

I sit on my stone slab and wait for her to come and find me. There is nowhere left to search. I'm afraid that, if I move, I will become like a ship looking for its neighbour at night, passing yards from its target without even realizing it is there.

Hour after hour has sunk before me and there is no sign of her in the crowd. It is so hot that I want to peel back my skin: sweat gathers and then settles on me. I find myself wishing for Imber's breezes.

A woman approaches with a cup of water and puts a shawl over my head. The cool of her shadow releases me momentarily from the heat. She passes me the cup and I lift it to my lips. But the silk of the water in my throat awakens – rather than quenches – my thirst. I pour some on my face, which is dry again in moments. 'Thank you,' I whisper, but she's already folded herself into the crowd.

How many hours would James have waited before getting up and searching again? I can't help thinking that I have given up before he would have. She met him at the festival on the Isle of Wight. They had barely known each other a few weeks but he wasted no time in introducing her to his family – all cordial and art-loving and as footloose as their son. They have had six homes since he was a child. Six. London, Jerusalem, Cambodia, Singapore, Thailand, Hong Kong. The names alone taste hot and green.

Six homes, stints in Asia and a mother whom Alice thinks is *just what she ought to be*. When Pete moved towns, it broke my heart. And yet these people skip from country to country as if they were pieces on a Monopoly board.

'I wonder what my dad would have thought of him,' she remarked, on the first and only time she brought James home. She often talked of her father in that way, as if he were dead. I hadn't the heart to tell her that he probably wouldn't have taken the time to form an opinion about James. Loving Pete was like pouring water into a plugless bath; the thought of him storing up our affection, or of letting us wallow in his own, was unsustainable.

Freda had always been quick to warn me about Pete. She saw him for what he was a long time before I did. And sometimes I wonder whether she made her mistake so that I wouldn't have to.

After her return to London in the wake of her falling-out with Mama, we wondered whether she would ever return to us. Granted, the war was over, but she had been so upset about Sam that we feared she would stay in London for good. Her telegram announcing her intention to move home came as a surprise to both of us.

In the August after the war ended, she arrived in Wiltshire with her silence and spread it throughout the house, just as she had done with Father's books. The afternoon of her arrival clenched into evening and the three of us assembled around the kitchen table for dinner. Mama ladled stew onto three plates and, after a short grace, entreated us to start eating. Freda and I sat on one side of the table, my mother on the other. My sister did not eat hers; instead, she drew patterns in the gravy. We might have grown accustomed to this habit, just as we had done with her larder raids when Father died, but she had been away for so long that Mama could not help but appear perturbed.

'Tell us your news, then, Freda,' my mother began, looking down at the untouched vegetables on my sister's plate. 'You mentioned that you had something important to tell us in your telegram. A reason for coming home.'

Freda swallowed air and glanced at me.

'I've . . . given notice at the hospital.'

This was not the news; it was simply the garnish. I could tell there was more to come.

'And I'm engaged.' She rushed through the words. There was no smile.

'To whom?' my mother enquired, lowering her fork.

'To Pete,' she answered.

When I think back to her words and my reaction, I am over-ridden by one feeling only: a sense that I had known what was coming and had always known. Perhaps it is just the way I have remembered it: enhancing the tell-tale signs of their attachment to each other as a means of protecting myself from feeling that incision of pain all over again.

'But how?' my mother stuttered. 'He's in love with Violet!'

'If he loved Violet, he would have proposed to her, not me.' She kept her words flat and plain, as if the logic of what she had announced was as simple as solving a sum.

'Freda, I cannot –' Mama stood up from her chair and put a hand to her head. 'You had such high notions . . . He's a farm-hand and one year your junior. I don't understand.'

'I was snobbish, Mama, that's what.'

'How could you do this? To your own sister?' she choked out. 'What would your father say?'

A tremor invaded my fingers. I removed them from the table and dropped them onto my lap so that they could not be seen.

'If you loved your sister, you would think twice about such spitefulness!' She took a breath and hung her head. 'The fact that you could be so unfeeling towards your own family . . . You can't love him, Freda. I won't believe it. It's malice.'

'Think what you like, Mama. It's settled.'

'Where will you live? What will you live on? For you shan't receive a penny from me.'

'We're to move to Leconfield. Pete's joined the RAF.'

Mama threw up her hands vaguely and turned towards the

sink. Finally, I felt capable of speech, the words emerging, lemon-sour, on my tongue.

'Has he told you he loves you?' I shifted in my chair and fixed my stare on her.

She did not return it. 'Of course.'

'And do you love him?'

She bowed her head in a vague nod.

'Then you should marry. I wouldn't want to get in the way of his happiness.'

'Violet!' exclaimed my mother. I stood up and tucked my chair under the table. Then I left the kitchen.

'Well, if Violet won't defend herself, I don't stand a chance of dissuading you,' hissed my mother, as I made my way towards the stairs. 'You can marry him if you like, but do remember that it's for life. *Life*, Freda. And that's a very long time to hold a grudge.'

Upstairs in the bedroom I longed for a lock and key. I tried to keep my composure. But I was unable to swallow my hopelessness any longer. It was all I could do to cry noiselessly into the back of the wardrobe, opening the doors to hide my face from anyone who might disturb me.

I was not angry: I couldn't make him love me any more than Mama could make Freda act judiciously. She was as stubborn as an ox at times. If she was truly bent on marrying Pete there would be no deterring her. I buried my swollen eyes among the hems of our dresses – hers mingling with mine on the rail.

'Whatever you think of me,' I heard Freda's voice at the door, 'I didn't accept him to spite you.'

I shut the wardrobe as if I had been looking for something inside it. I did not turn to face her.

'If I thought you could be happy with him,' she continued, 'if I thought there was even a chance of it . . . then I promise you I would have refused him, no matter what.'

'I should be the judge of my own happiness, Freda, not you,'

I murmured, into the oak face of the cupboard. Hearing her approaching steps, I backed away to the window.

'There are things he hasn't told you.'

I felt suddenly as absent as her reflection in the glass. *Please leave. I don't want to hear any more.*

'What things?' I asked, before I knew where the words had come from.

'Violet . . . I'm having a baby.' The words were barely audible. 'Please don't tell Mama.'

I looked up to the window and saw my sister's wet face reflected in the glass. She seemed spectral, as if she were disappearing.

'Why else do you think I'd marry him?' She muffled her tears in her sleeve. 'I'm so sorry.'

'It's not possible –' I turned to face her. 'You've been in London . . . all this time.'

I stared at her belly, still flat. The news, if true, must be fresh even to her.

'I wish it were impossible. I wish none of it had happened.' She put her head into her hands.

'Freda –'

'Don't pity me . . . whatever you do. It's my own fault.'

'Tell me what happened. Please?'

She paused, drew breath, as if to begin explaining, then sank into a fresh silence. Finally, after some time, she spoke.

'He came to London to see his mother. You won't know about her because he's never spoken of her to anyone. Months ago, unbeknown to you or any of us, she wrote, asking to see him. He'd wanted to meet her for so long that he accepted at the drop of a hat and travelled to the city.' When she had finished explaining about the other child, she looked at me with pleading eyes as if expecting me to respond, but I had so many questions there was nothing useful to say. 'Violet, you have to understand that he was hurt and alone in a place he didn't know and the only person he could think to contact was me. And so he made enquiries at the hospital . . .'

'I don't understand. Why didn't he tell me about her?' I blurted, finally.

'I don't know, Vi. Maybe he was embarrassed. We had everything – you and I – two parents who loved us dearly.'

I frowned. 'But what happened? What does his mother have to do with –' My eyes settled for a second time on her stomach.

Freda turned away from me. 'He asked to meet me after my shift . . . We only meant to have dinner together. But then it was announced that the war had ended in Europe for good. The whole city was alive with celebrations. There was dancing, which I thought would take his mind off his mother . . . I missed you and Mama terribly and he reminded me so much of home . . .'

The window-sill pressed into my back. I imagined what it would feel like to push backwards through the glass and fall down into the garden. There seemed nothing to exist for now. Just a hollow future, which loomed like an impossible drop. 'You could have had anyone, Freda. Any boy you liked. You know you could.'

'Please believe me. I never wanted it to happen . . . not with him. Violet, I promise you it was an accident. It was a lapse . . . a momentary lapse. He told me about the American on the night we won the war, you see . . . and, for a split second, I hated you for letting Mama forget Father. For looking on while she took off with that Yank.' Her voice dimmed until it was barely more than a rasp. 'But, most of all, I couldn't bear the thought that you had moved on without me . . . When I left, I thought everything would stay the same, that time would simply stop until I came back. It's madness, I know. But the evacuation and then the American – it was too much. I realized you were living your lives without me. Without Father. I was as dead to you as he was. It broke my heart to think of it . . . Pete was there, and I knew you loved him. I knew, and still I danced with him and took his hand and . . . I felt as if everything had been taken from me. It was my way of taking something back. Just for a night.'

I pushed my palms into the window-sill and tried to steady myself.

Freda caught her breath, eyes full, lips pressed into white. 'I know how much you love him, Vi. But it would have been a miserable existence. You belong here. Near Imber. With Father and Mama. Can you really imagine yourself trailing around the country after him while he takes to the skies in a plane?'

'He never gave me the chance.'

'It would be intolerable.'

'Please, stop speaking for me.' I raised my eyes and glared at her. The movement was so sudden and my stare so direct that she recoiled.

Freda began to flounder. 'Pete says you're like a limpet – you'll never let go of Imber. He couldn't understand your loyalty. It's so unflinching . . . but I understand. I know you better than he does –'

'Isn't it enough that you have him?' I interrupted, giving in to the quiver in my voice and turning back to the window. 'Isn't that enough?'

My sister walked to the door without speaking another word. Through the glass, I could trace the shadow of the bell on the lawn – the place where I had stood and watched her cry only a few months ago. The rust had encased its shape so thickly of late that it now resembled a rock more than a bell. I imagined its inner skin – the untouched metal inside it, hidden from the rain and wind. I saw it for a moment, impossible, at the top of Imber's tower: gleaming and pealing, as if new.

Chapter 35

The rebuilding has begun: it is time to plant what the wave uprooted. Stones are gathered; timber arrives; walls gain roofs and roofs gain walls. And out of the debris, the stirrings of a city are born.

The activity around me has shifted from an exodus to a homecoming. For the first time in days, people are not running but resettling. They scan each other's faces for something familiar – something solid that is not brick or stone to which they can cling. I look for Alice among them. But she isn't there.

There was a brief time when a return to Imber had seemed as possible and daunting as rebuilding this town. Imber's villagers had started to gather again, and word spread that if we could prove the existence of a military pledge before the war, we would be permitted to return home. For years I had lived for our homecoming. But to return to it in ruins, when I carried with me so many ruins of my own, seemed impossible.

Freda and Pete did not talk of their marriage in front of me. I learnt from Annie that they intended to marry in Wiltshire before leaving for Leconfield. Annie had married her fiancé only a few weeks before and was due to move north soon. Freda had asked her for advice on ceremonies and Annie had sent a telegram to warn me of their plans.

As for Pete, he avoided the house as much as he could; we had not spoken since Freda announced their engagement. But I could do little to avoid our encounter one morning in September when I was struck down with a headache and could not go into town with Mama as planned. Thinking I would be out, Freda brought Pete back to the house with her. I heard them open and close the front door and seat themselves in the living room just as I was boiling water to make tea. Neither of them realized that I was in the kitchen. Through the door, I could just see Pete, pulling Freda onto his knee in the armchair. This closeness took the breath out of my lungs. They were due to be married; they were allowed to touch. And yet I had convinced myself it was for entirely practical reasons: the pregnancy, the raising of their child. I watched his hand on her hip, his fingers taking hold of some of the material in her skirt. I heard her laughing. And I saw, with a slow intake of breath, how easily they had taken to each other. Freda might not have wanted a baby, but she had wanted Pete – and a feeling that was once momentary was now rooting. I could see it in her movements – the way she fitted easily onto his lap, and stayed there.

I tried to busy myself noiselessly in the kitchen but it was with hesitancy that I began to catch fragments of their conversation.

'Yes, but the letter from the War Office *implies* that we are to be allowed back after the war. That must count for something.'

'I'm telling you not to put too much weight on it.' Pete sighed. 'It certainly isn't going to happen overnight.'

'Mr Madigan as good as confirmed what I'd been thinking all along,' Freda said, 'that a verbal pledge, backed up indirectly by the evacuation letter, was made to us at the time of the eviction. The War Office must stand by their promise, and I'll be sure to hold them to it. They'll let us use the church, you mark my words. And then, later, Violet and Mama can move home.'

'Freda. Please.' Pete looked to check the door to the hall was shut. He failed to see me in the kitchen. 'The church is in a bad way. And if Violet ever found out . . .'

The sound of my name on his lips, which used to stir me, now felt alarming. My heart raced.

'You're forgetting it was my home too. Our home,' Freda interjected.

'I only thought – we've hurt her enough already.'

Freda went quiet. Or, at least, I did not hear her response. I moved closer to the kitchen door.

'Neither of us wanted this.' She laid a hand on her stomach and stood up from his lap. 'Ever since the accident, I knew I'd come back after the war and marry in Imber . . . with Father there. Violet knows it's what he would have wanted. Nothing has worked out the way we planned. The very least I can do is give my father the wedding he always hoped he'd see. At home. In St Giles's.'

'You haven't seen . . .' Pete ventured, his voice trailing off. I bent into the door. 'The place is in ruins . . . and what will we do for a vicar?'

'I've spoken to the vicar at Bratton. He was a colleague of Father's.'

Just then the water boiled. I had completely forgotten about it. I saw Pete look up and, afraid he had heard something, I rushed to quell the sound. I turned – kettle in hand – to see him staring at me from the kitchen door, Freda just behind him.

'I want to be there,' I murmured, before I even realized what I was saying. 'I want to come to the wedding.'

I looked up at Pete, whose eyes seemed to fidget under my gaze, not knowing where to direct themselves.

'Violet . . . what are you doing in here?' asked my sister.

'I – I don't know. I had a headache.'

'Violet,' began Pete, 'I don't know how much you heard –'

'I heard you.'

'It's highly unlikely that they'll let us marry there . . .'

'If they do,' I began, 'I would like to be there, if you'll have me. Freda's right.' I paused, waiting for my voice to regain its steadiness. 'Father always said he wanted to see at least one of us married in Imber.'

'Don't do this to yourself, Vi,' said Pete. 'We'll go somewhere else. Somewhere north where you don't have to know about it.'

'You'll need witnesses, and it'll be a chance for me to say goodbye,' I explained, with increasing resolve.

'To Imber?' intervened Pete. He seemed afraid of what I might be implying.

'To lots of things, my sister for one.' I glanced at Freda. 'I won't be seeing much of either of you once you're settled in Yorkshire, after all.'

Freda pursed her lips. She seemed on the edge of tears.

'What do you say, Freda?' Pete muttered, over his shoulder. She nodded her assent at the hallway floor.

Chapter 36

'You cannot be serious, Violet!' exclaimed Mama.

'They've tried everything – letters to the War Office, pleas to the council. Their only option is to break in at night.'

'But I can't believe you'd want to subject yourself to such a thing –'

'Will you come with me?'

'Certainly not. I know how you feel about that place – it was you who talked of getting married there, not Freda.'

'Please, Mama, I'm not asking you to come for my sake. Father wouldn't have wanted us to carry on like this.'

Before Mama knew how to put a stop to it, a plan had been forged. We were to drive cross-country from Chitterne to avoid the military barriers, then join the track on Fore Down, which led into Imber. The Reverend Mr Dalton, from Bratton, was to meet us at the church at just gone ten o'clock at night, and we had arranged to borrow a car from the landlady at the Pembroke Inn.

Freda put on her wedding clothes before we left. We did not have any money for a dress and Mama's had been destroyed by the damp. Before the war, Freda would have made a fuss about not wearing her own but she had no grounds for complaint in the circumstances. I asked Annie, who had recently worn her mother's dress to marry her officer in Devizes, if she would lend her wedding clothes to Freda. She refused at first, saying she was not going to play a part in helping my sister break my heart. But eventually my persistence paid off.

By now, Freda's stomach had begun to swell and the dress was not an easy fit. Mama kept silent on the subject but she must have guessed about the baby. On the night of the wedding, she threw Pete's coat over Freda to keep out the cold, eyes lingering on her waist. I pinned up my hair and masked my face in powder. Mama wore a hat and a frown.

As the car sidled across the Plain, the sky over Bowls Barrow stuttered like a chessboard between white and black; the army were firing thunder flashes again. Gunfire could be heard cackling across the Downs. I began to worry that they might be training in Imber but Pete had received word from one of the wardens that a practice was taking place on another part of the Plain. Each hill spoke the gunfire back to its neighbour, like a game of Chinese whispers. These sounds had become as common as gales during the war, embedding themselves in the fabric of our valley so that they were as inevitable to us as the wind.

It was difficult terrain – the tracks from Chitterne were not suited to vehicles and Mama refused to turn on the headlights for fear of being spotted; we could see barely more than a few feet ahead of us. Shortly before joining the track at Fore Down, the engine choked and brought us to a halt.

'Darn!' whispered Mama, leaping out of the driver's seat to turn the crank handle. She tried several times but to no avail. Pete took over but the car remained taciturn.

'What did I tell you? I knew it would struggle off the road,' she said.

'We'll walk,' said Pete. 'The church can't be more than a mile away.'

'A mile?' Freda protested. 'What about my dress?'

We climbed out of the Hillman Minx and I carried the back of Freda's dress to prevent it dragging in the mud. Approaching the village was different from how it had been on my dawn visit with Pete. Having confronted the ruins once before, I felt drawn back to them, like a moth to a flame, preferring to arrive and be burnt than turn and be forever cold. The grass beneath our feet – sodden with a full day's rain – inked into our boots and hems. I lifted Freda's dress higher off the ground.

Every now and then, the landscape lit up, lightning white, and we would have half a second to locate the church tower and alter our direction. Finally Pete stumbled across the fence encircling the church – barbed wire concertinaed around the rim. He hooked his fingers on to it and rattled it, the vibrations ricocheting across the Plain.

'There's no need,' Mama muttered fiercely, 'for a fence.'

'I suppose they wanted to protect it,' Freda bleated.

'There's a hole,' whispered Pete. 'I made it last time we were here.' He nodded in my direction. Mama transferred her glare from Pete to me, then back again, but refrained from asking how and why we had returned. Freda frowned at me before smoothing the pleats in her dress. 'Follow me,' Pete murmured.

Locating the hole in the fence, he held open the gap in the wire with one hand. 'After you,' he instructed Freda, guiding her through. I watched their touch, the way his eyes followed her to the other side. Once I had made my way through the fence, I saw Mama's gaze wander across the grass towards the parsonage. Despite the darkness, I could just make out the shape of our old home – as barren as a skull – on the other side of the field. Once she became aware that I was looking at her, she quickly turned her attention back to the fence.

The church stood shipwrecked in the graveyard. It was shrouded in moss and ivy, its windows as hollow as the craters on the Plain. We scrambled between the graves, now enveloped in grass and knapweed. Father's was on the far side of the church.

Mama took out the key to the vestry from the pocket of her dress and slotted it into the lock. Then Pete put a shoulder to the oak so that it groaned open in baritone. My sister started suddenly at a rattle of the fence behind us but it was only the vicar arriving from Bratton.

The church had always been dark, even in daylight. But the

ivy had since blocked out the little light that was left; it had low-ered itself over the windows like the slow blink of an eyelid. The lead frames were so high up on the walls that the sunlight used to enter the nave in shafts, missing the pews and illuminat-ing instead the paint on the opposite wall. My father would wonder why they had not built the church on the height of the Plain so that it could enjoy the sunlight. For a building sur-rounded by undulating Downs, it was strange that its architect had shut out the view. And yet a small part of him, he used to say – the part he carried with him from his childhood – knew why it had been built that way. Sitting in this small space for hours with the four walls cocooning him, it seemed more pos-sible to meet the God of the landscape outside. When eventually his eyes became hungry for the light, for the feel of the chalked wind on his skin, he would emerge from the church, surprised at how the land exceeded the image he'd had of it in his mind – at how its creator could sit with him for a moment, like a compan-ion, in a house built by human hands.

There was no separation between outside and inside any more. The old patterns of movement and stillness, weekdays and Sundays, of morning communion and evensong, had ceased to exist; the church stood timeless – an ancient cliff rebutting the drum of the sea. All that was left was a vast expanse of time – charted only by the growth of the creepers up the walls. I took a step towards the altar and disturbed a bird in the roof. It shook like a black rag through the gaping window and Mama turned to face me from the other end of the aisle. She was calm, not dis-traught as I had expected her to be. Maybe she sensed, like I did, that the bricks and stones were not everything.

Mama saw to Freda's outfit in the roofless vestry, smoothing the creases that the fabric had acquired during the walk. She straightened my sister's veil and whispered something to her that I could not hear. Freda seemed to tense. I wondered whether Mama had told her it was not too late to call it off.

She did not leave. She did not remove her veil. Instead, she stood before the altar and made her pledge, as erring as the ivy that moved from pew to pew. I listened with wonder as she took his hand and said that she would keep him for better or for worse, for richer or for poorer, in sickness and in health, till death parted them. For his sake, I willed it to be true. Pete's features were full of the stone that I had seen in them when I'd first met him. The affection that he had shown by the hole in the fence had vanished: the cold reality of his duty – a mother and her child – stood, immovable, before him. I knew then that, for them both, it was not a case of love but of nearly, nearly loving.

Once the vows were complete, Pete approached the one remaining bell in the tower and I had to call after him to stop him ringing it. I could not have borne the sound of that solitary knell, its dirge echoing across the Plain.

Freda lost her veil on the way out of the church – the wind ripping it clean from her head. We watched it snake over the barbed wire at the end of the churchyard. Nobody tried to stop it. Not even Pete.

Mama took Freda's flowers and put them on my father's grave. 'He would have liked to know that his daughter's wedding was in Imber,' she murmured, tugging at the weeds around his headstone.

'There's no such place,' I replied.

Chapter 37

Dusk comes. The sun slips, like a coin from a pocket, out of the sky and into someone else's morning. It is unfathomably dark. Somebody rigs up a lantern by the lost-and-found board where it bores a hole through the blackness. Crowds disperse and people in search of sleep crawl under scraps of metal or overturned cars, or scuttle away up the hill.

I pick up my suitcase, full of Alice's things, and plant it next to the lantern. Sitting just outside its glow, I watch the filament lure in finger-length dragon flies and other fist-sized bugs. They tether themselves to its yellow stain and butt blithely against the glass, always an inch away from settling into its impossible scorch.

At last I am free of the heat, and the cool of the evening settles on my skin. How many more nights will I spend like this, in the open air with no shelter, waiting for my daughter to come back to me? Right now, I could spend a million, anything to be away from the day with its sun and crowds and corpses. The dead are still here, lining the square. But, hidden as they are in the darkness, I can forget about them. They are not my own after all; and here, you must blot from your memory anything that is not your own.

I think of Freda, as unburied as those bodies, despite the grave we gave her. Mama wanted her to be laid to rest in Imber. But I could not bring myself to place her in another's tomb. So much had died there. We hardly needed to add to its toll.

I should have known that, like Imber, there would be no easy way of forgetting her – that Alice would grow into her likeness, not my own. I wish, for Alice's sake, that Freda had been happier with Pete. Perhaps then I would have passed on the truth to their daughter more easily. Wars begin and end. Things clash. And there are a thousand other beginnings and endings in between – things that, perhaps, would never have come into being, or simply would have carried on existing, untouched. Maybe, if Alice had come later when love had been given the chance to take root, events might have unfurled differently. But Pete knew from the onset that he had never had Freda's heart, just as I knew I lacked his. When his mother sent for him again in London, telling him she was sick and in need of his care, he deserted my sister – it was no life for her, with her fancy things and her unborn baby. He took his mother and her daughter to live with him in Leconfield and left Freda behind. She might have gone with him, if he had asked, but he didn't. He chose his mother over her – a single, barren act of loyalty.

After she died, I raised Alice as my own, as he had told me to do in his letter. But I knew I would have done the same, regardless of whether or not he had written. So many mistakes had come together to form her, and yet, when I held her, it was as if they could all be undone.

Sleep comes to me in the marketplace. Only a thin layer but I give in to it. The lantern flickers between itself and my vision of it until I don't know which is real. The sea unravels on the beach ahead, then rolls itself up again, inhaling whenever I inhale and breathing its rhythm into my dreams.

Just then, in the corner of the square, the darkness is disturbed by somebody else's light. A white orb sways in time with their step, growing from a pinprick into a cat's eye until it is the size of an apple. Closer and closer come the steps, the sea ssshing beneath their staccato.

Soon they adopt a shape and, once in range of my lantern, collect features and, finally, a face.

'Alice?' I test through the darkness.

'Who's that?' The shadow flinches back. I bend into the glow of the lantern and the torch is dropped. It falls and rolls and draws an arc in the dirt, like a needle spinning inside a compass.

Epilogue: I Lift Up My Eyes

What is the difference between an ocean and a sea? Where does one start and the other end? If you were to find the exact point – a hairline crack in the surface of the water running all the way down between the two – would you see any contrast between them? A variation in the colour or texture or thickness, perhaps?

Alice imagines oceans as blue and seas as grey and channels as a mingling of the two. She is as full of questions today as the sea is of waves.

Can a wave circumvent the earth without hitting land? If it did, would it keep on going and going and going, without ever arriving?

Maybe they're magnetic, I suggest, drawn to breaking in a place marked as theirs.

Was my wave meant for Kanyakumari? she asks. I tell her that is not what I meant to say. It is too big a thing not to have been meant, is her reply. My words or her wave: I do not know to which she is referring.

Alice's fingers shrink like sea anemones into balls each time a wave breaks at our feet. She is resisting the urge to run.

'It'll start off as nothing more than a smudge, Mum. You won't even notice because it keeps itself so close to the water.' She doesn't turn to face me but picks a point on the horizon and chisels at it with her eyes. 'Then, up it goes and rises. And the water next to the beach empties, like some massive washbasin.' It's the first time she's talked, given it words, assembled it into a story. 'And all the time you think you can outrun it because it doesn't look as if it will ever come. Do you know what I mean?'

I nod, not knowing.

The Indian Ocean is making inroads towards our feet. She recoils again. I stay still this time, letting the sea invade my shoes; Alice draws a breath. 'I didn't quite mean to marry James,' she confesses, the words seeping out of her as if she had been trying to say them for some time. 'But the wave. It binds things.' She pauses, turning to me. 'I'm not making sense.'

'A lot of things aren't meant,' I say, taking her hand. She does not lift her eyes from the water. I ask her about the letters I posted and she says that she has read them, that she understands.

I tell her that I was with her mother when she died. When they cut Alice out of Freda, the wound wouldn't heal. The infection invaded her blood. One night, after the doctor had implied there was nothing more he could do, she broke free of the house in Wilton and limped as far as the allotments. We found her an hour later – her face wet and shimmering in the grass. My mother had to carry her back to the house, she was so weak. I realized, then, where she was bent on going. I took her hand in mine and felt the hold leave each of her fingers. She parted her lips to let out a word but instead let go of her breath. The last flood of it pushed through her throat and divorced itself from her, the blink in her eyes fleeing quickly afterwards, then the heat from her hand. Pete wasn't there that night: they had separated before he even got to Yorkshire.

My daughter – my sister's daughter – is standing next to me on the beach, her feet within touching distance of the sea. She understands what it took for me to love her; she understands the cost. She has not kept secrets, as I have, but has left things unsaid. She tells me about Pete's sister, her visit to the house and how she had thought Alice was mine. He must have wanted it to be true, Alice says, to make his own sister believe such a thing. But I fear she is being too kind.

The waves break again over our feet. She knows. And has known for some time. What the water took away. And what it gave.

When I took her to the hospital to see James, she stood blinking, as I had done, at the opposite side of the ward. It didn't seem real – the sight of him there on the bed. He stayed sleeping, even as she lay down on the mattress beside him – her eyes level with his. For days after my Delhi train ride, I had dreamt I was still moving each time I closed my eyes. I pictured all the miles they had covered together – how every period of sleep must have felt like another journey. But afterwards, once the miles were complete, there was the comfort of waking, as James did now, to find her there, unmoving, beside him.

It is my turn, now, to settle my stare on the horizon. I think of the waves pulsing under its lip. There is one stored there whose magnet, I imagine, can draw it to my shore. I see it building, pouring itself upwards until it has grown as tall as the Downs. It is ready to break now, to crash into England's coast. To muscle into Wiltshire. To erase the chalk horse from West bury. To baptize the Plain. To fill the valley, like an overflowing jar, and burst open Imber's ruins. To lift the absent bells from their tower and plant them again in shards. Not here. But in somebody else's field.

Acknowledgements

Novels are more than solitary creations; they are the fruit of many conversations. This book belongs to lots of people. In particular, I would like to thank Juliet Annan and Sophie Missing, at Fig Tree, for their astute and sensitive editing; Cathryn Summerhayes and Becky Thomas, who represent me at WME; Commander Ed Brown, for his assistance in researching the Salisbury Plain military range; Rex Sawyer, for his insight into Imber's history; Mark and Ruth Devaraj, for their help with Tamil translation; Mrs Sen, for her memories of 1970s India; Ashley and Lin Rowlands, for their stories and photographs of the hippie trail; author Jennifer Potter, for her encouragement and wisdom throughout the writing of the novel; the London Library, for its endless supply of off-beat books and the quietness in which to write this one; the students and staff on the 2010/11 Warwick Writing MA; Becky Jones, Cat Rashid, Sarah Ritchie and Kath Wade, who are not only dear friends but my first readers; my wonderful family – Bill, Dad, Mum and Ian; and my maker, who, through every sea change, always stays the same.

For those interested in reading more about Imber and its evacuation, the following books were invaluable in helping me bring the village to life in the novel:

Henry Buckton, *The Lost Villages: In Search of Britain's Vanished Communities* (London: I.B. Tauris, 2008).

Peter Daniels and Rex Sawyer, *Images of England: Salisbury Plain* (Stroud, 1996).

Rex Sawyer, *Little Imber on the Down: Salisbury Plain's Ghost Village* (Salisbury: The Hobnob Press, 2001).

*

He just wanted a decent book to read ...

Not too much to ask, is it? It was in 1935 when Allen Lane, Managing Director of Bodley Head Publishers, stood on a platform at Exeter railway station looking for something good to read on his journey back to London. His choice was limited to popular magazines and poor-quality paperbacks – the same choice faced every day by the vast majority of readers, few of whom could afford hardbacks. Lane's disappointment and subsequent anger at the range of books generally available led him to found a company – and change the world.

'We believed in the existence in this country of a vast reading public for intelligent books at a low price, and staked everything on it'
Sir Allen Lane, 1902–1970, founder of Penguin Books

The quality paperback had arrived – and not just in bookshops. Lane was adamant that his Penguins should appear in chain stores and tobacconists, and should cost no more than a packet of cigarettes.

Reading habits (and cigarette prices) have changed since 1935, but Penguin still believes in publishing the best books for everybody to enjoy. We still believe that good design costs no more than bad design, and we still believe that quality books published passionately and responsibly make the world a better place.

So wherever you see the little bird – whether it's on a piece of prize-winning literary fiction or a celebrity autobiography, political tour de force or historical masterpiece, a serial-killer thriller, reference book, world classic or a piece of pure escapism – you can bet that it represents the very best that the genre has to offer.

Whatever you like to read – trust Penguin.